DEMOCRACY

HENRY ADAMS

DEMOCRACY

AN AMERICAN NOVEL

Introduction by Arthur Schlesinger, Jr.

THE MODERN LIBRARY

NEW YORK

LIBRARY OF CONGRESS CATALOGING-IN-PUBLICATION DATA
Adams, Henry, 1838–1918.
Democracy : an American novel / Henry Adams ; introduction by
Arthur Schlesinger, Jr.
p.   cm.
ISBN 0-375-76058-X
1. Washington (D.C.)—Fiction. 2. Legislators—Fiction.
3. Socialites—Fiction. 4. Widows—Fiction. I. Title.
PS1004.A4 D4 2002
813'.4—dc21   2002019645

Modern Library website address: www.modernlibrary.com

Printed in the United States of America

2   4   6   8   9   7   5   3   1

Henry Adams

Henry Brooks Adams was born in Boston on February 16, 1838, into one of America's most prominent intellectual and political families. His great-grandfather, John Adams, was the second president of the United States, and his grandfather, John Quincy Adams, was the sixth, and throughout his life Henry Adams would remain ambivalent about his legacy of privilege and patriotism. He graduated from Harvard College in 1858 and like many young wealthy men of his day set forth on a European grand tour, sailing on the Cunard line's *Persia*. Among the places he visited that decades later would influence his political and historical views was Berlin, where, according to *The Education of Henry Adams*, "He could never recall what he expected to find, but whatever he expected, it had no relation with what it turned out to be."

In 1861 President Abraham Lincoln appointed Adams's father minister to England. Henry joined him at the Court of St. James, working as his father's personal secretary and watching the Civil War from the far side of the Atlantic. Henry Adams returned to the United States in 1868, working for two years as a journalist in

Washington, D.C., a city he described as "rural, and its society was primitive." Despite this depiction, Adams was a man as much of Washington as of Braintree and Boston, and his first appointment in the nation's capital was with President Andrew Johnson.

In 1870 Harvard appointed Adams a professor of medieval history. During his academic years in the 1870s, Adams edited the influential *The North American Review,* Adams's first national platform. But life in the nation's innermost circles of political power lured Adams back to Washington in 1877, where he began writing a number of influential histories and biographies, including his nine-volume *History of the United States of America During the Administrations of Thomas Jefferson and James Madison* (1889–1891). During this period he also published anonymously *Democracy: An American Novel* (1880), a best-selling roman à clef that set off a flurry of speculation over the true identity of its author. Adams followed with a second novel, *Esther* (1884), published under the pseudonym Frances Snow Compton. In 1885 Adams's wife committed suicide, an event only briefly mentioned in his *Education.* In fact, in his autobiography Adams passes over almost entirely the years between 1872 and 1892, the two decades when he lived and worked among Washington's most powerful.

After the death of his wife, Adams began to travel around the world, voyaging to the South Seas and the Middle East. In 1904 he wrote his influential meditation upon medievalism and architecture, *Mont-Saint-Michel and Chartres.* In 1907 he finished his masterpiece, *The Education of Henry Adams,* a book that would go on to win the Pulitzer Prize and for the first time reveal Adams's true literary sensibility. It has long been regarded as one of the greatest works of autobiographical literature, and in 1999 the Modern Library Editorial Board named it the Best Nonfiction Book of the Twentieth Century written in the English language.

Adams died at his Washington home on March 27, 1918. After his death he was revealed as the author of *Democracy.*

CONTENTS

INTRODUCTION

Arthur Schlesinger, Jr.

The novelist swore the publisher to secrecy about his identity, instructed him to bring the book out on April Fool's Day 1880, and took care to be in Europe on that day. *Democracy: An American Novel,* its author anonymous, created a sensation and was a bestseller in the United States and England. The author was not to be disclosed for another thirty-five years. It was Henry Adams.

Edward Chalfant, his best biographer, believes that Adams began *Democracy* as early as 1867, in London, when he was secretary to his father, Charles Francis Adams, the American minister to the Court of St. James's. In 1868 the Adamses returned to the United States. Henry, thirty years old and in search of a career, supposed that political journalism might be the way to move his bewildered country in the right direction. The press, he conceded, was "an inferior pulpit; an anonymous schoolmaster; a cheap boarding-school; but it was still the nearest approach to a career for the literary survivor of a wrecked education."[1]

Where to establish a reputation? "Neither by temperament nor by education," Adams observed in his (third-person) *The Education of Henry Adams,* "was he fitted for Boston."[2] New York dazzled him, but he had no New York base, so he decided on Washington. In the nation's capital Adams found active and intelligent contemporaries, eager for reform, rallied by Secretary of the Treasury Hugh McCulloch—"the broadest, most liberal, most genial, and most practical public man in Washington"[3]—united by the conviction that, after the Civil War, the country's whole political fabric required rethinking and renewal "as much," Adams said, "as in 1789." He found himself at home with the young reformers, "more at home," he later wrote, "than he ever had been before, or was ever to be again."[4] He adored Washington, "the easiest society he had ever seen."[5]

Like other young reformers in 1868, Adams was thrilled when Ulysses S. Grant was elected president. People saw hopeful parallels between Grant and George Washington. Both were generals; both commanded national confidence; both had the capacity to improve the character of government. Then Adams heard the announcement of Grant's cabinet. When Adams learned that Hugh McCulloch, a man he admired, was to be replaced in the treasury by George W. Boutwell, a man he detested, he saw this as "a somewhat lugubrious joke" signifying "total extinction for anyone resembling Henry Adams"*[6] "To the end of his life," he recalled, toward the end of his life, "he wondered at the suddenness of the revolution which actually, within five minutes, changed his intended future into an absurdity so laughable as to make him ashamed of it." Disenchantment accelerated as fraud and scandal spread through the Grant administration. "The progress of evolution from President Washington to President Grant, was alone evidence enough to upset Darwin."[7]

What had gone wrong? As the old Henry Adams was to remark

---

*Adams was indifferent to the fact that Boutwell, who believed in civil rights for ex-slaves, was more of a reformer than McCulloch, who supported Andrew Johnson's Reconstruction policies.

about his younger self, "He needed to penetrate the political mystery."[8] If the Op Ed page had been invented, Henry Adams could have been the Walter Lippmann of his day. What he required was a New York daily, but no New York daily required him. Still, E. L. Godkin's weekly *Nation* and James Russell Lowell's quarterly *North American Review* were always available, and in Great Britain *The Edinburgh Review* and *The Westminster Review* took occasional Adams pieces.

In a series of powerful articles, young Adams did his best to set forth the tragic dilemmas of democracy. Popular government, he contended, was fatally threatened by the emerging power of the corporation. In a savage piece for *The North American Review,* published in July 1870 and entitled "The Session, 1869–1870," he emphasized the impotence of reform as a check on corporate aggression. While reformers in Congress rejoiced at carrying a small reduction in the tariff on pig-iron, Congress was creating a new Pacific railway—"an imperishable corporation with its own territory, an empire within the republic, more powerful than a sovereign State, and inconsistent with the purity of Republican institutions or with the safety of any government.... With the prodigious development of corporate and private wealth resistance must be in vain."[9] (The Democratic National Committee circulated Adams's article in a vain effort to stop Grant's reelection in 1872.)

Young Adams summed up his indictment of corporate power in "The New York Gold Conspiracy" for *The Westminster Review* in October 1870. The Erie Railroad, he wrote, "has shown its power for mischief, and has proved itself able to override and trample on law, custom, decency, and every restraint known to society, without scruple, and as yet without check." "The day is at hand," Adams continued, "when corporations far greater than the Erie ... swaying power such as has never in the world's history been trusted in the hands of private citizens ... after having created a system of quiet but irresistible corruption—will ultimately succeed in directing government itself. Under the American form of society no authority exists capable of effective resistance." The regulatory power of government "sooner or later is likely to fall into the hands it is trying to escape, and thus destroy the limits of its power only in order to make corruption omnipotent."[10]

"The tendency of our political system to corruption," he wrote in the October 1876 *North American Review,* had accelerated to the point where "unless the evil is checked, our political system must break down." Corporations dependent on legislation routinely bribed legislators and parties to assure profits and dividends. "So long as there is money to corrupt, there will be parties to hide the corruption and to receive their reward."[11] The domination of politics by the party system, Adams argued, crucially reinforced the tendency to corruption and constituted a mortal danger to democratic self-government.

Meanwhile, Harvard had offered Adams an assistant professorship in history and the editorship of *The North American Review,* and his family prevailed on the disillusioned young journalist to accept. His Harvard years were not especially happy—"several score of the best-educated, most agreeable, and personally the most sociable people in America united in Cambridge to make a social desert that would have starved a polar bear"[12]—and his concern for the American future did not abate. Confiding only in his wife, Marian Hooper (Clover) Adams, he quietly worked away in spare moments on his Washington novel.

In 1877, to his immense relief, he moved back to Washington. "I gravitate to a capital by a primary law of nature," he wrote a British friend. "This is the only place in America where society amuses me, or where life offers variety."[13] By now he had worked out the central conflicts of the Washington novel.

The protagonist is a New York woman, Mrs. Lightfoot Lee, thirty years old, whose husband and child have died and who has tried, and failed, to fill an empty life with good works. Nor does foreign travel help. She is American to the tips of her fingers, "but she meant to get all that American life had to offer, good or bad, and to drink it down to the dregs."

So Madeleine Lee decides to pass the winter in Washington. "She wanted to see with her own eyes the action of primary forces; to touch with her own hand the massive machinery of society; to measure with her own mind the capacity of the motive power. She was bent upon getting to the heart of the great American mystery of democracy. . . . What she wanted, was POWER." Like Henry Adams.

She comes to Washington at a propitious time for her quest. It is during an interregnum, the interval of four months (as it was until the twentieth amendment) between the election and the installation of a new president. Rumors abound in such transitions, and this time speculation centers on the relationship between the president-elect, a one-term governor of Indiana, and Senator Silas P. Ratcliffe of Illinois, the "Prairie Giant," whom the unknown Indiana farmer had beaten by three votes for the presidential nomination. But Senator Ratcliffe retains his power in Congress and in the party, and the new president must somehow come to terms with him.

Madeleine Lee rents a house on Lafayette Square, opposite the White House. Soon politicians and diplomats flock to her soirees, Ratcliffe among them. He is an impressive figure, masculine, confident, eloquent, talking naturally, shrewdly, humorously. "There was a certain bigness about the man; a keen practical sagacity; a bold freedom of self-assertion; a broad way of dealing with what he knew."

He talks to Madeleine with astonishing freedom about his own political situation, making her complicit by discussing his strategy toward the president-elect. She sees Ratcliffe as "the high-priest of American politics; he was charged with the meaning of the mysteries, the clue to political hieroglyphics. . . . If there was good or bad in him, she meant to find its meaning." Each is soon fascinated with the other, and the reciprocal fascination has sexual overtones. Senator Ratcliffe decides that to complete his life he must marry Mrs. Lee; he already sees her as his partner in the White House.

Much of *Democracy* is taken up with elegant social comedy and witty set pieces; but darker themes lie underneath. "Surely," Madeleine cries to Ratcliffe, "something can be done to check corruption. Are we for ever to be at the mercy of thieves and ruffians? Is a respectable government impossible in a democracy?" "No representative government," Ratcliffe replies sententiously, "can long be much better or much worse than the society it represents. Purify society and you purify the government. But try to purify the government artificially and you only aggravate failure."

"You Americans believe yourselves to be excepted from the operation of general laws," is the sour observation of Baron Jacobi, the cynical Bulgarian minister. ". . . Rome, Paris, Vienna, Petersburg, London, all are corrupt; only Washington is pure! Well, I declare to you that in all my experience I have found no society which has had elements of corruption like the United States. The children in the street are corrupt, and know how to cheat me. The cities are all corrupt, and also the towns and the counties and the States' legislatures and the judges. Everywhere men betray trusts both public and private, steal money, run away with public funds."

Mrs. Lee pursues the question of corruption with Ratcliffe. He freely admits that "in politics we cannot keep our hands clean. I have done many things in my political career that are not defensible." In the worst days of the Civil War, he confides to Madeleine, it had seemed almost certain that Illinois would be carried by the peace party in the 1864 election. Ratcliffe, an old abolitionist, was governor; and he believed that "had Illinois been lost then, we should certainly have lost the Presidential election, and with it probably the Union. At any rate, I believed the fate of the war to depend on the result." So he had the northern counties delay election returns until he knew the precise number of votes needed to give President Lincoln a majority in the state. Then "we telegraphed to our northern returning officers to make the vote of their districts such and such." Ratcliffe concludes his recital, "I am not proud of the transaction, but I would do it again, and worse than that, if I thought it would save this country from disunion." Madeleine's silence conveys approval.

For Ratcliffe, loyalty to his party is the highest political morality. "Believing as I do," he tells Madeleine, "that great results can only be accomplished by great parties, I have uniformly yielded my own personal opinions where they have failed to obtain general assent." Madeleine: " 'Have you never refused to go with your party?' 'Never!' was Ratcliffe's firm reply."

Ratcliffe decides to accept the president-elect's offer of the Treasury Department, rapidly comes to dominate the cabinet, and soon tells Madeleine that the new president's incompetence is becoming notorious and that the odds are two to one that the secretary of the treasury would get his party's nomination the next time around. Finally, Ratcliffe's strong will prevails on Madeleine's unacknowledged ambition. She makes up her mind to marry him.

This decision sets in motion an anti-Ratcliffe conspiracy propelled by John Carrington, who is vainly in love with Madeleine, and by her own younger sister, Sybil. Their weapon is the charge that Ratcliffe has accepted a bribe of one hundred thousand dollars (probably equal to nearly two million dollars in today's degraded currency) for enactment of legislation benefiting a steamship company. Madeleine is at first shocked and angered. On second thought she feels she has no right to be angry; Ratcliffe "had never deceived her." She is angry at herself for ever having believed in him.

Confronting Ratcliffe with the accusation, she is met by ready explanations. He harks back to the 1864 election. "Our defeat meant that the government must pass into the blood-stained hands of rebels. . . . Money was freely spent, even to an amount much in excess of our resources." The head of the national committee told him that he must, for the party's sake, abandon his opposition to the steamship subsidy bill. The hundred thousand was paid to the national committee; "I received no money"; the Union was saved.

Ratcliffe continues: "Did I not tell you then that I had even violated the sanctity of a great popular election and reversed its result? . . . In comparison with it, this is a trifle! Who is injured by a steamship company subscribing one or ten hundred thousand dollars to a campaign fund?" He reminds Madeleine that she had not uttered a word of criticism for depriving a million people of their votes. "Why are you now so severe upon the smaller crime?"

With the power of a revelation, Madeleine suddenly sees Ratcliffe as a "moral lunatic" talking about "virtue and vice as a man who is colour-blind talks about red and green." Coldly she rejects Ratcliffe, rejects Washington, rejects democratic politics, preferring "the true democracy of life, her paupers and her prisons, her schools and her hospitals," and, democracy having shaken her nerves to pieces, goes off to Egypt to recuperate. "The bitterest part of all this horrid story," Madeleine concludes, "is that nine out of ten of our countrymen would say I had made a mistake."

At the time of publication, people rushed to read *Democracy* as a roman à clef and gossiped about the personalities satirized—and gossiped even more about the anonymous author who dared produce such a scandalous book. Clover Adams, Henry's wife, wrote her father, "I am much amused but not surprised at your suspecting me of having written *Democracy,* as I find I am on the 'black list' here"; she named half a dozen other suspects, including John Hay.[14] James G. Blaine, widely supposed, even by himself, to be the model for Ratcliffe, cut Clarence King as the suspected author, and later blamed Clover Adams. "I understand," Henry wrote Hay, ". . . that Hon. J. G. Blaine at a dinner party in New York said that Mrs. H. A. 'acknowledges' to have written *Democracy.* You know how I have always admired Mr. Blaine's powers of invention!"[15]

Adams remained a tease about the authorship. "The riddle," he told the publisher, "is more amusing . . . than the solution would be."[16] "I am glad that the secret is at last coming out," he wrote Hay. "I was always confident that you wrote that book."[17] In 1911, Adams even told a correspondent, "Really, of course Henry James wrote it, in connection with his brother Willy, to illustrate Pragmatism."[18] There were other contenders. William Dean Howells and Charles Dudley Warner decided that John W. DeForest, the gifted author of a couple of Washington novels, had written the book.[19] No one, except for the British novelist Mrs. Humphry Ward, detected Henry Adams's hand in *Democracy*.[20]

People today read *Democracy* not as a roman à clef but as a gallery of political types and as a novel of political ideas. Adams detested Blaine, but he was less interested in portraying real personages than in defining Washington types—the unscrupulous politician, the naïve idealist, the lightweight reformer, the cynical diplomat, the cunning lobbyist, the congressional hangers-on. The cast of Adams's *Democracy* populates Washington today, which is why the book is still in print.

As a novel of political ideas, *Democracy* is intermittently brilliant but ultimately unsatisfactory. There is no question that Henry Adams thinks that Madeleine is right in her rejection of Washington and her withdrawal from politics. But why then does he give the more powerful arguments to Ratcliffe? Madeleine herself admits to Ratcliffe, "I have no doubt that you can overcome me in argument." And where does Adams stand on Madeleine's key question: "Is a respectable government impossible in a democracy?" His support of Madeleine's decision suggests that his answer would be yes.

There is a minor figure in the novel, a historian and diplomat, Nathan Gore, inspired somewhat by John Lothrop Motley, the historian of the Netherlands and minister to England in 1869–70. Grant's secretary of state, Hamilton Fish, once told Adams that

Grant recalled Motley from London because he parted his hair in the middle; Nathan Gore, Adams's fictional historian of Spain, was not kept on as minister to Spain because, he tells Madeleine, the new president objected to the cut of his hair. After Baron Jacobi's rant about corruption in America, Madeleine turns to Nathan Gore: "I must know whether America is right or wrong. . . . Do you yourself think democracy the best government, and universal suffrage a success?"

Gore, goaded by Madeleine, affirms his political creed: "I believe in democracy. I accept it. I will faithfully serve and defend it. I believe in it because it appears to me the inevitable consequence of what has gone before it. Democracy asserts the fact that the masses are now raised to a higher intelligence than formerly. All our civilisation aims at this mark. We want to do what we can to help it. I myself want to see the result. I grant it is an experiment, but it is the only direction society can take that is worth its taking. . . . Every other possible step is backward, and I do not care to repeat the past."

"And supposing your experiment fails," Madeleine asks; "suppose society destroys itself with universal suffrage, corruption, and communism." "Let us be true to our time, Mrs. Lee!" Gore replies. "If our age is to be beaten, let us die in the ranks. If it is to be victorious, let us be first to lead the column. Anyway, let us not be skulkers or grumblers."

Nathan Gore, most students of *Democracy* agree, was speaking for Henry Adams. Yet Adams endorses Mrs. Lee's decision to retreat from the challenges of her age. How to reconcile participation with rejection? Perhaps Adams, in his desire to get the novel out in time to stop the nomination of James G. Blaine, rushed the final chapters and did not think through his political creed.

The neglected figure in *Democracy* is the widow of the lobbyist who extracted Ratcliffe's one hundred thousand dollars from the steamship company. As Edward Chalfant points out, it is Mrs. Sam Baker who really understood the action of primary forces in Washington. "I knew half the members of Congress intimately," Mrs. Baker tells Mrs. Lee, "and all of them by sight. I knew where they came from and what they liked best. . . . We had more congressional business than all the other agents put together." Mrs. Lee had seen duchesses as vulgar, so why did she "draw back from this interesting lobbyist with such babyish repulsion?" Perhaps because she sensed that Mrs. Baker had really got to the heart of the great American mystery of democracy and really exerted "POWER."

Someone who, unlike Madeleine Lee, embraced the challenges of his age was a young acquaintance of Henry Adams, though neither cared much for the other. "The other day I was reading *Democracy*," Theodore Roosevelt wrote Henry Cabot Lodge in September 1905, "that novel which made a great furor among the educated incompetents and the pessimists generally about twenty-five years ago. It was written by Godkin, perhaps with assistance from Mrs. Henry Adams. It had a superficial and rotten cleverness, but it was essentially false, essentially mean and base, and it is amusing to read it now and see how completely events have given it the lie."[21]

Events may have given *Democracy* the lie in Theodore Roosevelt's Progressive Era, at the beginning of the twentieth century. But Henry Adams's novel is all too true for Washington under corporate domination at the beginning of the twenty-first century.

—

ARTHUR SCHLESINGER, JR., was born in 1917 in Columbus, Ohio, and was educated at Harvard and Cambridge Universities. He is a historian who has taken an active role in politics, culminating in his service as special assistant to President John F. Kennedy, from 1961 to 1963. He has taught at Harvard University and the City University of New York and has won two Pulitzer Prizes and received the National Humanities Medal.

SOURCE NOTES

1. Henry Adams. *The Education of Henry Adams*, 1918, ch. XIV.

2. Ibid., ch. XVI.

3. Ibid.

4. Ibid.

5. Ibid., ch. XVII.

6. Ibid.

7. Ibid.

8. Ibid., ch. XVIII.

9. Henry Adams. "The Session, 1869–1870," *The North American Review*, July 1870.

10. ———. "The New York Gold Conspiracy," *The Westminster Review*, October 1870.

11. ———. " 'Independents' in the Canvass," *The North American Review*, October 1876.

12. ———. *Education*, ch. XX.

13. J. C. Levinson, et al., eds. *The Letters of Henry Adams*, 6 vols. (Harvard University Press, 1982–88), vol. 2, p. 326.

14. Edward Chalfant, *Better in Darkness: A Biography of Henry Adams, His Second Life, 1852–1891* (Archon Books, 1994), p. 411. Volume two of a trilogy of the life of Henry Adams.

15. Adams, *Letters*, vol. 2, p. 488.

16. Ibid., vol. 3, p. 192.

17. Ibid., vol. 2, p. 459.

18. Ibid., vol. 6, pp. 457–58.

19. Ibid., vol. 2, p. 472.

20. Ibid., p. 468.

21. Elting E. Morison, ed. *The Letters of Theodore Roosevelt*, 8 vols. (Harvard University Press, 1951–54), vol. 5, p. 10.

A NOTE ON THE TEXT

Democracy: An American Novel was first published anonymously in 1880 (New York: Henry Holt & Co.). This Modern Library Paperback Classics edition has been set from that edition with one important change. The first edition skipped from chapter XI to chapter XIII. The editors have renumbered the chapters sequentially, and hence chapters XIII and XIV have been renumbered as chapter XII and chapter XIII.

DEMOCRACY

CHAPTER I

For reasons which many persons thought ridiculous, Mrs. Lightfoot Lee decided to pass the winter in Washington. She was in excellent health, but she said that the climate would do her good. In
New York she had troops of friends, but she suddenly became eager
to see again the very small number of those who lived on the Potomac. It was only to her closest intimates that she honestly acknowledged herself to be tortured by *ennui*. Since her husband's
death, five years before, she had lost her taste for New York society;
she had felt no interest in the price of stocks, and very little in the
men who dealt in them; she had become serious. What was it all
worth, this wilderness of men and women as monotonous as the
brown stone houses they lived in? In her despair she had resorted to
desperate measures. She had read philosophy in the original German, and the more she read, the more she was disheartened that so
much culture should lead to nothing—nothing. After talking of
Herbert Spencer for an entire evening with a very literary transcendental commission-merchant, she could not see that her time
had been better employed than when in former days she had passed

it in flirting with a very agreeable young stock-broker; indeed, there was an evident proof to the contrary, for the flirtation might lead to something—had, in fact, led to marriage; while the philosophy could lead to nothing, unless it were perhaps to another evening of the same kind, because transcendental philosophers are mostly elderly men, usually married, and, when engaged in business, somewhat apt to be sleepy towards evening. Nevertheless Mrs. Lee did her best to turn her study to practical use. She plunged into philanthropy, visited prisons, inspected hospitals, read the literature of pauperism and crime, saturated herself with the statistics of vice, until her mind had nearly lost sight of virtue. At last it rose in rebellion against her, and she came to the limit of her strength. This path, too, seemed to lead nowhere. She declared that she had lost the sense of duty, and that, so far as concerned her, all the paupers and criminals in New York might henceforward rise in their majesty and manage every railway on the continent. Why should she care? What was the city to her? She could find nothing in it that seemed to demand salvation. What gave peculiar sanctity to numbers? Why were a million people, who all resembled each other, any way more interesting than one person? What aspiration could she help to put into the mind of this great million-armed monster that would make it worth her love or respect? Religion? A thousand powerful churches were doing their best, and she could see no chance for a new faith of which she was to be the inspired prophet. Ambition? High popular ideals? Passion for whatever is lofty and pure? The very words irritated her. Was she not herself devoured by ambition, and was she not now eating her heart out because she could find no one object worth a sacrifice?

Was it ambition—real ambition—or was it mere restlessness that made Mrs. Lightfoot Lee so bitter against New York and Philadelphia, Baltimore and Boston, American life in general and all life in particular? What did she want? Not social position, for she herself was an eminently respectable Philadelphian by birth; her father a famous clergyman; and her husband had been equally irreproachable, a descendant of one branch of the Virginia Lees, which had drifted to New York in search of fortune, and had found it, or enough of it to keep the young man there. His widow had her own place in society which no one disputed. Though not brighter than her neighbours, the world persisted in classing her among clever women; she had wealth, or at least enough of it to give her all that money can give by way of pleasure to a sensible woman in an American city; she had her house and her carriage; she dressed well; her table was good, and her furniture was never allowed to fall behind the latest standard of decorative art. She had travelled in Europe, and after several visits, covering some years of time, had returned home, carrying in one hand, as it were, a green-grey landscape, a remarkably pleasing specimen of Corot, and in the other some bales of Persian and Syrian rugs and embroideries, Japanese bronzes and porcelain. With this she declared Europe to be exhausted, and she frankly avowed that she was American to the tips of her fingers; she neither knew nor greatly cared whether America or Europe were best to live in; she had no violent love for either, and she had no objection to abusing both; but she meant to get all that American life had to offer, good or bad, and to drink it down to the dregs, fully determined that whatever there was in it she would have, and that whatever could be made out of it she would manufacture. "I know," said she, "that America produces petroleum and pigs; I have seen both on the steamers; and I am told it produces silver and gold. There is choice enough for any woman."

Yet, as has been already said, Mrs. Lee's first experience was not a success. She soon declared that New York might represent the petroleum or the pigs, but the gold of life was not to be discovered there by her eyes. Not but that there was variety enough; a variety of people, occupations, aims, and thoughts; but that all these, after growing to a certain height, stopped short. They found nothing to hold them up. She knew, more or less intimately, a dozen men whose fortunes ranged between one million and forty millions. What did they do with their money? What could they do with it that was different from what other men did? After all, it is absurd to spend more money than is enough to satisfy all one's wants; it is vulgar to live in two houses in the same street, and to drive six horses abreast. Yet, after setting aside a certain income sufficient for all one's wants, what was to be done with the rest? To let it accumulate was to own one's failure; Mrs. Lee's great grievance was that it did accumulate, without changing or improving the quality of its owners. To spend it in charity and public works was doubtless praiseworthy, but was it wise? Mrs. Lee had read enough political economy and pauper reports to be nearly convinced that public work should be public duty, and that great benefactions do harm as well as good. And even supposing it spent on these objects, how could it do more than increase and perpetuate that same kind of human nature which was her great grievance? Her New York friends could not meet this question except by falling back upon their native commonplaces, which she recklessly trampled upon, averring that, much as she admired the genius of the famous traveller, Mr. Gulliver, she never had been able, since she became a widow, to accept the Brobdingnagian doctrine that he who made two blades of grass grow where only one grew before deserved better of mankind than the whole race of politicians. She would not find fault with the philosopher had he required that the grass should be of an improved quality; "but," said she, "I cannot honestly pretend that I should be pleased to see two New York men where I now see one; the idea is too ridiculous; more than one and a half would be fatal to me."

Then came her Boston friends, who suggested that higher education was precisely what she wanted; she should throw herself into a crusade for universities and art-schools. Mrs. Lee turned upon them with a sweet smile; "Do you know," said she, "that we have in New York already the richest university in America, and that its only trouble has always been that it can get no scholars even by paying for them? Do you want me to go out into the streets and waylay boys? If the heathen refuse to be converted, can you give me power over the stake and the sword to compel them to come in? And suppose you can? Suppose I march all the boys in Fifth Avenue down to the university and have them all properly taught Greek and Latin, English literature, ethics, and German philosophy. What then? You do it in Boston. Now tell me honestly what comes of it. I suppose you have there a brilliant society; numbers of poets, scholars, philosophers, statesmen, all up and down Beacon Street. Your evenings must be sparkling. Your press must scintillate. How is it that we New Yorkers never hear of it? We don't go much into your society; but when we do, it doesn't seem so very much better than our own. You are just like the rest of us. You grow six inches high, and then you stop. Why will not somebody grow to be a tree and cast a shadow?"

The average member of New York society, although not unused to this contemptuous kind of treatment from his leaders, retaliated in his blind, common-sense way. "What does the woman want?" he said. "Is her head turned with the Tuileries and Marlborough House? Does she think herself made for a throne? Why does she not lecture for women's rights? Why not go on the stage? If she cannot be contented like other people, what need is there for abusing us just because she feels herself no taller than we are? What does she expect to get from her sharp tongue? What does she know, any way?"

Mrs. Lee certainly knew very little. She had read voraciously and promiscuously one subject after another. Ruskin and Taine had danced merrily through her mind, hand in hand with Darwin and Stuart Mill, Gustave Droz and Algernon Swinburne. She had even laboured over the literature of her own country. She was perhaps, the only woman in New York who knew something of American history. Certainly she could not have repeated the list of Presidents in their order, but she knew that the Constitution divided the government into Executive, Legislative, and Judiciary; she was aware that the President, the Speaker, and the Chief Justice were important personages, and instinctively she wondered whether they might not solve her problem; whether they were the shade trees which she saw in her dreams.

Here, then, was the explanation of her restlessness, discontent, ambition,—call it what you will. It was the feeling of a passenger on an ocean steamer whose mind will not give him rest until he has been in the engine-room and talked with the engineer. She wanted to see with her own eyes the action of primary forces; to touch with her own hand the massive machinery of society; to measure with her own mind the capacity of the motive power. She was bent upon getting to the heart of the great American mystery of democracy and government. She cared little where her pursuit might lead her, for she put no extravagant value upon life, having already, as she said, exhausted at least two lives, and being fairly hardened to insensibility in the process. "To lose a husband and a baby," said she, "and keep one's courage and reason, one must become very hard or very soft. I am now pure steel. You may beat my heart with a trip-hammer and it will beat the trip-hammer back again."

Perhaps after exhausting the political world she might try again elsewhere; she did not pretend to say where she might then go, or what she should do; but at present she meant to see what amusement there might be in politics. Her friends asked what kind of amusement she expected to find among the illiterate swarm of ordinary people who in Washington represented constituencies so dreary that in comparison New York was a New Jerusalem, and Broad Street a grove of Academe. She replied that if Washington society were so bad as this, she should have gained all she wanted, for it would be a pleasure to return,—precisely the feeling she longed for. In her own mind, however, she frowned on the idea of seeking for men. What she wished to see, she thought, was the clash of interests, the interests of forty millions of people and a whole continent, centering at Washington; guided, restrained, controlled, or unrestrained and uncontrollable, by men of ordinary mould; the tremendous forces of government, and the machinery of society, at work. What she wanted, was POWER.

Perhaps the force of the engine was a little confused in her mind with that of the engineer, the power with the men who wielded it. Perhaps the human interest of politics was after all what really attracted her, and, however strongly she might deny it, the passion for exercising power, for its own sake, might dazzle and mislead a woman who had exhausted all the ordinary feminine resources. But why speculate about her motives? The stage was before her, the curtain was rising, the actors were ready to enter; she had only to go quietly on among the supernumeraries and see how the play was acted and the stage effects were produced; how the great tragedians mouthed, and the stage-manager swore.

CHAPTER II

On the first of December, Mrs. Lee took the train for Washington, and before five o'clock that evening she was entering her newly hired house on Lafayette Square. She shrugged her shoulders with a mingled expression of contempt and grief at the curious barbarism of the curtains and the wall-papers, and her next two days were occupied with a life-and-death struggle to get the mastery over her surroundings. In this awful contest the interior of the doomed house suffered as though a demon were in it; not a chair, not a mirror, not a carpet, was left untouched, and in the midst of the worst confusion the new mistress sat, calm as the statue of Andrew Jackson in the square under her eyes, and issued her orders with as much decision as that hero had ever shown. Towards the close of the second day, victory crowned her forehead. A new era, a nobler conception of duty and existence, had dawned upon that benighted and heathen residence. The wealth of Syria and Persia was poured out upon the melancholy Wilton carpets; embroidered comets and woven gold from Japan and Teheran depended from and covered over every sad stuff-curtain; a strange medley of sketches, paintings, fans, embroideries, and porcelain was hung, nailed, pinned, or stuck against the wall; finally the domestic altar-piece, the mystical Corot landscape, was hoisted to its place over the parlour fire, and then all was over. The setting sun streamed softly in at the windows, and peace reigned in that redeemed house and in the heart of its mistress.

"I think it will do now, Sybil," said she, surveying the scene.

"It must," replied Sybil. "You haven't a plate or a fan or coloured scarf left. You must send out and buy some of these old negro-women's bandannas if you are going to cover anything else. What *is* the use? Do you suppose any human being in Washington will like it? They will think you demented."

"There is such a thing as self-respect," replied her sister, calmly.

Sybil—Miss Sybil Ross—was Madeleine Lee's sister. The keen-est psychologist could not have detected a single feature or quality which they had in common, and for that reason they were devoted friends. Madeleine was thirty, Sybil twenty-four. Madeleine was indescribable; Sybil was transparent. Madeleine was of medium height with a graceful figure, a well-set head, and enough golden-brown hair to frame a face full of varying expression. Her eyes were never for two consecutive hours of the same shade, but were more often blue than grey. People who envied her smile said that she cultivated a sense of humour in order to show her teeth. Perhaps they were right; but there was no doubt that her habit of talking with gesticulation would never have grown upon her unless she had known that her hands were not only beautiful but expressive. She dressed as skilfully as New York women do, but in growing older she began to show symptoms of dangerous unconventionality. She had been heard to express a low opinion of her countrywomen who blindly fell down before the golden calf of Mr. Worth, and she had even fought a battle of great severity, while it lasted, with one of her best-dressed friends who had been invited—and had gone—to Mr. Worth's afternoon tea-parties. The secret was that Mrs. Lee had artistic tendencies, and unless they were checked in time, there was no knowing what might be the consequence. But as yet they had done no harm; indeed, they rather helped to give her that sort of atmosphere which belongs only to certain women; as indescribable as the after-glow; as impalpable as an Indian summer mist; and non-existent except to people who feel rather than reason. Sybil had none of it. The imagination gave up all attempts to soar where she came. A more straightforward, downright, gay, sympathetic, shallow, warm-hearted, sternly practical young woman has rarely touched this planet. Her mind had room for neither grave-stones nor guide-books; she could not have lived in the past or the future if she had spent her days in churches and her nights in tombs. "She was not clever, like Madeleine, thank Heaven." Madeleine was not an orthodox member of the church; sermons bored her, and clergymen never failed to irritate every nerve in her excitable system. Sybil was a simple and devout worshipper at the ritualistic altar; she bent humbly before the Paulist fathers. When she went to a ball she always had the best partner in the room, and took it as a matter of course; but then, she always prayed for one; somehow it strengthened her faith. Her sister took care never to laugh at her on this score, or to shock her religious opinions. "Time enough," said she, "for her to forget religion when religion fails her." As for regular attendance at church, Madeleine was able to reconcile their habits without trouble. She herself had not entered a church for years; she said it gave her unchristian feelings; but Sybil had a voice of excellent quality, well trained and cultivated: Madeleine insisted that she should sing in the choir, and by this little manœuvre, the divergence of their paths was made less evident. Madeleine did not sing, and therefore could not go to church with Sybil. This outrageous fallacy seemed perfectly to answer its purpose, and Sybil accepted it, in good faith, as a fair working principle which explained itself.

Madeleine was sober in her tastes. She wasted no money. She

made no display. She walked rather than drove, and wore neither diamonds nor brocades. But the general impression she made was nevertheless one of luxury. On the other hand, her sister had her dresses from Paris, and wore them and her ornaments according to all the formulas; she was good-naturedly correct, and bent her round white shoulders to whatever burden the Parisian autocrat chose to put upon them. Madeleine never interfered, and always paid the bills.

Before they had been ten days in Washington, they fell gently into their place and were carried along without an effort on the stream of social life. Society was kind; there was no reason for its being otherwise. Mrs. Lee and her sister had no enemies, held no offices, and did their best to make themselves popular. Sybil had not passed summers at Newport and winters in New York in vain; and neither her face nor her figure, her voice nor her dancing, needed apology. Politics were not her strong point. She was induced to go once to the Capitol and to sit ten minutes in the gallery of the Senate. No one ever knew what her impressions were; with feminine tact she managed not to betray herself. But, in truth, her notion of legislative bodies was vague, floating between her experience at church and at the opera, so that the idea of a performance of some kind was never out of her head. To her mind the Senate was a place where people went to recite speeches, and she naïvely assumed that the speeches were useful and had a purpose, but as they did not interest her she never went again. This is a very common conception of Congress; many Congressmen share it.

Her sister was more patient and bolder. She went to the Capitol nearly every day for at least two weeks. At the end of that time her interest began to flag, and she thought it better to read the debates every morning in the *Congressional Record*. Finding this a laborious and not always an instructive task, she began to skip the dull parts; and in the absence of any exciting question, she at last resigned herself to skipping the whole. Nevertheless she still had energy to visit the Senate gallery occasionally when she was told that a splendid orator was about to speak on a question of deep interest to his country. She listened with a little disposition to admire, if she could; and, whenever she could, she did admire. She said nothing, but she listened sharply. She wanted to learn how the machinery of government worked, and what was the quality of the men who controlled it. One by one, she passed them through her crucibles, and tested them by acids and by fire. A few survived her tests and came out alive, though more or less disfigured, where she had found impurities. Of the whole number, only one retained under this process enough character to interest her.

In these early visits to Congress, Mrs. Lee sometimes had the company of John Carrington, a Washington lawyer about forty years old, who, by virtue of being a Virginian and a distant connection of her husband, called himself a cousin, and took a tone of semi-intimacy, which Mrs. Lee accepted because Carrington was a man whom she liked, and because he was one whom life had treated hardly. He was of that unfortunate generation in the south which began existence with civil war, and he was perhaps the more unfortunate because, like most educated Virginians of the old Washington school, he had seen from the first that, whatever issue the war took, Virginia and he must be ruined. At twenty-two he had gone into the rebel army as a private and carried his musket modestly through a campaign or two, after which he slowly rose to the rank of senior captain in his regiment, and closed his services on the staff of a major-general, always doing scrupulously enough what he conceived to be his duty, and never doing it with enthusiasm. When the rebel armies surrendered, he rode away to his family plantation—not a difficult thing to do, for it was only a few miles from Appomatox—and at once began to study law; then, leaving his mother and sisters to do what they could with the worn-out plantation, he began the practice of law in Washington, hoping thus to support himself and them. He had succeeded after a fashion, and for the first time the future seemed not absolutely dark. Mrs. Lee's house was an oasis to him, and he found himself, to his surprise, almost gay in her company. The gaiety was of a very quiet kind, and Sybil, while friendly with him, averred that he was certainly dull; but this dulness had a fascination for Madeleine, who, having tasted many more kinds of the wine of life than Sybil, had learned to value certain delicacies of age and flavour that were lost upon younger and coarser palates. He talked rather slowly and almost with effort, but he had something of the dignity—others call it stiffness—of the old Virginia school, and twenty years of constant responsibility and deferred hope had added a touch of care that bordered closely on sadness. His great attraction was that he never talked or seemed to think of himself. Mrs. Lee trusted in him by instinct. "He is a type!" said she; "he is my idea of George Washington at thirty."

One morning in December, Carrington entered Mrs. Lee's parlour towards noon, and asked if she cared to visit the Capitol.

"You will have a chance of hearing to-day what may be the last great speech of our greatest statesman," said he; "you should come."

"A splendid sample of our na-tive raw material, sir?" asked she, fresh from a reading of Dickens, and his famous picture of American statesmanship.

"Precisely so," said Carrington; "the Prairie Giant of Peonia, the Favourite Son of Illinois; the man who came within three votes of getting the party nomination for the Presidency last spring, and was only defeated because ten small intriguers are sharper than one big one. The Honourable Silas P. Ratcliffe, Senator from Illinois; he will be run for the Presidency yet."

"What does the P. stand for?" asked Sybil.

"I don't remember ever to have heard his middle name," said Carrington. "Perhaps it is Peonia or Prairie; I can't say."

"He is the man whose appearance struck me so much when we

were in the Senate last week, is he not? A great, ponderous man, over six feet high, very senatorial and dignified, with a large head and rather good features?" inquired Mrs. Lee.

"The same," replied Carrington. "By all means hear him speak. He is the stumbling-block of the new President, who is to be allowed no peace unless he makes terms with Ratcliffe; and so every one thinks that the Prairie Giant of Peonia will have the choice of the State or Treasury Department. If he takes either it will be the Treasury, for he is a desperate political manager, and will want the patronage for the next national convention."

Mrs. Lee was delighted to hear the debate, and Carrington was delighted to sit through it by her side, and to exchange running comments with her on the speeches and the speakers.

"Have you ever met the Senator?" asked she.

"I have acted several times as counsel before his committees. He is an excellent chairman, always attentive and generally civil."

"Where was he born?"

"The family is a New England one, and I believe respectable. He came, I think, from some place in the Connecticut Valley, but whether Vermont, New Hampshire, or Massachusetts, I don't know."

"Is he an educated man?"

"He got a kind of classical education at one of the country colleges there. I suspect he has as much education as is good for him. But he went West very soon after leaving college, and being then young and fresh from that hot-bed of abolition, he threw himself into the anti-slavery movement in Illinois, and after a long struggle he rose with the wave. He would not do the same thing now."

"Why not?"

"He is older, more experienced, and not so wise. Besides, he has no longer the time to wait. Can you see his eyes from here? I call them Yankee eyes."

"Don't abuse the Yankees," said Mrs. Lee; "I am half Yankee myself."

"Is that abuse? Do you mean to deny that they have eyes?"

"I concede that there may be eyes among them; but Virginians are not fair judges of their expression."

"Cold eyes," he continued; "steel grey, rather small, not unpleasant in good-humour, diabolic in a passion, but worst when a little suspicious; then they watch you as though you were a young rattlesnake, to be killed when convenient."

"Does he not look you in the face?"

"Yes; but not as though he liked you. His eyes only seem to ask the possible uses you might be put to. Ah, the vice-president has given him the floor; now we shall have it. Hard voice, is it not? like his eyes. Hard manner, like his voice. Hard all through."

"What a pity he is so dreadfully senatorial!" said Mrs. Lee; "otherwise I rather admire him."

"Now he is settling down to his work," continued Carrington. "See how he dodges all the sharp issues. What a thing it is to be a Yankee! What a genius the fellow has for leading a party! Do you see how well it is all done? The new President flattered and conciliated, the party united and given a strong lead. And now we shall see how the President will deal with him. Ten to one on Ratcliffe. Come, there is that stupid ass from Missouri getting up. Let us go."

As they passed down the steps and out into the Avenue, Mrs. Lee turned to Carrington as though she had been reflecting deeply and had at length reached a decision.

"Mr. Carrington," said she, "I want to know Senator Ratcliffe."

"You will meet him to-morrow evening," replied Carrington, "at your senatorial dinner."

The Senator from New York, the Honourable Schuyler Clinton, was an old admirer of Mrs. Lee, and his wife was a cousin of hers, more or less distant. They had lost no time in honouring the letter of credit she thus had upon them, and invited her and her sister to a solemn dinner, as imposing as political dignity could make it. Mr. Carrington, as a connection of hers, was one of the party, and almost the only one among the twenty persons at table who had neither an office, nor a title, nor a constituency. Senator Clinton received Mrs. Lee and her sister with tender enthusiasm, for they were attractive specimens of his constituents. He pressed their hands and evidently restrained himself only by an effort from embracing them, for the Senator had a marked regard for pretty women, and had made love to every girl with any pretensions to beauty that had appeared in the State of New York for fully half a century. At the same time he whispered an apology in her ear; he regretted so much that he was obliged to forego the pleasure of taking her to dinner; Washington was the only city in America where this could have happened, but it was a fact that ladies here were very great sticklers for etiquette; on the other hand he had the sad consolation that she would be the gainer, for he had allotted to her Lord Skye, the British Minister, "a most agreeable man and not married, as I have the misfortune to be;" and on the other side "I have ventured to place Senator Ratcliffe, of Illinois, whose admirable speech I saw you listening to with such rapt attention yesterday. I thought you might like to know him. Did I do right?" Madeleine assured him that he had divined her inmost wishes, and he turned with even more warmth of affection to her sister: "As for you, my dear—dear Sybil, what can I do to make your dinner agreeable? If I give your sister a coronet, I am only sorry not to have a diadem for you. But I have done everything in my power. The first Secretary of the Russian Legation, Count Popoff, will take you in; a charming young man, my dear Sybil; and on your other side I have placed the Assistant Secretary of State, whom you know." And so, after the due delay, the party settled themselves at the dinner-table, and Mrs. Lee found Senator Ratcliffe's grey eyes resting on her face for a moment as they sat down.

Lord Skye was very agreeable, and, at almost any other moment of her life, Mrs. Lee would have liked nothing better than to talk with him from the beginning to the end of her dinner. Tall, slender, bald-headed, awkward, and stammering with his elaborate British stammer whenever it suited his convenience to do so; a sharp observer who had wit which he commonly concealed; a humourist who was satisfied to laugh silently at his own humour; a diplomatist who used the mask of frankness with great effect; Lord Skye was one of the most popular men in Washington. Every one knew that he was a ruthless critic of American manners, but he had the art to combine ridicule with good-humour, and he was all the more popular accordingly. He was an outspoken admirer of American women in everything except their voices, and he did not even shrink from occasionally quizzing a little the national peculiarities of his own countrywomen; a sure piece of flattery to their American cousins. He would gladly have devoted himself to Mrs. Lee, but decent civility required that he should pay some attention to his hostess, and he was too good a diplomatist not to be attentive to a hostess who was the wife of a Senator, and that Senator the chairman of the committee of foreign relations.

The moment his head was turned, Mrs. Lee dashed at her Peonia Giant, who was then consuming his fish, and wishing he understood why the British Minister had worn no gloves, while he himself had sacrificed his convictions by wearing the largest and whitest pair of French kids that could be bought for money on Pennsylvania Avenue. There was a little touch of mortification in the idea that he was not quite at home among fashionable people, and at this instant he felt that true happiness was only to be found among the simple and honest sons and daughters of toil. A certain secret jealousy of the British Minister is always lurking in the breast of every American Senator, if he is truly democratic; for democracy, rightly understood, is the government of the people, by the people, for the benefit of Senators, and there is always a danger that the British

Minister may not understand this political principle as he should. Lord Skye had run the risk of making two blunders; of offending the Senator from New York by neglecting his wife, and the Senator from Illinois by engrossing the attention of Mrs. Lee. A young Englishman would have done both, but Lord Skye had studied the American constitution. The wife of the Senator from New York now thought him most agreeable, and at the same moment the Senator from Illinois awoke to the conviction that after all, even in frivolous and fashionable circles, true dignity is in no danger of neglect; an American Senator represents a sovereign state; the great state of Illinois is as big as England—with the convenient omission of Wales, Scotland, Ireland, Canada, India, Australia, and a few other continents and islands; and in short, it was perfectly clear that Lord Skye was not formidable to him, even in light society; had not Mrs. Lee herself as good as said that no position equalled that of an American Senator?

In ten minutes Mrs. Lee had this devoted statesman at her feet. She had not studied the Senate without a purpose. She had read with unerring instinct one general characteristic of all Senators, a boundless and guileless thirst for flattery, engendered by daily draughts from political friends or dependents, then becoming a necessity like a dram, and swallowed with a heavy smile of ineffable content. A single glance at Mr. Ratcliffe's face showed Madeleine that she need not be afraid of flattering too grossly; her own self-respect, not his, was the only restraint upon her use of this feminine bait.

She opened upon him with an apparent simplicity and gravity, a quiet repose of manner, and an evident consciousness of her own strength, which meant that she was most dangerous.

"I heard your speech yesterday, Mr. Ratcliffe. I am glad to have a chance of telling you how much I was impressed by it. It seemed to me masterly. Do you not find that it has had a great effect?"

"I thank you, madam. I hope it will help to unite the party, but as yet we have had no time to measure its results. That will require several days more." The Senator spoke in his senatorial manner, elaborate, condescending, and a little on his guard.

"Do you know," said Mrs. Lee, turning towards him as though he were a valued friend, and looking deep into his eyes, "Do you know that every one told me I should be shocked by the falling off in political ability at Washington? I did not believe them, and since hearing your speech I am sure they are mistaken. Do you yourself think there is less ability in Congress than there used to be?"

"Well, madam, it is difficult to answer that question. Government is not so easy now as it was formerly. There are different customs. There are many men of fair abilities in public life; many more than there used to be; and there is sharper criticism and more of it."

"Was I right in thinking that you have a strong resemblance to Daniel Webster in your way of speaking? You come from the same neighbourhood, do you not?"

Mrs. Lee here hit on Ratcliffe's weak point; the outline of his head had, in fact, a certain resemblance to that of Webster, and he prided himself upon it, and on a distant relationship to the Expounder of the Constitution; he began to think that Mrs. Lee was a very intelligent person. His modest admission of the resemblance gave her the opportunity to talk of Webster's oratory, and the conversation soon spread to a discussion of the merits of Clay and Calhoun. The Senator found that his neighbour—a fashionable New York woman, exquisitely dressed, and with a voice and manner seductively soft and gentle—had read the speeches of Webster and Calhoun. She did not think it necessary to tell him that she had persuaded the honest Carrington to bring her the volumes and to mark such passages as were worth her reading; but she took care to lead the conversation, and she criticised with some skill and more humour the weak points in Websterian oratory, saying with a little laugh and a glance into his delighted eyes:

"My judgment may not be worth much, Mr. Senator, but it does seem to me that our fathers thought too much of themselves, and till you teach me better I shall continue to think that the passage in your speech of yesterday which began with, 'Our strength lies in this twisted and tangled mass of isolated principles, the hair of the half-sleeping giant of Party,' is both for language and imagery quite equal to anything of Webster's."

The Senator from Illinois rose to this gaudy fly like a huge, two-hundred-pound salmon; his white waistcoat gave out a mild silver reflection as he slowly came to the surface and gorged the hook. He made not even a plunge, not one perceptible effort to tear out the barbed weapon, but, floating gently to her feet, allowed himself to be landed as though it were a pleasure. Only miserable casuists will ask whether this was fair play on Madeleine's part; whether flattery so gross cost her conscience no twinge, and whether any woman can without self-abasement be guilty of such shameless falsehood. She, however, scorned the idea of falsehood. She would have defended herself by saying that she had not so much praised Ratcliffe as depreciated Webster, and that she was honest in her opinion of the old-fashioned American oratory. But she could not deny that she had wilfully allowed the Senator to draw conclusions very different from any she actually held. She could not deny that she had intended to flatter him to the extent necessary for her pur-pose, and that she was pleased at her success. Before they rose from table the Senator had quite unbent himself; he was talking natu-rally, shrewdly, and with some humour; he had told her Illinois stories; spoken with extraordinary freedom about his political situa-tion; and expressed the wish to call upon Mrs. Lee, if he could ever hope to find her at home.

"I am always at home on Sunday evenings," said she.

To her eyes he was the high-priest of American politics; he was charged with the meaning of the mysteries, the clue to political hieroglyphics. Through him she hoped to sound the depths of statesmanship and to bring up from its oozy bed that pearl of which she was in search; the mysterious gem which must lie hidden somewhere in politics. She wanted to understand this man; to turn him inside out; to experiment on him and use him as young physiologists use frogs and kittens. If there was good or bad in him, she meant to find its meaning.

And he was a western widower of fifty; his quarters in Washington were in gaunt boarding-house rooms, furnished only with public documents and enlivened by western politicians and office-seekers. In the summer he retired to a solitary, white framehouse with green blinds, surrounded by a few feet of uncared-for grass and a white fence; its interior more dreary still, with iron stoves, oil-cloth carpets, cold white walls, and one large engraving of Abraham Lincoln in the parlour; all in Peonia, Illinois! What equality was there between these two combatants? what hope for him? what risk for her? And yet Madeleine Lee had fully her match in Mr. Silas P. Ratcliffe.

CHAPTER III

Mrs. Lee soon became popular. Her parlour was a favourite haunt of certain men and women who had the art of finding its mistress at home; an art which seemed not to be within the powers of everybody. Carrington was apt to be there more often than any one else, so that he was looked on as almost a part of the family, and if Madeleine wanted a book from the library, or an extra man at her dinner-table, Carrington was pretty certain to help her to the one or the other. Old Baron Jacobi, the Bulgarian minister, fell madly in love with both sisters, as he commonly did with every pretty face and neat figure. He was a witty, cynical, broken-down Parisian *roué*, kept in Washington for years past by his debts and his salary; always grumbling because there was no opera, and mysteriously disappearing on visits to New York; a voracious devourer of French and German literature, especially of novels; a man who seemed to have met every noted or notorious personage of the century, and whose mind was a magazine of amusing information; an excellent musical critic, who was not afraid to criticise Sybil's singing; a connoisseur in bric-à-brac, who laughed at Madeleine's display of odds and ends, and occasionally brought her a Persian plate or a bit of embroidery, which he said was good and would do her credit. This old sinner believed in everything that was perverse and wicked, but he accepted the prejudices of Anglo-Saxon society, and was too clever to obtrude his opinions upon others. He would have married both sisters at once more willingly than either alone, but as he feelingly said, "If I were forty years younger, mademoiselle, you should not sing to me so calmly." His friend Popoff, an intelligent, vivacious Russian, with very Calmuck features, susceptible as a girl, and passionately fond of music, hung over Sybil's piano by the hour; he brought Russian airs which he taught her to sing, and, if the truth were known, he bored Madeleine desperately, for she undertook to act the part of duenna to her younger sister.

A very different visitor was Mr. C. C. French, a young member of Congress from Connecticut, who aspired to act the part of the educated gentleman in politics, and to purify the public tone. He had reform principles and an unfortunately conceited manner; he was rather wealthy, rather clever, rather well-educated, rather honest, and rather vulgar. His allegiance was divided between Mrs. Lee and her sister, whom he infuriated by addressing as "Miss Sybil" with patronising familiarity. He was particularly strong in what he called "badinaige," and his playful but ungainly attempts at wit drove Mrs. Lee beyond the bounds of patience. When in a solemn mood, he talked as though he were practising for the ear of a college debating society, and with a still worse effect on the patience; but with all this he was useful, always bubbling with the latest political gossip, and deeply interested in the fate of party stakes.

Quite another sort of person was Mr. Hartbeest Schneidekoupon, a citizen of Philadelphia, though commonly resident in New York, where he had fallen a victim to Sybil's charms, and made efforts to win her young affections by instructing her in the mysteries of currency and protection, to both which subjects he was devoted. To forward these two interests and to watch over Miss

Ross's welfare, he made periodical visits to Washington, where he closeted himself with committee-men and gave expensive dinners to members of Congress. Mr. Schneidekoupon was rich, and about thirty years old, tall and thin, with bright eyes and smooth face, elaborate manners and much loquacity. He had the reputation of turning rapid intellectual somersaults, partly to amuse himself and partly to startle society. At one moment he was artistic, and discoursed scientifically about his own paintings; at another he was literary, and wrote a book on "Noble Living," with a humanitarian purpose; at another he was devoted to sport, rode a steeplechase, played polo, and set up a four-in-hand; his last occupation was to establish in Philadelphia the *Protective Review,* a periodical in the interests of American industry, which he edited himself, as a stepping-stone to Congress, the Cabinet, and the Presidency. At about the same time he bought a yacht, and heavy bets were pending among his sporting friends whether he would manage to sink first his Review or his yacht. But he was an amiable and excellent fellow through all his eccentricities, and he brought to Mrs. Lee the simple outpourings of the amateur politician.

A much higher type of character was Mr. Nathan Gore, of Massachusetts, a handsome man with a grey beard, a straight, sharply-cut nose, and a fine, penetrating eye; in his youth a successful poet whose satires made a noise in their day, and are still remembered for the pungency and wit of a few verses; then a deep student in Europe for many years, until his famous "History of Spain in America" placed him instantly at the head of American historians, and made him minister at Madrid, where he remained four years to his entire satisfaction, this being the nearest approach to a patent of nobility and a government pension which the American citizen can attain. A change of administration had reduced him to private life again, and after some years of retirement he was now in Washington, willing to be restored to his old mission. Every President thinks it respectable to have at least one literary man in his pay, and

Mr. Gore's prospects were fair for obtaining his object, as he had the active support of a majority of the Massachusetts delegation. He was abominably selfish, colossally egoistic, and not a little vain; but he was shrewd; he knew how to hold his tongue; he could flatter dexterously, and he had learned to eschew satire. Only in confidence and among friends he would still talk freely, but Mrs. Lee was not yet on those terms with him.

These were all men, and there was no want of women in Mrs. Lee's parlour; but, after all, they are able to describe themselves better than any poor novelist can describe them.

Generally two currents of conversation ran on together—one round Sybil, the other about Madeleine.

"Mees Ross," said Count Popoff, leading in a handsome young foreigner, "I have your permission to present to you my friend Count Orsini, Secretary of the Italian Legation. Are you at home this afternoon? Count Orsini sings also."

"We are charmed to see Count Orsini. It is well you came so late, for I have this moment come in from making Cabinet calls. They were so queer! I have been crying with laughter for an hour past."

"Do you find these calls amusing?" asked Popoff, gravely and diplomatically.

"Indeed I do! I went with Julia Schneidekoupon, you know, Madeleine; the Schneidekoupons are descended from all the Kings of Israel, and are prouder than Solomon in his glory. And when we got into the house of some dreadful woman from Heaven knows where, imagine my feelings at overhearing this conversation: 'What may be your family name, ma'am?' 'Schneidekoupon is my name,' replies Julia, very tall and straight. 'Have you any friends whom I should likely know?' 'I think not,' says Julia, severely. 'Wal! I don't seem to remember of ever having heerd the name. But I s'pose it's all right. I like to know who calls.' I almost had hysterics when we got into the street, but Julia could not see the joke at all."

Count Orsini was not quite sure that he himself saw the joke, so he only smiled becomingly and showed his teeth. For simple, child-like vanity and self-consciousness nothing equals an Italian Secretary of Legation at twenty-five. Yet conscious that the effect of his personal beauty would perhaps be diminished by permanent silence, he ventured to murmur presently: "Do you not find it very strange, this society in America?"

"Society!" laughed Sybil with gay contempt. "There are no snakes in America, any more than in Norway."

"Snakes, mademoiselle!" repeated Orsini, with the doubtful expression of one who is not quite certain whether he shall risk walking on thin ice, and decides to go softly: "Snakes! Indeed they would rather be doves I would call them."

A kind laugh from Sybil strengthened into conviction his hope that he had made a joke in this unknown tongue. His face brightened, his confidence returned; once or twice he softly repeated to himself: "Not snakes; they would be doves!"

But Mrs. Lee's sensitive ear had caught Sybil's remark, and detected in it a certain tone of condescension which was not to her taste. The impassive countenances of these bland young Secretaries of Legation seemed to acquiesce far too much as a matter of course in the idea that there was no society except in the old world. She broke into the conversation with an emphasis that fluttered the dove-cote:

"Society in America? Indeed there is society in America, and very good society too; but it has a code of its own, and new-comers seldom understand it. I will tell you what it is, Mr. Orsini, and you will never be in danger of making any mistake. 'Society' in America means all the honest, kindly mannered, pleasant-voiced women, and all the good, brave, unassuming men, between the Atlantic and the Pacific. Each of these has a free pass in every city and village, 'good for this generation only,' and it depends on each to make use of this pass or not as it may happen to suit his or her fancy. To this rule there are *no* exceptions, and those who say 'Abraham is our father' will surely furnish food for that humour which is the staple product of our country."

The alarmed youths, who did not in the least understand the meaning of this demonstration, looked on with a feeble attempt at acquiescence, while Mrs. Lee brandished her sugar-tongs in the act of transferring a lump of sugar to her cup, quite unconscious of the slight absurdity of the gesture, while Sybil stared in amazement, for it was not often that her sister waved the stars and stripes so energetically. Whatever their silent criticisms might be, however, Mrs. Lee was too much in earnest to be conscious of them, or, indeed, to care for anything but what she was saying. There was a moment's pause when she came to the end of her speech, and then the thread of talk was quietly taken up again where Sybil's incipient sneer had broken it.

Carrington came in.

"What have you been doing at the Capitol?" asked Madeleine.

"Lobbying!" was the reply, given in the semi-serious tone of Carrington's humour.

"So soon, and Congress only two days old?" exclaimed Mrs. Lee.

"Madam," rejoined Carrington, with his quietest malice, "Congressmen are like birds of the air, which are caught only by the early worm."

"Good afternoon, Mrs. Lee. Miss Sybil, how do you do again? Which of these gentlemen's hearts are you feeding upon now?" This was the refined style of Mr. French, indulging in what he was pleased to term "badinaige." He, too, was on his way from the Capitol, and had come in for a cup of tea and a little human society. Sybil made a face which plainly expressed a longing to inflict on Mr. French some grievous personal wrong, but she pretended not to hear. He sat down by Madeleine, and asked, "Did you see Ratcliffe yesterday?"

"Yes," said Madeleine; "he was here last evening with Mr. Carrington and one or two others."

"Did he say anything about politics?"

"Not a word. We talked mostly about books."

"Books! What does he know about books?"

"You must ask him."

"Well, this is the most ridiculous situation we are all in. No one knows anything about the new President. You could take your oath that everybody is in the dark. Ratcliffe says he knows as little as the rest of us, but it can't be true; he is too old a politician not to have wires in his hand; and only to-day one of the pages of the Senate told my colleague Cutter that a letter sent off by him yesterday was directed to Sam Grimes, of North Bend, who, as every one knows, belongs to the President's particular crowd.—Why, Mr. Schneidekoupon! How do you do? When did you come on?"

"Thank you; this morning," replied Mr. Schneidekoupon, just entering the room. "So glad to see you again, Mrs. Lee. How do you and your sister like Washington? Do you know I have brought Julia on for a visit? I thought I should find her here."

"She has just gone. She has been all the afternoon with Sybil, making calls. She says you want her here to lobby for you, Mr. Schneidekoupon. Is it true?"

"So I did," replied he, with a laugh, "but she is precious little use. So I've come to draft you into the service."

"Me!"

"Yes; you know we all expect Senator Ratcliffe to be Secretary of the Treasury, and it is very important for us to keep him straight on the currency and the tariff. So I have come on to establish more intimate relations with him, as they say in diplomacy. I want to get him to dine with me at Welckley's, but as I know he keeps very shy of politics I thought my only chance was to make it a ladies' dinner, so I brought on Julia. I shall try and get Mrs. Schuyler Clinton, and I depend upon you and your sister to help Julia out."

"Me! at a lobby dinner! Is that proper?"

"Why not? You shall choose the guests."

"I never heard of such a thing; but it would certainly be amusing. Sybil must not go, but I might."

"Excuse me; Julia depends upon Miss Ross, and will not go to table without her."

"Well," assented Mrs. Lee, hesitatingly, "perhaps if you get Mrs. Clinton, and if your sister is there—— And who else?"

"Choose your own company."

"I know no one."

"Oh yes; here is French, not quite sound on the tariff, but good for what we want just now. Then we can get Mr. Gore; he has his little hatchet to grind too, and will be glad to help grind ours. We only want two or three more, and I will have an extra man or so to fill up."

"Do ask the Speaker. I want to know him."

"I will, and Carrington, and my Pennsylvania Senator. That will do nobly. Remember, Welckley's, Saturday at seven."

Meanwhile Sybil had been at the piano, and when she had sung for a time, Orsini was induced to take her place, and show that it was possible to sing without injury to one's beauty. Baron Jacobi came in and found fault with them both. Little Miss Dare—commonly known among her male friends as little Daredevil—who was always absorbed in some flirtation with a Secretary of Legation, came in, quite unaware that Popoff was present, and retired with him into a corner, while Orsini and Jacobi bullied poor Sybil, and fought with each other at the piano; everybody was talking with very little reference to any reply, when at last Mrs. Lee drove them all out of the room: "We are quiet people," said she, "and we dine at half-past six."

Senator Ratcliffe had not failed to make his Sunday evening call upon Mrs. Lee. Perhaps it was not strictly correct to say that they had talked books all the evening, but whatever the conversation was, it had only confirmed Mr. Ratcliffe's admiration for Mrs. Lee, who, without intending to do so, had acted a more dangerous part than if she had been the most accomplished of coquettes. Nothing could be more fascinating to the weary politician in his solitude than the repose of Mrs. Lee's parlour, and when Sybil sang for him one or two simple airs—she said they were foreign hymns, the Senator being, or being considered, orthodox—Mr. Ratcliffe's heart yearned toward the charming girl quite with the sensations of a father, or even of an elder brother.

His brother senators very soon began to remark that the Prairie Giant had acquired a trick of looking up to the ladies' gallery. One day Mr. Jonathan Andrews, the special correspondent of the New York *Sidereal System,* a very friendly organ, approached Senator Schuyler Clinton with a puzzled look on his face.

"Can you tell me," said he, "what has happened to Silas P. Ratcliffe? Only a moment ago I was talking with him at his seat on a very important subject, about which I must send his opinions off to New York to-night, when, in the middle of a sentence, he stopped short, got up without looking at me, and left the Senate Chamber, and now I see him in the gallery talking with a lady whose face I don't know."

Senator Clinton slowly adjusted his gold eyeglasses and looked up at the place indicated: "Ah! Mrs. Lightfoot Lee! I think I will say a word to her myself;" and turning his back on the special correspondent, he skipped away with youthful agility after the Senator from Illinois.

"Devil!" muttered Mr. Andrews; "what has got into the old fools?" and in a still less audible murmur as he looked up to Mrs. Lee, then in close conversation with Ratcliffe: "Had I better make an item of that?"

When young Mr. Schneidekoupon called upon Senator Ratcliffe to invite him to the dinner at Welckley's, he found that gentleman overwhelmed with work, as he averred, and very little disposed to converse. No! he did not now go out to dinner. In the present condition of the public business he found it impossible to spare the time for such amusements. He regretted to decline Mr. Schneidekoupon's civility, but there were imperative reasons why he should abstain for the present from social entertainments; he had made but one exception to his rule, and only at the pressing request of his old friend Senator Clinton, and on a very special occasion.

Mr. Schneidekoupon was deeply vexed—the more, he said, because he had meant to beg Mr. and Mrs. Clinton to be of the party, as well as a very charming lady who rarely went into society, but who had almost consented to come.

"Who is that?" inquired the Senator.

"A Mrs. Lightfoot Lee, of New York. Probably you do not know her well enough to admire her as I do; but I think her quite the most intelligent woman I ever met."

The Senator's cold eyes rested for a moment on the young man's open face with a peculiar expression of distrust. Then he solemnly said, in his deepest senatorial tones:

"My young friend, at my time of life men have other things to occupy them than women, however intelligent they may be. Who else is to be of your party?"

Mr. Schneidekoupon named his list.

"And for Saturday evening at seven, did you say?"

"Saturday at seven."

"I fear there is little chance of my attending, but I will not absolutely decline. Perhaps when the moment arrives, I may find myself able to be there. But do not count upon me—do not count upon me. Good day, Mr. Schneidekoupon."

Schneidekoupon was rather a simple-minded young man, who saw no deeper than his neighbours into the secrets of the universe, and he went off swearing roundly at "the infernal airs these senators give themselves." He told Mrs. Lee all the conversation, as indeed he was compelled to do under penalty of bringing her to his party under false pretences.

"Just my luck," said he; "here I am forced to ask no end of people to meet a man, who at the same time says he shall probably not come. Why, under the stars, couldn't he say, like other people, whether he was coming or not? I've known dozens of senators, Mrs. Lee, and they're all like that. They never think of any one but themselves."

Mrs. Lee smiled rather a forced smile, and soothed his wounded feelings; she had no doubt the dinner would be very agreeable whether the Senator were there or not; at any rate she would do all she could to carry it off well, and Sybil should wear her newest dress. Still she was a little grave, and Mr. Schneidekoupon could only declare that she was a trump; that he had told Ratcliffe she was the cleverest woman he ever met, and he might have added the most obliging, and Ratcliffe had only looked at him as though he were a green ape. At all which Mrs. Lee laughed good-naturedly, and sent him away as soon as she could.

When he was gone, she walked up and down the room and thought. She saw the meaning of Ratcliffe's sudden change in tone. She had no more doubt of his coming to the dinner than she had of the reason why he came. And was it possible that she was being drawn into something very near a flirtation with a man twenty years her senior; a politician from Illinois; a huge, ponderous, grey-eyed, bald senator, with a Websterian head, who lived in Peonia? The idea was almost too absurd to be credited; but on the whole the thing itself was rather amusing. "I suppose senators can look out for themselves like other men," was her final conclusion. She thought only of his danger, and she felt a sort of compassion for him as she reflected on the possible consequences of a great, absorbing love at his time of life. Her conscience was a little uneasy; but of herself she never thought. Yet it is a historical fact that elderly senators have had a curious fascination for young and handsome women. Had *they* looked out for themselves too? And which parties most needed to be looked after?

When Madeleine and her sister arrived at Welckley's the next Saturday evening, they found poor Schneidekoupon in a temper very unbecoming a host.

"He won't come! I told you he wouldn't come!" said he to Madeleine, as he handed her into the house. "If I ever turn communist, it will be for the fun of murdering a senator."

Madeleine consoled him gently, but he continued to use, behind Mr. Clinton's back, language the most offensive and improper towards the Senate, and at last, ringing the bell, he sharply ordered the head waiter to serve dinner. At that very moment the door opened, and Senator Ratcliffe's stately figure appeared on the threshold. His eye instantly caught Madeleine's, and she almost laughed aloud, for she saw that the Senator was dressed with very unsenatorial neatness; that he had actually a flower in his button-hole and no gloves!

After the enthusiastic description which Schneidekoupon had given of Mrs. Lee's charms, he could do no less than ask Senator Ratcliffe to take her in to dinner, which he did without delay. Either this, or the champagne, or some occult influence, had an extraordinary effect upon him. He appeared ten years younger than usual; his face was illuminated; his eyes glowed; he seemed bent on proving his kinship to the immortal Webster by rivalling his convivial powers. He dashed into the conversation; laughed, jested, and ridiculed; told stories in Yankee and Western dialect; gave sharp little sketches of amusing political experiences.

"Never was more surprised in my life," whispered Senator Krebs, of Pennsylvania, across the table to Schneidekoupon. "Hadn't an idea that Ratcliffe was so entertaining."

And Mr. Clinton, who sat by Madeleine on the other side, whispered low into her ear: "I am afraid, my dear Mrs. Lee, that you are responsible for this. He never talks so to the Senate."

Nay, he even rose to a higher flight, and told the story of President Lincoln's death-bed with a degree of feeling that brought tears into their eyes. The other guests made no figure at all. The Speaker consumed his solitary duck and his lonely champagne in a corner without giving a sign. Even Mr. Gore, who was not wont to hide his light under any kind of extinguisher, made no attempt to claim the floor, and applauded with enthusiasm the conversation of his opposite neighbour. Ill-natured people might say that Mr. Gore saw in Senator Ratcliffe a possible Secretary of State; be this as it may, he certainly said to Mrs. Clinton, in an aside that was perfectly audible to every one at the table: "How brilliant! what an original mind! what a sensation he would make abroad!" And it was quite true, apart from the mere momentary effect of dinner-table talk, that there was a certain bigness about the man; a keen practical sagacity; a bold freedom of self-assertion; a broad way of dealing with what he knew. Carrington was the only person at table who looked on with a perfectly cool head, and who criticised in a hostile spirit. Carrington's impression of Ratcliffe was perhaps beginning to be warped by a shade of jealousy, for he was in a peculiarly bad temper this evening, and his irritation was not wholly concealed.

"If one only had any confidence in the man!" he muttered to French, who sat by him.

This unlucky remark set French to thinking how he could draw Ratcliffe out, and accordingly, with his usual happy manner, combining self-conceit and high principles, he began to attack the Senator with some "badinaige" on the delicate subject of Civil Service Reform, a subject almost as dangerous in political conversation at Washington as slavery itself in old days before the war. French was a reformer, and lost no occasion of impressing his views; but unluckily he was a very light weight, and his manner was a little ridiculous, so that even Mrs. Lee, who was herself a warm reformer, sometimes went over to the other side when he talked. No sooner had he now shot his little arrow at the Senator, than that astute man saw his opportunity, and promised himself the pleasure of administering to Mr. French punishment such as he knew would delight the company. Reformer as Mrs. Lee was, and a little alarmed at the roughness of Ratcliffe's treatment, she could not blame the Prairie Giant, as she ought, who, after knocking poor French down, rolled him over and over in the mud.

"Are you financier enough, Mr. French, to know what are the most famous products of Connecticut?"

Mr. French modestly suggested that he thought its statesmen best answered that description.

"No, sir! even there you're wrong. The showmen beat you on your own ground. But every child in the union knows that the most famous products of Connecticut are Yankee notions, nutmegs made of wood and clocks that won't go. Now, your Civil Service Reform is just such another Yankee notion; it's a wooden nutmeg; it's a clock with a show case and sham works. And you know it! You are precisely the old-school Connecticut peddler. You have gone about peddling your wooden nutmegs until you have got yourself into Congress, and now you pull them out of your pockets and not only want us to take them at your own price, but you lecture us on our sins if we don't. Well! we don't mind your doing that at home. Abuse us as much as you like to your constituents. Get as many votes as you can. But don't electioneer here, because we know you intimately, and we've all been a little in the wooden nutmeg business ourselves."

Senator Clinton and Senator Krebs chuckled high approval over this punishment of poor French, which was on the level of their idea of wit. They were all in the nutmeg business, as Ratcliffe said. The victim tried to make head against them; he protested that his nutmegs were genuine; he sold no goods that he did not guarantee; and that this particular article was actually guaranteed by the national conventions of both political parties.

"Then what you want, Mr. French, is a common school education. You need a little study of the alphabet. Or if you won't believe me, ask my brother senators here what chance there is for your Reforms so long as the American citizen is what he is."

"You'll not get much comfort in my State, Mr. French," growled the senator from Pennsylvania, with a sneer; "suppose you come and try."

"Well, well!" said the benevolent Mr. Schuyler Clinton, gleaming benignantly through his gold spectacles; "don't be too hard on French. He means well. Perhaps he's not very wise, but he does good. I know more about it than any of you, and I don't deny that the thing is all bad. Only, as Mr. Ratcliffe says, the difficulty is in the people, not in us. Go to work on them, French, and let us alone."

French repented of his attack, and contented himself by muttering to Carrington: "What a set of damned old reprobates they are!"

"They are right, though, in one thing," was Carrington's reply: "their advice is good. Never ask one of them to reform anything; if you do, you will be reformed yourself."

The dinner ended as brilliantly as it began, and Schneidekoupon was delighted with his success. He had made himself particularly agreeable to Sybil by confiding in her all his hopes and fears about the tariff and the finances. When the ladies left the table, Ratcliffe could not stay for a cigar; he must get back to his rooms, where he knew several men were waiting for him; he would take his leave of the ladies and hurry away. But when the gentlemen came up nearly an hour afterwards they found Ratcliffe still taking his leave of the ladies, who were delighted at his entertaining conversation; and when at last he really departed, he said to Mrs. Lee, as though it were quite a matter of course: "You are at home as usual tomorrow evening?" Madeleine smiled, bowed, and he went his way.

As the two sisters drove home that night, Madeleine was unusually silent. Sybil yawned convulsively and then apologized:

"Mr. Schneidekoupon is very nice and good-natured, but a whole evening of him goes a long way; and that horrid Senator Krebs would not say a word, and drank a great deal too much wine, though it couldn't make him any more stupid than he is. I don't think I care for senators." Then, wearily, after a pause: "Well, Maude, I do hope you've got what you wanted. I'm sure you must have had politics enough. Haven't you got to the heart of your great American mystery yet?"

"Pretty near it, I think," said Madeleine, half to herself.

CHAPTER IV

Sunday evening was stormy, and some enthusiasm was required to make one face its perils for the sake of society. Nevertheless, a few intimates made their appearance as usual at Mrs. Lee's. The faithful Popoff was there, and Miss Dare also ran in to pass an hour with her dear Sybil; but as she passed the whole evening in a corner with Popoff, she must have been disappointed in her object. Carrington came, and Baron Jacobi. Schneidekoupon and his sister dined with Mrs. Lee, and remained after dinner, while Sybil and Julia Schneidekoupon compared conclusions about Washington society. The happy idea also occurred to Mr. Gore that, inasmuch as Mrs. Lee's house was but a step from his hotel, he might as well take the chance of amusement there as the certainty of solitude in his rooms. Finally, Senator Ratcliffe duly made his appearance, and, having established himself with a cup of tea by Madeleine's side, was soon left to enjoy a quiet talk with her, the rest of the party by common consent occupying themselves with each other. Under cover of the murmur of conversation in the room, Mr. Ratcliffe quickly became confidential.

"I came to suggest that, if you want to hear an interesting debate, you should come up to the Senate to-morrow. I am told that Garrard, of Louisiana, means to attack my last speech, and I shall probably in that case have to answer him. With you for a critic I shall speak better."

"Am I such an amiable critic?" asked Madeleine.

"I never heard that amiable critics were the best," said he; "justice is the soul of good criticism, and it is only justice that I ask and expect from you."

"What good does this speaking do?" inquired she. "Are you any nearer the end of your difficulties by means of your speeches?"

"I hardly know yet. Just now we are in dead water; but this can't last long. In fact, I am not afraid to tell you, though of course you will not repeat it to any human being, that we have taken measures to force an issue. Certain gentlemen, myself among the rest, have written letters meant for the President's eye, though not addressed directly to him, and intended to draw out an expression of some sort that will show us what to expect."

"Oh!" laughed Madeleine, "I knew about that a week ago."

"About what?"

"About your letter to Sam Grimes, of North Bend."

"What have you heard about my letter to Sam Grimes, of North Bend?" ejaculated Ratcliffe, a little abruptly.

"Oh, you do not know how admirably I have organised my secret service bureau," said she. "Representative Cutter cross-questioned one of the Senate pages, and obliged him to confess that he had received from you a letter to be posted, which letter was addressed to Mr. Grimes, of North Bend."

"And, of course, he told this to French, and French told you," said Ratcliffe; "I see. If I had known this I would not have let French off so gently last night, for I prefer to tell you my own story without his embellishments. But it was my fault. I should not have trusted a page. Nothing is a secret here long. But one thing that

Mr. Cutter did not find out was that several other gentlemen wrote letters at the same time, for the same purpose. Your friend, Mr. Clinton, wrote; Krebs wrote; and one or two members."

"I suppose I must not ask what you said?"

"You may. We agreed that it was best to be very mild and conciliatory, and to urge the President only to give us some indication of his intentions, in order that we might not run counter to them. I drew a strong picture of the effect of the present situation on the party, and hinted that I had no personal wishes to gratify."

"And what do you think will be the result?"

"I think we shall somehow manage to straighten things out," said Ratcliffe. "The difficulty is only that the new President has little experience, and is suspicious. He thinks we shall intrigue to tie his hands, and he means to tie ours in advance. I don't know him personally, but those who do, and who are fair judges, say that, though rather narrow and obstinate, he is honest enough, and will come round. I have no doubt I could settle it all with him in an hour's talk, but it is out of the question for me to go to him unless I am asked, and to ask me to come would be itself a settlement."

"What, then, is the danger you fear?"

"That he will offend all the important party leaders in order to conciliate unimportant ones, perhaps sentimental ones, like your friend French; that he will make foolish appointments without taking advice. By the way, have you seen French to-day?"

"No," replied Madeleine; "I think he must be sore at your treatment of him last evening. You were very rude to him."

"Not a bit," said Ratcliffe; "these reformers need it. His attack on me was meant for a challenge. I saw it in his manner."

"But is reform really so impossible as you describe it? Is it quite hopeless?"

"Reform such as he wants is utterly hopeless, and not even desirable."

Mrs. Lee, with much earnestness of manner, still pressed her question: "Surely something can be done to check corruption. Are we for ever to be at the mercy of thieves and ruffians? Is a respectable government impossible in a democracy?"

Her warmth attracted Jacobi's attention, and he spoke across the room. "What is that you say, Mrs. Lee? What is it about corruption?"

All the gentlemen began to listen and gather about them.

"I am asking Senator Ratcliffe," said she, "what is to become of us if corruption is allowed to go unchecked."

"And may I venture to ask permission to hear Mr. Ratcliffe's reply?" asked the baron.

"My reply," said Ratcliffe, "is that no representative government can long be much better or much worse than the society it represents. Purify society and you purify the government. But try to purify the government artificially and you only aggravate failure."

"A very statesmanlike reply," said Baron Jacobi, with a formal bow, but his tone had a shade of mockery. Carrington, who had listened with a darkening face, suddenly turned to the baron and asked him what conclusion he drew from the reply.

"Ah!" exclaimed the baron, with his wickedest leer, "what for is my conclusion good? You Americans believe yourselves to be excepted from the operation of general laws. You care not for experience. I have lived seventy-five years, and all that time in the midst of corruption. I am corrupt myself, only I do have courage to proclaim it, and you others have it not. Rome, Paris, Vienna, Petersburg, London, all are corrupt; only Washington is pure! Well, I declare to you that in all my experience I have found no society which has had elements of corruption like the United States. The children in the street are corrupt, and know how to cheat me. The cities are all corrupt, and also the towns and the counties and the States' legislatures and the judges. Everywhere men betray trusts both public and private, steal money, run away with public funds. Only in the Senate men take no money. And you gentlemen in the Senate very well declare that your great United States, which is the head of the civilized world, can never learn anything from the example of corrupt Europe. You are right—quite right! The great United States needs not an example. I do much regret that I have not yet one hundred years to live. If I could then come back to this city, I should find myself very content—much more than now. I am always content where there is much corruption, and *ma parole d'honneur!*" broke out the old man with fire and gesture, "the United States will then be more corrupt than Rome under Caligula; more corrupt than the Church under Leo X.; more corrupt than France under the Regent!"

As the baron closed his little harangue, which he delivered directly at the senator sitting underneath him, he had the satisfaction to see that every one was silent and listening with deep attention. He seemed to enjoy annoying the senator, and he had the satisfaction of seeing that the senator was visibly annoyed. Ratcliffe looked sternly at the baron and said, with some curtness, that he saw no reason to accept such conclusions. Conversation flagged, and all except the baron were relieved when Sybil, at Schneidekoupon's request, sat down at the piano to sing what she called a hymn. So soon as the song was over, Ratcliffe, who seemed to have been curiously thrown off his balance by Jacobi's harangue, pleaded urgent duties at his rooms, and retired. The others soon afterwards went off in a body, leaving only Carrington and Gore, who had seated himself by Madeleine, and was at once dragged by her into a discussion of the subject which perplexed her, and for the moment threw over her mind a net of irresistible fascination.

"The baron discomfited the senator," said Gore, with a certain hesitation. "Why did Ratcliffe let himself be trampled upon in that manner?"

"I wish you would explain why," replied Mrs. Lee; "tell me, Mr. Gore—you who represent cultivation and literary taste hereabouts—please tell me what to think about Baron Jacobi's speech. Who and what is to be believed? Mr. Ratcliffe seems honest and wise. Is he a corruptionist? He believes in the people, or says he does. Is he telling the truth or not?"

Gore was too experienced in politics to be caught in such a trap as this. He evaded the question. "Mr. Ratcliffe has a practical piece of work to do; his business is to make laws and advise the President; he does it extremely well. We have no other equally good practical politician; it is unfair to require him to be a crusader besides."

"No!" interposed Carrington, curtly; "but he need not obstruct crusades. He need not talk virtue and oppose the punishment of vice."

"He is a shrewd practical politician," replied Gore, "and he feels first the weak side of any proposed political tactics."

With a sigh of despair Madeleine went on: "Who, then, is right? How *can* we all be right? Half of our wise men declare that the world is going straight to perdition; the other half that it is fast becoming perfect. Both cannot be right. There is only one thing in life," she went on, laughing, "that I must and will have before I die. I must know whether America is right or wrong. Just now this question is a very practical one, for I really want to know whether to believe in Mr. Ratcliffe. If I throw him overboard, everything must go, for he is only a specimen."

"Why not believe in Mr. Ratcliffe?" said Gore; "I believe in him myself, and am not afraid to say so."

Carrington, to whom Ratcliffe now began to represent the spirit of evil, interposed here, and observed that he imagined Mr. Gore had other guides besides, and steadier ones than Ratcliffe, to believe in; while Madeleine, with a certain feminine perspicacity, struck at a much weaker point in Mr. Gore's armour, and asked point-blank whether he believed also in what Ratcliffe represented: "Do you yourself think democracy the best government, and universal suffrage a success?"

Mr. Gore saw himself pinned to the wall, and he turned at bay with almost the energy of despair:

"These are matters about which I rarely talk in society; they are like the doctrine of a personal God; of a future life; of revealed religion; subjects which one naturally reserves for private reflection. But since you ask for my political creed, you shall have it. I only condition that it shall be for you alone, never to be repeated or quoted as mine. I believe in democracy. I accept it. I will faithfully serve and defend it. I believe in it because it appears to me the inevitable consequence of what has gone before it. Democracy asserts the fact that the masses are now raised to a higher intelligence than formerly. All our civilisation aims at this mark. We want to do what we can to help it. I myself want to see the result. I grant it is an experiment, but it is the only direction society can take that is worth its taking; the only conception of its duty large enough to satisfy its instincts; the only result that is worth an effort or a risk. Every other possible step is backward, and I do not care to repeat the past. I am glad to see society grapple with issues in which no one can afford to be neutral."

"And supposing your experiment fails," said Mrs. Lee; "suppose society destroys itself with universal suffrage, corruption, and communism."

"I wish, Mrs. Lee, you would visit the Observatory with me some evening, and look at Sirius. Did you ever make the acquaintance of a fixed star? I believe astronomers reckon about twenty millions of them in sight, and an infinite possibility of invisible millions, each one of which is a sun, like ours, and may have satellites like our planet. Suppose you see one of these fixed stars suddenly increase in brightness, and are told that a satellite has fallen into it and is burning up, its career finished, its capacities exhausted? Curious, is it not; but what does it matter? Just as much as the burning up of a moth at your candle."

Madeleine shuddered a little. "I cannot get to the height of your philosophy," said she. "You are wandering among the infinites, and I am finite."

"Not at all! But I have faith; not perhaps in the old dogmas, but in the new ones; faith in human nature; faith in science; faith in the survival of the fittest. Let us be true to our time, Mrs. Lee! If our age is to be beaten, let us die in the ranks. If it is to be victorious, let us be first to lead the column. Anyway, let us not be skulkers or grumblers. There! have I repeated my catechism correctly? You would have it! Now oblige me by forgetting it. I should lose my character at home if it got out. Good night!"

Mrs. Lee duly appeared at the Capitol the next day, as she could not but do after Senator Ratcliffe's pointed request. She went alone, for Sybil had positively refused to go near the Capitol again, and Madeleine thought that on the whole this was not an occasion for enrolling Carrington in her service. But Ratcliffe did not speak. The debate was unexpectedly postponed. He joined Mrs. Lee in the gallery, however, sat with her as long as she would allow, and became still more confidential, telling her that he had received the expected reply from Grimes, of North Bend, and that it had enclosed a letter written by the President-elect to Mr. Grimes in regard to the advances made by Mr. Ratcliffe and his friends.

"It is not a handsome letter," said he; "indeed, a part of it is positively insulting. I would like to read you one extract from it, and hear your opinion as to how it should be treated." Taking the letter from his pocket, he sought out the passage, and read as follows: " 'I cannot lose sight, too, of the consideration that these three Senators' (he means Clinton, Krebs, and me) 'are popularly considered to be the most influential members of that so-called senatorial ring, which has acquired such general notoriety. While I shall always receive their communications with all due respect, I must continue to exercise complete freedom of action in consulting other political advisers as well as these, and I must in all cases make it my first object to follow the wishes of the people, not always most truly represented by their nominal representatives.' What say you to that precious piece of presidential manners?"

"At least I like his courage," said Mrs. Lee.

"Courage is one thing; common sense is another. This letter is a studied insult. He has knocked me off the track once. He means to do it again. It is a declaration of war. What ought I to do?"

"Whatever is most for the public good," said Madeleine, gravely.

Ratcliffe looked into her face with such undisguised delight— there was so little possibility of mistaking or ignoring the expression of his eyes, that she shrank back with a certain shock. She was not prepared for so open a demonstration. He hardened his features at once, and went on:

"But what *is* most for the public good?"

"That you know better than I," said Madeleine; "only one thing is clear to me. If you let yourself be ruled by your private feelings, you will make a greater mistake than he. Now I must go, for I have visits to make. The next time I come, Mr. Ratcliffe, you must keep your word better."

When they next met, Ratcliffe read to her a part of his reply to Mr. Grimes, which ran thus: "It is the lot of every party leader to suffer from attacks and to commit errors. It is true, as the President says, that I have been no exception to this law. Believing as I do that great results can only be accomplished by great parties, I have uniformly yielded my own personal opinions where they have failed to obtain general assent. I shall continue to follow this course, and the President may with perfect confidence count upon my disinterested support of all party measures, even though I may not be consulted in originating them."

Mrs. Lee listened attentively, and then said: "Have you never refused to go with your party?"

"Never!" was Ratcliffe's firm reply.

Madeleine still more thoughtfully inquired again: "Is nothing more powerful than party allegiance?"

"Nothing, except national allegiance," replied Ratcliffe, still more firmly.

CHAPTER V

To tie a prominent statesman to her train and to lead him about like a tame bear, is for a young and vivacious woman a more certain amusement than to tie herself to him and to be dragged about like an Indian squaw. This fact was Madeleine Lee's first great political discovery in Washington, and it was worth to her all the German philosophy she had ever read, with even a complete edition of Herbert Spencer's works into the bargain. There could be no doubt that the honours and dignities of a public career were no fair consideration for its pains. She made a little daily task for herself of reading in succession the lives and letters of the American Presidents, and of their wives, when she could find that there was a trace of the latter's existence. What a melancholy spectacle it was, from George Washington down to the last incumbent; what vexations, what disappointments, what grievous mistakes, what very objectionable manners! Not one of them, who had aimed at high purpose, but had been thwarted, beaten, and habitually insulted! What a gloom lay on the features of those famous chieftains, Calhoun, Clay, and Webster; what varied expression of defeat and unsatis-

fied desire; what a sense of self-importance and senatorial magnilo-
quence; what a craving for flattery; what despair at the sentence of
fate! And what did they amount to, after all?

They were practical men, these! they had no great problems of
thought to settle, no questions that rose above the ordinary rules
of common morals and homely duty. How they had managed to
befog the subject! What elaborate show-structures they had built
up, with no result but to obscure the horizon! Would not the country have done better without them? Could it have done worse?
What deeper abyss could have opened under the nation's feet, than
that to whose verge they brought it?

Madeleine's mind wearied with the monotony of the story. She
discussed the subject with Ratcliffe, who told her frankly that
the pleasure of politics lay in the possession of power. He agreed
that the country would do very well without him. "But here I am,"
said he, "and here I mean to stay." He had very little sympathy for
thin moralising, and a statesman-like contempt for philosophical
politics. He loved power, and he meant to be President. That was
enough.

Sometimes the tragic and sometimes the comic side was uppermost in her mind, and sometimes she did not herself know whether
to cry or to laugh. Washington more than any other city in the
world swarms with simple-minded exhibitions of human nature;
men and women curiously out of place, whom it would be cruel to
ridicule and ridiculous to weep over. The sadder exhibitions are
fortunately seldom seen by respectable people; only the little social
accidents come under their eyes. One evening Mrs. Lee went to the
President's first evening reception. As Sybil flatly refused to face
the crowd, and Carrington mildly said that he feared he was not
sufficiently reconstructed to appear at home in that august presence, Mrs. Lee accepted Mr. French for an escort, and walked
across the Square with him to join the throng that was pouring into
the doors of the White House. They took their places in the line of

citizens and were at last able to enter the reception-room. There Madeleine found herself before two seemingly mechanical figures, which might be wood or wax, for any sign they showed of life. These two figures were the President and his wife; they stood stiff and awkward by the door, both their faces stripped of every sign of intelligence, while the right hands of both extended themselves to the column of visitors with the mechanical action of toy dolls. Mrs. Lee for a moment began to laugh, but the laugh died on her lips. To the President and his wife this was clearly no laughing matter. There they stood, automata, representatives of the society which streamed past them. Madeleine seized Mr. French by the arm.

"Take me somewhere at once," said she, "where I can look at it. Here! in the corner. I had no conception how shocking it was!"

Mr. French supposed she was thinking of the queer-looking men and women who were swarming through the rooms, and he made, after his own delicate notion of humour, some uncouth jests on those who passed by. Mrs. Lee, however, was in no humour to explain or even to listen. She stopped him short:—

"There, Mr. French! Now go away and leave me. I want to be alone for half an hour. Please come for me then." And there she stood, with her eyes fixed on the President and his wife, while the endless stream of humanity passed them, shaking hands.

What a strange and solemn spectacle it was, and how the deadly fascination of it burned the image in upon her mind! What a horrid warning to ambition! And in all that crowd there was no one besides herself who felt the mockery of this exhibition. To all the others this task was a regular part of the President's duty, and there was nothing ridiculous about it. They thought it a democratic institution, this droll aping of monarchical forms. To them the deadly dulness of the show was as natural and proper as ever to the courtiers of the Philips and Charleses seemed the ceremonies of the Escurial. To her it had the effect of a nightmare, or of an opium-eater's vision. She felt a sudden conviction that this was to be the end of

American society; its realisation and dream at once. She groaned in spirit.

"Yes! at last I have reached the end! We shall grow to be wax images, and our talk will be like the squeaking of toy dolls. We shall all wander round and round the earth and shake hands. No one will have any object in this world, and there will be no other. It is worse than anything in the 'Inferno.' What an awful vision of eternity!"

Suddenly, as through a mist, she saw the melancholy face of Lord Skye approaching. He came to her side, and his voice recalled her to reality.

"Does it amuse you, this sort of thing?" he asked in a vague way.

"We take our amusement sadly, after the manner of our people," she replied; "but it certainly interests me."

They stood for a time in silence, watching the slowly eddying dance of Democracy, until he resumed:

"Whom do you take that man to be—the long, lean one, with a long woman on each arm?"

"That man," she replied, "I take to be a Washington department-clerk, or perhaps a member of Congress from Iowa, with a wife and wife's sister. Do they shock your nobility?"

He looked at her with comical resignation. "You mean to tell me that they are quite as good as dowager-countesses. I grant it. My aristocratic spirit is broken, Mrs. Lee. I will even ask them to dinner if you bid me, and if you will come to meet them. But the last time I asked a member of Congress to dine, he sent me back a note in pencil on my own envelope that he would bring two of his friends with him, very respectable constituents from Yahoo city, or some such place; nature's noblemen, he said."

"You should have welcomed them."

"I did. I wanted to see two of nature's noblemen, and I knew they would probably be pleasanter company than their representative. They came; very respectable persons, one with a blue necktie, the other with a red one: both had diamond pins in their shirts, and were carefully brushed in respect to their hair. They said nothing, ate little, drank less, and were much better behaved than I am. When they went away, they unanimously asked me to stay with them when I visited Yahoo city."

"You will not want guests if you always do that."

"I don't know. I think it was pure ignorance on their part. They knew no better, and they seemed modest enough. My only complaint was that I could get nothing out of them. I wonder whether their wives would have been more amusing."

"Would they be so in England, Lord Skye?"

He looked down at her with half-shut eyes, and drawled: "You know my countrywomen?"

"Hardly at all."

"Then let us discuss some less serious subject."

"Willingly. I have waited for you to explain to me why you have to-night an expression of such melancholy."

"Is that quite friendly, Mrs. Lee? Do I really look melancholy?"

"Unutterably, as I feel. I am consumed with curiosity to know the reason."

The British minister coolly took a complete survey of the whole room, ending with a prolonged stare at the President and his wife, who were still mechanically shaking hands; then he looked back into her face, and said never a word.

She insisted: "I must have this riddle answered. It suffocates me. I should not be sad at seeing these same people at work or at play, if they ever do play; or in a church or a lecture-room. Why do they weigh on me like a horrid phantom here?"

"I see no riddle, Mrs. Lee. You have answered your own question; they are neither at work nor at play."

"Then please take me home at once. I shall have hysterics. The sight of those two suffering images at the door is too mournful to be borne. I am dizzy with looking at these stalking figures. I don't believe they're real. I wish the house would take fire. I want an earthquake. I wish some one would pinch the President, or pull his wife's hair."

Mrs. Lee did not repeat the experiment of visiting the White House, and indeed for some time afterwards she spoke with little enthusiasm of the presidential office. To Senator Ratcliffe she expressed her opinions strongly. The Senator tried in vain to argue that the people had a right to call upon their chief magistrate, and that he was bound to receive them; this being so, there was no less objectionable way of proceeding than the one which had been chosen. "Who gave the people any such right?" asked Mrs. Lee. "Where does it come from? What do they want it for? You know better, Mr. Ratcliffe! Our chief magistrate is a citizen like any one else. What puts it into his foolish head to cease being a citizen and to ape royalty? Our governors never make themselves ridiculous. Why cannot the wretched being content himself with living like the rest of us, and minding his own business? Does he know what a figure of fun he is?" And Mrs. Lee went so far as to declare that she would like to be the President's wife only to put an end to this folly; nothing should ever induce *her* to go through such a performance; and if the public did not approve of this, Congress might impeach her, and remove her from office; all she demanded was the right to be heard before the Senate in her own defence.

Nevertheless, there was a very general impression in Washington that Mrs. Lee would like nothing better than to be in the White House. Known to comparatively few people, and rarely discussing even with them the subjects which deeply interested her, Madeleine passed for a clever, intriguing woman who had her own objects to gain. True it is, beyond peradventure, that all residents of Washington may be assumed to be in office or candidates for office; unless they avow their object, they are guilty of an attempt—and a stupid one—to deceive; yet there is a small class of apparent exceptions destined at last to fall within the rule. Mrs. Lee was properly assumed to be a candidate for office. To the Washingtonians it was a matter of course that Mrs. Lee should marry Silas P. Ratcliffe. That he should be glad to get a fashionable and intelligent wife, with twenty or thirty thousand dollars a year, was not surprising. That she should accept the first public man of the day, with a flattering chance for the Presidency—a man still comparatively young and not without good looks—was perfectly natural, and in her undertaking she had the sympathy of all well-regulated Washington women who were not possible rivals; for to them the President's wife is of more consequence than the President; and, indeed, if America only knew it, they are not very far from the truth.

Some there were, however, who did not assent to this good-natured though worldly view of the proposed match. These ladies were severe in their comments upon Mrs. Lee's conduct, and did not hesitate to declare their opinion that she was the calmest and most ambitious minx who had ever come within their observation. Unfortunately it happened that the respectable and proper Mrs. Schuyler Clinton took this view of the case, and made little attempt to conceal her opinion. She was justly indignant at her cousin's gross worldliness, and possible promotion in rank.

"If Madeleine Ross marries that coarse, horrid old Illinois politician," said she to her husband, "I never will forgive her so long as I live."

Mr. Clinton tried to excuse Madeleine, and even went so far as to suggest that the difference of age was no greater than in their own case; but his wife trampled ruthlessly on his argument.

"At any rate," said she, "I never came to Washington as a widow on purpose to set my cap for the first candidate for the Presidency, and I never made a public spectacle of my indecent eagerness in the very galleries of the Senate; and Mrs. Lee ought to be ashamed of herself. She is a cold-blooded, heartless, unfeminine cat."

Little Victoria Dare, who babbled like the winds and streams, with utter indifference as to what she said or whom she addressed, used to bring choice bits of this gossip to Mrs. Lee. She always affected a little stammer when she said anything uncommonly impudent, and put on a manner of languid simplicity. She felt keenly the satisfaction of seeing Madeleine charged with her own besetting sins. For years all Washington had agreed that Victoria was little better than one of the wicked; she had done nothing but violate every rule of propriety and scandalise every well-regulated family in the city, and there was no good in her. Yet it could not be denied that Victoria was amusing, and had a sort of irregular fascination; consequently she was universally tolerated. To see Mrs. Lee thrust down to her own level was an unmixed pleasure to her, and she carefully repeated to Madeleine the choice bits of dialogue which she picked up in her wanderings.

"Your cousin, Mrs. Clinton, says you are a ca-ca-cat, Mrs. Lee."

"I don't believe it, Victoria. Mrs. Clinton never said anything of the sort."

"Mrs. Marston says it is because you have caught a ra-ra-rat, and Senator Clinton was only a m-m-mouse!"

Naturally all this unexpected publicity irritated Mrs. Lee not a little, especially when short and vague paragraphs, soon followed by longer and more positive ones, in regard to Senator Ratcliffe's matrimonial prospects, began to appear in newspapers, along with descriptions of herself from the pens of enterprising female correspondents for the press, who had never so much as seen her. At the first sight of one of these newspaper articles, Madeleine fairly cried with mortification and anger. She wanted to leave Washington the next day, and she hated the very thought of Ratcliffe. There was something in the newspaper style so inscrutably vulgar, something so inexplicably revolting to the sense of feminine decency, that she shrank under it as though it were a poisonous spider. But after the first acute shame had passed, her temper was roused, and she vowed that she would pursue her own path just as she had begun, without regard to all the malignity and vulgarity in the wide United States. She did not care to marry Senator Ratcliffe; she liked his society and was flattered by his confidence; she rather hoped to prevent him from ever making a formal offer, and if not, she would at least push it off to the last possible moment; but she was not to be frightened from marrying him by any amount of spitefulness or gossip, and she did not mean to refuse him except for stronger reasons than these. She even went so far in her desperate courage as to laugh at her cousin, Mrs. Clinton, whose venerable husband she allowed and even encouraged to pay her such public attention and to express sentiments of such youthful ardour as she well knew would inflame and exasperate the excellent lady his wife.

Carrington was the person most unpleasantly affected by the course which this affair had taken. He could no longer conceal from himself the fact that he was as much in love as a dignified Virginian could be. With him, at all events, she had shown no coquetry, nor had she ever either flattered or encouraged him. But Carrington, in his solitary struggle against fate, had found her a warm friend; always ready to assist where assistance was needed, generous with her money in any cause which he was willing to vouch for, full of sympathy where sympathy was more than money, and full of resource and suggestion where money and sympathy failed. Carrington knew her better than she knew herself. He selected her books; he brought the last speech or the last report from the Capitol or the departments; he knew her doubts and her vagaries, and as far as he understood them at all, helped her to solve them. Carrington was too modest, and perhaps too shy, to act the part of a declared lover, and he was too proud to let it be thought that he wanted to exchange his poverty for her wealth. But he was all the more anxious when he saw the evident attraction which Ratcliffe's strong will and unscrupulous energy exercised over her. He saw that Ratcliffe was steadily pushing his advances; that he flattered all Mrs. Lee's weaknesses by the confidence and deference with which he treated her; and that in a very short time, Madeleine must either marry him or find herself looked upon as a heartless coquette. He had his own reasons for thinking ill of Senator Ratcliffe, and he meant to prevent a marriage; but he had an enemy to deal with not easily driven from the path, and quite capable of routing any number of rivals.

Ratcliffe was afraid of no one. He had not fought his own way in life for nothing, and he knew all the value of a cold head and dogged self-assurance. Nothing but this robust Americanism and his strong will carried him safely through the snares and pitfalls of Mrs. Lee's society, where rivals and enemies beset him on every hand. He was little better than a schoolboy, when he ventured on their ground, but when he could draw them over upon his own territory of practical life he rarely failed to trample on his assailants. It was this practical sense and cool will that won over Mrs. Lee, who was woman enough to assume that all the graces were well enough employed in decorating her, and it was enough if the other sex felt her superiority. Men were valuable only in proportion to their strength and their appreciation of women. If the senator had only been strong enough always to control his temper, he would have done very well, but his temper was under a great strain in these times, and his incessant effort to control it in politics made him less watchful in private life. Mrs. Lee's tacit assumption of superior refinement irritated him, and sometimes made him show his teeth like a bull-dog, at the cost of receiving from Mrs. Lee a quick stroke in return such as a well-bred tortoise-shell cat administers to check over-familiarity; innocent to the eye, but drawing blood. One evening when he was more than commonly out of sorts, after sitting some time in moody silence, he roused himself, and, taking up a book that lay on her table, he glanced at its title and turned over the leaves. It happened by ill luck to be a volume of Darwin that Mrs. Lee had just borrowed from the library of Congress.

"Do you understand this sort of thing?" asked the Senator abruptly, in a tone that suggested a sneer.

"Not very well," replied Mrs. Lee, rather curtly.

"Why do you want to understand it?" persisted the Senator. "What good will it do you?"

"Perhaps it will teach us to be modest," answered Madeleine, quite equal to the occasion.

"Because it says we descend from monkeys?" rejoined the Senator, roughly. "Do you think you are descended from monkeys?"

"Why not?" said Madeleine.

"Why not?" repeated Ratcliffe, laughing harshly. "I don't like the connection. Do you mean to introduce your distant relations into society?"

"They would bring more amusement into it than most of its present members," rejoined Mrs. Lee, with a gentle smile that threatened mischief.

But Ratcliffe would not be warned; on the contrary, the only effect of Mrs. Lee's defiance was to exasperate his ill-temper, and whenever he lost his temper he became senatorial and Websterian. "Such books," he began, "disgrace our civilization; they degrade and stultify our divine nature; they are only suited for Asiatic despotisms where men are reduced to the level of brutes; that they should be accepted by a man like Baron Jacobi, I can understand; he and his masters have nothing to do in the world but to trample on human rights. Mr. Carrington, of course, would approve those ideas; he believes in the divine doctrine of flogging negroes; but that you, who profess philanthropy and free principles, should go with them, is astonishing; it is incredible; it is unworthy of you."

"You are very hard on the monkeys," replied Madeleine, rather sternly, when the Senator's oration was ended. "The monkeys never did you any harm; they are not in public life; they are not even voters; if they were, you would be enthusiastic about their intelligence and virtue. After all, we ought to be grateful to them, for what would men do in this melancholy world if they had not in-herited gaiety from the monkeys—as well as oratory."

Ratcliffe, to do him justice, took punishment well, at least when it came from Mrs. Lee's hands, and his occasional outbursts of in-subordination were sure to be followed by improved discipline; but if he allowed Mrs. Lee to correct his faults, he had no notion of let-ting himself be instructed by her friends, and he lost no chance of telling them so. But to do this was not always enough. Whether it were that he had few ideas outside of his own experience, or that he would not trust himself on doubtful ground, he seemed compelled to bring every discussion down to his own level. Madeleine puzzled herself in vain to find out whether he did this because he knew no better, or because he meant to cover his own ignorance.

"The Baron has amused me very much with his account of Bucha-rest society," Mrs. Lee would say: "I had no idea it was so gay."

"I would like to show him our society in Peonia," was Ratcliffe's reply; "he would find a very brilliant circle there of nature's true noblemen."

"The Baron says their politicians are precious sharp chaps," added Mr. French.

"Oh, there are politicians in Bulgaria, are there?" asked the Sena-tor, whose ideas of the Roumanian and Bulgarian neighbourhood were vague, and who had a general notion that all such people lived in tents, wore sheepskins with the wool inside, and ate curds: "Oh, they have politicians there! I would like to see them try their sharp-ness in the west."

"Really!" said Mrs. Lee. "Think of Attila and his hordes running an Indiana caucus?"

"Anyhow," cried French with a loud laugh, "the Baron said that a set of bigger political scoundrels than his friends couldn't be found in all Illinois."

"Did he say that?" exclaimed Ratcliffe angrily.

"Didn't he, Mrs. Lee? but I don't believe it; do you? What's your candid opinion, Ratcliffe? What you don't know about Illinois politics isn't worth knowing; do you really think those Bulgrascals couldn't run an Illinois state convention?"

Ratcliffe did not like to be chaffed, especially on this subject, but he could not resent French's liberty which was only a moderate return for the wooden nutmeg. To get the conversation away from Europe, from literature, from art, was his great object, and chaff was a way of escape.

Carrington was very well aware that the weak side of the Senator lay in his blind ignorance of morals. He flattered himself that Mrs. Lee must see this and be shocked by it sooner or later, so that nothing more was necessary than to let Ratcliffe expose himself. Without talking very much, Carrington always aimed at drawing him out. He soon found, however, that Ratcliffe understood such tactics perfectly, and instead of injuring, he rather improved his position. At times the man's audacity was startling, and even when Carrington thought him hopelessly entangled, he would sweep away all the hunter's nets with a sheer effort of strength, and walk off bolder and more dangerous than ever.

When Mrs. Lee pressed him too closely, he frankly admitted her charges. "What you say is in great part true. There is much in politics that disgusts and disheartens; much that is coarse and bad. I grant you there is dishonesty and corruption. We must try to make the amount as small as possible."

"You should be able to tell Mrs. Lee how she must go to work," said Carrington; "you have had experience. I have heard, it seems to me, that you were once driven to very hard measures against corruption."

Ratcliffe looked ill-pleased at this compliment, and gave Carrington one of his cold glances that meant mischief. But he took up the challenge on the spot:—

"Yes, I was, and am very sorry for it. The story is this, Mrs. Lee; and it is well-known to every man, woman, and child in the State of

Illinois, so that I have no reason for softening it. In the worst days of the war there was almost a certainty that my State would be carried by the peace party, by fraud, as we thought, although, fraud or not, we were bound to save it. Had Illinois been lost then, we should certainly have lost the Presidential election, and with it probably the Union. At any rate, I believed the fate of the war to depend on the result. I was then Governor, and upon me the responsibility rested. We had entire control of the northern counties and of their returns. We ordered the returning officers in a certain number of counties to make no returns until they heard from us, and when we had received the votes of all the southern counties and learned the precise number of votes we needed to give us a majority, we telegraphed to our northern returning officers to make the vote of their districts such and such, thereby overbalancing the adverse returns and giving the State to us. This was done, and as I am now senator I have a right to suppose that what I did was approved. I am not proud of the transaction, but I would do it again, and worse than that, if I thought it would save this country from disunion. But of course I did not expect Mr. Carrington to approve it. I believe he was then carrying out his reform principles by bearing arms against the government."

"Yes!" said Carrington drily; "you got the better of me, too. Like the old Scotchman, you didn't care who made the people's wars provided you made its ballots."

Carrington had missed his point. The man who has committed a murder for his country, is a patriot and not an assassin, even when he receives a seat in the Senate as his share of the plunder. Women cannot be expected to go behind the motives of that patriot who saves his country and his election in times of revolution.

Carrington's hostility to Ratcliffe was, however, mild, when compared with that felt by old Baron Jacobi. Why the baron should have taken so violent a prejudice it is not easy to explain, but a diplomatist and a senator are natural enemies, and Jacobi, as an

avowed admirer of Mrs. Lee, found Ratcliffe in his way. This prejudiced and immoral old diplomatist despised and loathed an American senator as the type which, to his bleared European eyes,
combined the utmost pragmatical self-assurance and overbearing
temper with the narrowest education and the meanest personal
experience that ever existed in any considerable government. As
Baron Jacobi's country had no special relations with that of the
United States, and its Legation at Washington was a mere job to
create a place for Jacobi to fill, he had no occasion to disguise his
personal antipathies, and he considered himself in some degree as
having a mission to express that diplomatic contempt for the Senate which his colleagues, if they felt it, were obliged to conceal.
He performed his duties with conscientious precision. He never
missed an opportunity to thrust the sharp point of his dialectic
rapier through the joints of the clumsy and hide-bound senatorial
self-esteem. He delighted in skilfully exposing to Madeleine's eyes
some new side of Ratcliffe's ignorance. His conversation at such
times sparkled with historical allusions, quotations in half a dozen
different languages, references to well-known facts which an old
man's memory could not recall with precision in all their details,
but with which the Honourable Senator was familiarly acquainted,
and which he could readily supply. And his Voltairean face leered
politely as he listened to Ratcliffe's reply, which showed invariable
ignorance of common literature, art, and history. The climax of his
triumph came one evening when Ratcliffe unluckily, tempted by
some allusion to Molière which he thought he understood, made
reference to the unfortunate influence of that great man on the religious opinions of his time. Jacobi, by a flash of inspiration, divined
that he had confused Molière with Voltaire, and assuming a manner of extreme suavity, he put his victim on the rack, and tortured
him with affected explanations and interrogations, until Madeleine
was in a manner forced to interrupt and end the scene. But even
when the senator was not to be lured into a trap, he could not es-

cape assault. The baron in such a case would cross the lines and attack him on his own ground, as on one occasion, when Ratcliffe was defending his doctrine of party allegiance, Jacobi silenced him by sneering somewhat thus: "Your principle is quite correct, Mr. Senator. I, too, like yourself, was once a good party man: my party was that of the Church; I was ultramontane. Your party system is one of your thefts from our Church; your National Convention is our Œcumenic Council; you abdicate reason, as we do, before its decisions; and you yourself, Mr. Ratcliffe, you are a Cardinal. They are able men, those cardinals; I have known many; they were our best friends, but they were not reformers. Are you a reformer, Mr. Senator?"

Ratcliffe grew to dread and hate the old man, but all his ordinary tactics were powerless against this impenetrable eighteenth century cynic. If he resorted to his Congressional practise of browbeating and dogmatism, the Baron only smiled and turned his back, or made some remark in French which galled his enemy all the more, because, while he did not understand it, he knew well that Madeleine did, and that she tried to repress her smile. Ratcliffe's grey eyes grew colder and stonier than ever as he gradually perceived that Baron Jacobi was carrying on a set scheme with malignant ingenuity, to drive him out of Madeleine's house, and he swore a terrible oath that he would not be beaten by that monkey-faced foreigner. On the other hand Jacobi had little hope of success: "What can an old man do?" said he with perfect sincerity to Carrington; "If I were forty years younger, that great oaf should not have his own way. Ah! I wish I were young again and we were in Vienna!" From which it was rightly inferred by Carrington that the venerable diplomatist would, if such acts were still in fashion, have coolly insulted the Senator, and put a bullet through his heart.

Chapter VI

In February the weather became warmer and summer-like. In Virginia there comes often at this season a deceptive gleam of summer, slipping in between heavy storm-clouds of sleet and snow; days and sometimes weeks when the temperature is like June; when the earliest plants begin to show their hardy flowers, and when the bare branches of the forest trees alone protest against the conduct of the seasons. Then men and women are languid; life seems, as in Italy, sensuous and glowing with colour; one is conscious of walking in an atmosphere that is warm, palpable, radiant with possibilities; a delicate haze hangs over Arlington, and softens even the harsh white glare of the Capitol; the struggle of existence seems to abate; Lent throws its calm shadow over society; and youthful diplomatists, unconscious of their danger, are lured into asking foolish girls to marry them; the blood thaws in the heart and flows out into the veins, like the rills of sparkling water that trickle from every lump of ice or snow, as though all the ice and snow on earth, and all the hardness of heart, all the heresy and schism, all the works of the devil, had yielded to the force of love and to the fresh warmth of innocent, lamb-like, confiding virtue. In such a world there should be no guile—but there is a great deal of it notwithstanding. Indeed, at no other season is there so much. This is the moment when the two whited sepulchres at either end of the Avenue reek with the thick atmosphere of bargain and sale. The old is going; the new is coming. Wealth, office, power are at auction. Who bids highest? who hates with most venom? who intrigues with most skill? who has done the dirtiest, the meanest, the darkest, and the most, political work? He shall have his reward.

Senator Ratcliffe was absorbed and ill at ease. A swarm of applicants for office dogged his steps and beleaguered his rooms in quest of his endorsement of their paper characters. The new President was to arrive on Monday. Intrigues and combinations, of which the Senator was the soul, were all alive, awaiting this arrival. Newspaper correspondents pestered him with questions. Brother senators called him to conferences. His mind was pre-occupied with his own interests. One might have supposed that, at this instant, nothing could have drawn him away from the political gaming-table, and yet when Mrs. Lee remarked that she was going to Mount Vernon on Saturday with a little party, including the British Minister and an Irish gentleman staying as a guest at the British Legation, the Senator surprised her by expressing a strong wish to join them. He explained that, as the political lead was no longer in his hands, the chances were nine in ten that if he stirred at all he should make a blunder; that his friends expected him to do something when, in fact, nothing could be done; that every preparation had already been made, and that for him to go on an excursion to Mount Vernon, at this moment, with the British Minister, was, on the whole, about the best use he could make of his time, since it would hide him for one day at least.

Lord Skye had fallen into the habit of consulting Mrs. Lee when his own social resources were low, and it was she who had suggested this party to Mount Vernon, with Carrington for a guide and Mr.

Gore for variety, to occupy the time of the Irish friend whom Lord Skye was bravely entertaining. This gentleman, who bore the title of Dunbeg, was a dilapidated peer, neither wealthy nor famous. Lord Skye brought him to call on Mrs. Lee, and in some sort put him under her care. He was young, not ill-looking, quite intelligent, rather too fond of facts, and not quick at humour. He was given to smiling in a deprecatory way, and when he talked, he was either absent or excited; he made vague blunders, and then smiled in deprecation of offence, or his words blocked their own path in their rush. Perhaps his manner was a little ridiculous, but he had a good heart, a good head, and a title. He found favour in the eyes of Sybil and Victoria Dare, who declined to admit other women to the party, although they offered no objection to Mr. Ratcliffe's admission. As for Lord Dunbeg, he was an enthusiastic admirer of General Washington, and, as he privately intimated, eager to study phases of American society. He was delighted to go with a small party, and Miss Dare secretly promised herself that she would show him a phase.

The morning was warm, the sky soft, the little steamer lay at the quiet wharf with a few negroes lazily watching her preparations for departure. Carrington, with Mrs. Lee and the young ladies, arrived first, and stood leaning against the rail, waiting the arrival of their companions. Then came Mr. Gore, neatly attired and gloved, with a light spring overcoat; for Mr. Gore was very careful of his personal appearance, and not a little vain of his good looks. Then a pretty woman, with blue eyes and blonde hair, dressed in black, and leading a little girl by the hand, came on board, and Carrington went to shake hands with her. On his return to Mrs. Lee's side, she asked about his new acquaintance, and he replied with a half-laugh, as though he were not proud of her, that she was a client, a pretty widow, well known in Washington. "Any one at the Capitol would tell you all about her. She was the wife of a noted lobbyist, who died about two years ago. Congressmen can refuse nothing to a pretty face, and she was their idea of feminine perfection. Yet she is a silly little woman, too. Her husband died after a very short illness, and, to my great surprise, made me executor under his will. I think he had an idea that he could trust me with his papers, which were important and compromising, for he seems to have had no time to go over them and destroy what were best out of the way. So, you see, I am left with his widow and child to look after. Luckily, they are well provided for."

"Still you have not told me her name."

"Her name is Baker—Mrs. Sam Baker. But they are casting off, and Mr. Ratcliffe will be left behind. I'll ask the captain to wait."

About a dozen passengers had arrived, among them the two Earls, with a footman carrying a promising lunch-basket, and the planks were actually hauled in when a carriage dashed up to the wharf, and Mr. Ratcliffe leaped out and hurried on board. "Off with you as quick as you can!" said he to the negro-hands, and in another moment the little steamer had begun her journey, pounding the muddy waters of the Potomac and sending up its small column of smoke as though it were a newly invented incense-burner approaching the temple of the national deity. Ratcliffe explained in great glee how he had barely managed to escape his visitors by telling them that the British Minister was waiting for him, and that he would be back again presently. "If they had known where I was going," said he, "you would have seen the boat swamped with office-seekers. Illinois alone would have brought you to a watery grave." He was in high spirits, bent upon enjoying his holiday, and as they passed the arsenal with its solitary sentry, and the navy-yard, with its one unseaworthy wooden war-steamer, he pointed out these evidences of national grandeur to Lord Skye, threatening, as the last terror of diplomacy, to send him home in an American frigate. They were thus indulging in senatorial humour on one side of the boat, while Sybil and Victoria, with the aid of Mr. Gore and Carrington, were improving Lord Dunbeg's mind on the other.

Miss Dare, finding for herself at last a convenient seat where she could repose and be mistress of the situation, put on a more than usually demure expression and waited with gravity until her noble neighbour should give her an opportunity to show those powers which, as she believed, would supply a phase in his existence. Miss Dare was one of those young persons, sometimes to be found in America, who seem to have no object in life, and while apparently devoted to men, care nothing about them, but find happiness only in violating rules; she made no parade of whatever virtues she had, and her chief pleasure was to make fun of all the world and herself.

"What a noble river!" remarked Lord Dunbeg, as the boat passed out upon the wide stream; "I suppose you often sail on it?"

"I never was here in my life till now," replied the untruthful Miss Dare; "we don't think much of it; it's too small; we're used to so much larger rivers."

"I am afraid you would not like our English rivers then; they are mere brooks compared with this."

"Are they indeed?" said Victoria, with an appearance of vague surprise; "how curious! I don't think I care to be an Englishwoman then. I could not live without big rivers."

Lord Dunbeg stared, and hinted that this was almost unreasonable.

"Unless I were a Countess!" continued Victoria, meditatively, looking at Alexandria, and paying no attention to his lordship; "I think I could manage if I were a C-c-countess. It is such a pretty title!"

"Duchess is commonly thought a prettier one," stammered Dunbeg, much embarrassed. The young man was not used to chaff from women.

"I should be satisfied with Countess. It sounds well. I am surprised that you don't like it." Dunbeg looked about him uneasily for some means of escape but he was barred in. "I should think you would feel an awful responsibility in selecting a Countess. How do you do it?"

Lord Dunbeg nervously joined in the general laughter as Sybil ejaculated: "Oh, Victoria!" but Miss Dare continued without a smile or any elevation of her monotonous voice:

"Now, Sybil, don't interrupt me, please. I am deeply interested in Lord Dunbeg's conversation. He understands that my interest is purely scientific, but my happiness requires that I should know how Countesses are selected. Lord Dunbeg, how would you recommend a friend to choose a Countess?"

Lord Dunbeg began to be amused by her impudence, and he even tried to lay down for her satisfaction one or two rules for selecting Countesses, but long before he had invented his first rule, Victoria had darted off to a new subject.

"Which would you rather be, Lord Dunbeg? an Earl or George Washington?"

"George Washington, certainly," was the Earl's courteous though rather bewildered reply.

"Really?" she asked with a languid affectation of surprise; "it is awfully kind of you to say so, but of course you can't mean it."

"Indeed I do mean it."

"Is it possible? I never should have thought it."

"Why not, Miss Dare?"

"You have not the air of wishing to be George Washington."

"May I again ask, why not?"

"Certainly. Did you ever see George Washington?"

"Of course not. He died fifty years before I was born."

"I thought so. You see you don't know him. Now, will you give us an idea of what you imagine General Washington to have looked like?"

Dunbeg gave accordingly a flattering description of General Washington, compounded of Stuart's portrait and Greenough's statue of Olympian Jove with Washington's features, in the Capitol Square. Miss Dare listened with an expression of superiority not unmixed with patience, and then she enlightened him as follows:

"All you have been saying is perfect stuff—excuse the vulgarity of the expression. When I am a Countess I will correct my language. The truth is that General Washington was a raw-boned country farmer, very hard-featured, very awkward, very illiterate and very dull; very bad tempered, very profane, and generally tipsy after dinner."

"You shock me, Miss Dare!" exclaimed Dunbeg.

"Oh! I know all about General Washington. My grandfather knew him intimately, and often stayed at Mount Vernon for weeks together. You must not believe what you read, and not a word of what Mr. Carrington will say. He is a Virginian and will tell you no end of fine stories and not a syllable of truth in one of them. We are all patriotic about Washington and like to hide his faults. If I weren't quite sure you would never repeat it, I would not tell you this. The truth is that even when George Washington was a small boy, his temper was so violent that no one could do anything with him. He once cut down all his father's fruit-trees in a fit of passion, and then, just because they wanted to flog him, he threatened to brain his father with the hatchet. His aged wife suffered agonies from him. My grandfather often told me how he had seen the General pinch and swear at her till the poor creature left the room in tears; and how once at Mount Vernon he saw Washington, when quite an old man, suddenly rush at an unoffending visitor, and chase him off the place, beating him all the time over the head with a great stick with knots in it, and all just because he heard the poor man stammer; he never could abide s-s-stammering."

Carrington and Gore burst into shouts of laughter over this description of the Father of his country, but Victoria continued in her gentle drawl to enlighten Lord Dunbeg in regard to other subjects with information equally mendacious, until he decided that she was quite the most eccentric person he had ever met. The boat arrived at Mount Vernon while she was still engaged in a description of the society and manners of America, and especially of the rules which

made an offer of marriage necessary. According to her, Lord Dunbeg was in imminent peril; gentlemen, and especially foreigners,
were expected, in all the States south of the Potomac, to offer
themselves to at least one young lady in every city: "and I had only
yesterday," said Victoria, "a letter from a lovely girl in North Caro-
lina, a dear friend of mine, who wrote me that she was right put out
because her brothers had called on a young English visitor with
shot guns, and she was afraid he wouldn't recover, and, after all, she
says she should have refused him."

Meanwhile Madeleine, on the other side of the boat, undisturbed by the laughter that surrounded Miss Dare, chatted soberly
and seriously with Lord Skye and Senator Ratcliffe. Lord Skye, too,
a little intoxicated by the brilliancy of the morning, broke out into
admiration of the noble river, and accused Americans of not appre-
ciating the beauties of their own country.

"Your national mind," said he, "has no eyelids. It requires a broad
glare and a beaten road. It prefers shadows which you can cut out
with a knife. It doesn't know the beauty of this Virginia winter soft-
ness."

Mrs. Lee resented the charge. America, she maintained, had not
worn her feelings threadbare like Europe. She had still her story to
tell; she was waiting for her Burns and Scott, her Wordsworth and
Byron, her Hogarth and Turner. "You want peaches in spring," said
she. "Give us our thousand years of summer, and then complain, if
you please, that our peach is not as mellow as yours. Even our voices
may be soft then," she added, with a significant look at Lord Skye.

"We are at a disadvantage in arguing with Mrs. Lee," said he to
Ratcliffe; "when she ends as counsel, she begins as witness. The fa-
mous Duchess of Devonshire's lips were not half as convincing as
Mrs. Lee's voice."

Ratcliffe listened carefully, assenting whenever he saw that Mrs.
Lee wished it. He wished he understood precisely what tones and
half-tones, colours and harmonies, were.

They arrived and strolled up the sunny path. At the tomb they halted, as all good Americans do, and Mr. Gore, in a tone of subdued sorrow, delivered a short address—

"It might be much worse if they improved it," he said, surveying its proportions with the æsthetic eye of a cultured Bostonian. "As it stands, this tomb is a simple misfortune which might befall any of us; we should not grieve over it too much. What would our feelings be if a Congressional committee reconstructed it of white marble with Gothic pepper-pots, and gilded it inside on machine-moulded stucco!"

Madeleine, however, insisted that the tomb, as it stood, was the only restless spot about the quiet landscape, and that it contradicted all her ideas about repose in the grave. Ratcliffe wondered what she meant.

They passed on, wandering across the lawn, and through the house. Their eyes, weary of the harsh colours and forms of the city, took pleasure in the worn wainscots and the stained walls. Some of the rooms were still occupied; fires were burning in the wide fireplaces. All were tolerably furnished, and there was no uncomfortable sense of repair or newness. They mounted the stairs, and Mrs. Lee fairly laughed when she was shown the room in which General Washington slept, and where he died.

Carrington smiled too. "Our old Virginia houses were mostly like this," said he; "suites of great halls below, and these gaunt barracks above. The Virginia house was a sort of hotel. When there was a race or a wedding, or a dance, and the house was full, they thought nothing of packing half a dozen people in one room, and if the room was large, they stretched a sheet across to separate the men from the women. As for toilet, those were not the mornings of cold baths. With our ancestors a little washing went a long way."

"Do you still live so in Virginia?" asked Madeleine.

"Oh no, it is quite gone. We live now like other country people, and try to pay our debts, which that generation never did. They lived from hand to mouth. They kept a stable-full of horses. The young men were always riding about the country, betting on horse-races, gambling, drinking, fighting, and making love. No one knew exactly what he was worth until the crash came about fifty years ago, and the whole thing ran out."

"Just what happened in Ireland!" said Lord Dunbeg, much interested and full of his article in the *Quarterly;* "the resemblance is perfect, even down to the houses."

Mrs. Lee asked Carrington bluntly whether he regretted the destruction of this old social arrangement.

"One can't help regretting," said he, "whatever it was that produced George Washington, and a crowd of other men like him. But I think we might produce the men still if we had the same field for them."

"And would you bring the old society back again if you could?" asked she.

"What for? It could not hold itself up. General Washington himself could not save it. Before he died he had lost his hold on Virginia, and his power was gone."

The party for a while separated, and Mrs. Lee found herself alone in the great drawing-room. Presently the blonde Mrs. Baker entered, with her child, who ran about making more noise than Mrs. Washington would have permitted. Madeleine, who had the usual feminine love of children, called the girl to her and pointed out the shepherds and shepherdesses carved on the white Italian marble of the fireplace; she invented a little story about them to amuse the child, while the mother stood by and at the end thanked the story-teller with more enthusiasm than seemed called for. Mrs. Lee did not fancy her effusive manner, or her complexion, and was glad when Dunbeg appeared at the doorway.

"How do you like General Washington at home?" asked she.

"Really, I assure you I feel quite at home myself," replied Dunbeg, with a more beaming smile than ever. "I am sure General

Washington was an Irishman. I know it from the look of the place. I mean to look it up and write an article about it."

"Then if you have disposed of him," said Madeleine, "I think we will have luncheon, and I have taken the liberty to order it to be served outside."

There a table had been improvised, and Miss Dare was inspecting the lunch, and making comments upon Lord Skye's cuisine and cellar.

"I hope it is very dry champagne," said she, "the taste for sweet champagne is quite awfully shocking."

The young woman knew no more about dry and sweet champagne than of the wine of Ulysses, except that she drank both with equal satisfaction, but she was mimicking a Secretary of the British Legation who had provided her with supper at her last evening party. Lord Skye begged her to try it, which she did, and with great gravity remarked that it was about five per cent. she presumed. This, too, was caught from her Secretary, though she knew no more what it meant than if she had been a parrot.

The luncheon was very lively and very good. When it was over, the gentlemen were allowed to smoke, and conversation fell into a sober strain, which at last threatened to become serious.

"You want half-tones!" said Madeleine to Lord Skye: "are there not half-tones enough to suit you on the walls of this house?"

Lord Skye suggested that this was probably owing to the fact that Washington, belonging, as he did, to the universe, was in his taste an exception to local rules.

"Is not the sense of rest here captivating?" she continued. "Look at that quaint garden, and this ragged lawn, and the great river in front, and the superannuated fort beyond the river! Everything is peaceful, even down to the poor old General's little bed-room. One would like to lie down in it and sleep a century or two. And yet that dreadful Capitol and its office-seekers are only ten miles off."

"No! that is more than I can bear!" broke in Miss Victoria in a stage whisper, "that dreadful Capitol! Why, not one of us would be here without that dreadful Capitol! except, perhaps, myself."

"You would appear very well as Mrs. Washington, Victoria."

"Miss Dare has been so very obliging as to give us her views of General Washington's character this morning," said Dunbeg, "but I have not yet had time to ask Mr. Carrington for his."

"Whatever Miss Dare says is valuable," replied Carrington, "but her strong point is facts."

"Never flatter! Mr. Carrington," drawled Miss Dare; "I do not need it, and it does not become your style. Tell me, Lord Dunbeg, is not Mr. Carrington a little your idea of General Washington restored to us in his prime?"

"After your account of General Washington, Miss Dare, how can I agree with you?"

"After all," said Lord Skye, "I think we must agree that Miss Dare is in the main right about the charms of Mount Vernon. Even Mrs. Lee, on the way up, agreed that the General, who is the only permanent resident here, has the air of being confoundedly bored in his tomb. I don't myself love your dreadful Capitol yonder, but I prefer it to a bucolic life here. And I account in this way for my want of enthusiasm for your great General. He liked no kind of life but this. He seems to have been greater in the character of a homesick Virginia planter than as General or President. I forgive him his inordinate dulness, for he was not a diplomatist and it was not his business to lie, but he might once in a way have forgotten Mount Vernon."

Dunbeg here burst in with an excited protest; all his words seemed to shove each other aside in their haste to escape first. "All our greatest Englishmen have been home-sick country squires. I am a home-sick country squire myself."

"How interesting!" said Miss Dare under her breath.

Mr. Gore here joined in: "It is all very well for you gentlemen to measure General Washington according to your own private twelve-inch carpenter's rule. But what will you say to us New Englanders who never were country gentlemen at all, and never had any liking for Virginia? What did Washington ever do for us? He never even pretended to like us. He never was more than barely civil to us. I'm not finding fault with him; everybody knows that he never cared for anything but Mount Vernon. For all that, we idolize him. To us he is Morality, Justice, Duty, Truth; half a dozen Roman gods with capital letters. He is austere, solitary, grand; he ought to be deified. I hardly feel easy, eating, drinking, smoking here on his portico without his permission, taking liberties with his house, criticising his bed-rooms in his absence. Suppose I heard his horse now trotting up on the other side, and he suddenly appeared at this door and looked at us. I should abandon you to his indignation. I should run away and hide myself on the steamer. The mere thought unmans me."

Ratcliffe seemed amused at Gore's half-serious notions. "You recall to me," said he, "my own feelings when I was a boy and was made by my father to learn the Farewell Address by heart. In those days General Washington was a sort of American Jehovah. But the West is a poor school for Reverence. Since coming to Congress I have learned more about General Washington, and have been surprised to find what a narrow base his reputation rests on. A fair military officer, who made many blunders, and who never had more men than would make a full army-corps under his command, he got an enormous reputation in Europe because he did not make himself king, as though he ever had a chance of doing it. A respectable, painstaking President, he was treated by the Opposition with an amount of deference that would have made government easy to a baby, but it worried him to death. His official papers are fairly done, and contain good average sense such as a hundred thousand men in the United States would now write. I suspect that half of his attachment to this spot rose from his consciousness of inferior powers and his dread of responsibility. This government can show to-day a dozen men of equal abilities, but we don't deify them. What I most wonder at in him is not his military or political genius at all, for I doubt whether he had much, but a curious Yankee shrewdness in money matters. He thought himself a very rich man, yet he never spent a dollar foolishly. He was almost the only Virginian I ever heard of, in public life, who did not die insolvent."

During this long speech, Carrington glanced across at Madeleine, and caught her eye. Ratcliffe's criticism was not to her taste. Carrington could see that she thought it unworthy of him, and he knew that it would irritate her. "I will lay a little trap for Mr. Ratcliffe," thought he to himself; "we will see whether he gets out of it." So Carrington began, and all listened closely, for, as a Virginian, he was supposed to know much about the subject, and his family had been deep in the confidence of Washington himself.

"The neighbours hereabout had for many years, and may have still, some curious stories about General Washington's closeness in money matters. They said he never bought anything by weight but he had it weighed over again, nor by tale but he had it counted, and if the weight or number were not exact, he sent it back. Once, during his absence, his steward had a room plastered, and paid the plasterer's bill. On the General's return, he measured the room, and found that the plasterer had charged fifteen shillings too much. Meanwhile the man had died, and the General made a claim of fifteen shillings on his estate, which was paid. Again, one of his tenants brought him the rent. The exact change of fourpence was required. The man tendered a dollar, and asked the General to credit him with the balance against the next year's rent. The General refused and made him ride nine miles to Alexandria and back for the fourpence. On the other hand, he sent to a shoemaker in Alexandria to come and measure him for shoes. The man returned word that he did not go to any one's house to take measures, and the General mounted his horse and rode the nine miles to him. One of his rules was to pay at taverns the same sum for his servants' meals as for his own. An inn-keeper brought him a bill of three-and-ninepence for his own breakfast, and three shillings for his servant. He insisted upon adding the extra ninepence, as he did not doubt that the servant had eaten as much as he. What do you say to these anecdotes? Was this meanness or not?"

Ratcliffe was amused. "The stories are new to me," he said. "It is just as I thought. These are signs of a man who thinks much of trifles; one who fusses over small matters. We don't do things in that way now that we no longer have to get crops from granite, as they used to do in New Hampshire when I was a boy."

Carrington replied that it was unlucky for Virginians that they had not done things in that way then: if they had, they would not have gone to the dogs.

Gore shook his head seriously; "Did I not tell you so?" said he. "Was not this man an abstract virtue? I give you my word I stand in awe before him, and I feel ashamed to pry into these details of his life. What is it to us how he thought proper to apply his principles to nightcaps and feather dusters? We are not his body servants, and we care nothing about his infirmities. It is enough for us to know that he carried his rules of virtue down to a pin's point, and that we ought, one and all, to be on our knees before his tomb."

Dunbeg, pondering deeply, at length asked Carrington whether all this did not make rather a clumsy politician of the father of his country.

"Mr. Ratcliffe knows more about politics than I. Ask him," said Carrington.

"Washington was no politician at all, as we understand the word," replied Ratcliffe abruptly. "He stood outside of politics. The thing couldn't be done to-day. The people don't like that sort of royal airs."

"I don't understand!" said Mrs. Lee. "Why could you not do it now?"

"Because I should make a fool of myself," replied Ratcliffe, pleased to think that Mrs. Lee should put him on a level with Washington. She had only meant to ask why the thing could not be done, and this little touch of Ratcliffe's vanity was inimitable.

"Mr. Ratcliffe means that Washington was too respectable for our time," interposed Carrington.

This was deliberately meant to irritate Ratcliffe, and it did so all the more because Mrs. Lee turned to Carrington, and said, with some bitterness: "Was he then the only honest public man we ever had?"

"Oh, no!" replied Carrington cheerfully; "there have been one or two others."

"If the rest of our Presidents had been like him," said Gore, "we should have had fewer ugly blots on our short history."

Ratcliffe was exasperated at Carrington's habit of drawing discussion to this point. He felt the remark as a personal insult, and he knew it to be intended. "Public men," he broke out, "cannot be dressing themselves to-day in Washington's old clothes. If Washington were President now, he would have to learn our ways or lose his next election. Only fools and theorists imagine that our society can be handled with gloves or long poles. One must make one's self a part of it. If virtue won't answer our purpose, we must use vice, or our opponents will put us out of office, and this was as true in Washington's day as it is now, and always will be."

"Come," said Lord Skye, who was beginning to fear an open quarrel; "the conversation verges on treason, and I am accredited to this government. Why not examine the grounds?"

A kind of natural sympathy led Lord Dunbeg to wander by the side of Miss Dare through the quaint old garden. His mind being much occupied by the effort of stowing away the impressions he had just received, he was more than usually absent in his manner, and this want of attention irritated the young lady. She made some comments on flowers; she invented some new species with startling names; she asked whether these were known in Ireland; but Lord

Dunbeg was for the moment so vague in his answers that she saw her case was perilous.

"Here is an old sun-dial. Do you have sun-dials in Ireland, Lord Dunbeg?"

"Yes; oh, certainly! What! sun-dials? Oh, yes! I assure you there are a great many sun-dials in Ireland, Miss Dare."

"I am so glad. But I suppose they are only for ornament. Here it is just the other way. Look at this one! they all behave like that. The wear and tear of our sun is too much for them; they don't last. My uncle, who has a place at Long Branch, had five sun-dials in ten years."

"How very odd! But really now, Miss Dare, I don't see how a sun-dial could wear out."

"Don't you? How strange! Don't you see, they get soaked with sunshine so that they can't hold shadow. It's like me, you know. I have such a good time all the time that I can't be unhappy. Do you ever read the *Burlington Hawkeye*, Lord Dunbeg?"

"I don't remember; I think not. Is it an American serial?" gasped Dunbeg, trying hard to keep pace with Miss Dare in her reckless dashes across country.

"No, not serial at all!" replied Virginia; "but I am afraid you would find it very hard reading. I shouldn't try."

"Do you read it much, Miss Dare?"

"Oh, always! I am not really as light as I seem. But then I have an advantage over you because I know the language."

By this time Dunbeg was awake again, and Miss Dare, satisfied with her success, allowed herself to become more reasonable, until a slight shade of sentiment began to flicker about their path.

The scattered party, however, soon had to unite again. The boat rang its bell for return, they filed down the paths and settled themselves in their old places. As they steamed away, Mrs. Lee watched the sunny hill-side and the peaceful house above, until she could see them no more, and the longer she looked, the less she was pleased with herself. Was it true, as Victoria Dare said, that she could not live in so pure an air? Did she really need the denser fumes of the city? Was she, unknown to herself, gradually becoming tainted with the life about her? or was Ratcliffe right in accepting the good and the bad together, and in being of his time since he was in it? Why was it, she said bitterly to herself, that everything Washington touched, he purified, even down to the associations of his house? and why is it that everything we touch seems soiled? Why do I feel unclean when I look at Mount Vernon? In spite of Mr. Ratcliffe, is it not better to be a child and to cry for the moon and stars?

The little Baker girl came up to her where she stood, and began playing with her parasol.

"Who is your little friend?" asked Ratcliffe.

Mrs. Lee rather vaguely replied that she was the daughter of that pretty woman in black; she believed her name was Baker.

"Baker, did you say?" repeated Ratcliffe.

"Baker—Mrs. Sam Baker; at least so Mr. Carrington told me; he said she was a client of his."

In fact Ratcliffe soon saw Carrington go up to her and remain by her side during the rest of the trip. Ratcliffe watched them sharply and grew more and more absorbed in his own thoughts as the boat drew nearer and nearer the shore.

Carrington was in high spirits. He thought he had played his cards with unusual success. Even Miss Dare deigned to acknowledge his charms that day. She declared herself to be the moral image of Martha Washington, and she started a discussion whether Carrington or Lord Dunbeg would best suit her in the *rôle* of the General.

"Mr. Carrington is exemplary," she said, "but oh, what joy to be Martha Washington and a Countess too!"

Chapter VII

When he reached his rooms that afternoon, Senator Ratcliffe found there, as he expected, a choice company of friends and admirers, who had beguiled their leisure hours since noon by cursing him in every variety of profane language that experience could suggest and impatience stimulate. On his part, had he consulted his own feelings only, he would then and there have turned them out, and locked the doors behind them. So far as silent maledictions were concerned, no profanity of theirs could hold its own against the intensity and deliberation with which, as he found himself approaching his own door, he expressed between his teeth his views in respect to their eternal interests. Nothing could be less suited to his present humour than the society which awaited him in his rooms. He groaned in spirit as he sat down at his writing-table and looked about him. Dozens of office-seekers were besieging the house; men whose patriotic services in the last election called loudly for recognition from a grateful country. They brought their applications to the Senator with an entreaty that he would endorse and take charge of them. Several members and senators who felt that Ratcliffe had no reason for existence except to fight their battle for patronage, were lounging about his room, reading newspapers, or beguiling their time with tobacco in various forms; at long intervals making dull remarks, as though they were more weary than their constituents of the atmosphere that surrounds the grandest government the sun ever shone upon. Several newspaper correspondents, eager to barter their news for Ratcliffe's hints or suggestions, appeared from time to time on the scene, and, dropping into a chair by Ratcliffe's desk, whispered with him in mysterious tones.

Thus the Senator worked on, hour after hour, mechanically doing what was required of him, signing papers without reading them, answering remarks without hearing them, hardly looking up from his desk, and appearing immersed in labour. This was his protection against curiosity and garrulity. The pretence of work was the curtain he drew between himself and the world. Behind this curtain his mental operations went on, undisturbed by what was about him, while he heard all that was said, and said little or nothing himself. His followers respected this privacy, and left him alone. He was their prophet, and had a right to seclusion. He was their chieftain, and while he sat in his monosyllabic solitude, his ragged tail reclined in various attitudes about him, and occasionally one man spoke, or another swore. Newspapers and tobacco were their resource in periods of absolute silence.

A shade of depression rested on the faces and the voices of Clan Ratcliffe that evening, as is not unusual with forces on the eve of battle. Their remarks came at longer intervals, and were more pointless and random than usual. There was a want of elasticity in their bearing and tone, partly coming from sympathy with the evident depression of their chief, partly from the portents of the time. The President was to arrive within forty-eight hours, and as yet there was no sign that he properly appreciated their services; there were signs only too unmistakeable that he was painfully misled and deluded, that his countenance was turned wholly in another direction, and that all their sacrifices were counted as worthless. There was reason to believe that he came with a deliberate purpose of making war upon Ratcliffe and breaking him down; of refusing to bestow patronage on them, and of bestowing it wherever it would injure them most deeply. At the thought that their honestly earned harvest of foreign missions and consulates, department-bureaus, custom-house and revenue offices, postmasterships, Indian agencies, and army and navy contracts, might now be wrung from their grasp by the selfish greed of a mere accidental intruder—a man whom nobody wanted and every one ridiculed—their natures rebelled, and they felt that such things must not be; that there could be no more hope for democratic government if such things were possible. At this point they invariably became excited, lost their equanimity, and swore. Then they fell back on their faith in Ratcliffe: if any man could pull them through, he could; after all, the President must first reckon with him, and he was an uncommon tough customer to tackle.

Perhaps, however, even their faith in Ratcliffe might have been shaken, could they at that moment have looked into his mind and understood what was passing there. Ratcliffe was a man vastly their superior, and he knew it. He lived in a world of his own and had instincts of refinement. Whenever his affairs went unfavourably, these instincts revived, and for the time swept all his nature with them. He was now filled with disgust and cynical contempt for every form of politics. During long years he had done his best for his party; he had sold himself to the devil, coined his heart's blood, toiled with a dogged persistence that no day-labourer ever conceived; and all for what? To be rejected as its candidate; to be put under the harrow of a small Indiana farmer who made no secret of the intention to "corral" him, and, as he elegantly expressed it, to "take his hide and tallow." Ratcliffe had no great fear of losing his hide, but he felt aggrieved that he should be called upon to defend it, and that this should be the result of twenty years' devotion. Like

most men in the same place, he did not stop to cast up both
columns of his account with the party, nor to ask himself the question that lay at the heart of his grievance: How far had he served his
party and how far himself? He was in no humour for self-analysis:
this requires more repose of mind than he could then command. As
for the President, from whom he had not heard a whisper since the
insolent letter to Grimes, which he had taken care not to show, the
Senator felt only a strong impulse to teach him better sense and
better manners. But as for political life, the events of the last six
months were calculated to make any man doubt its value. He was
quite out of sympathy with it. He hated the sight of his tobacco-
chewing, newspaper-reading satellites, with their hats tipped at
every angle except the right one, and their feet everywhere except
on the floor. Their conversation bored him and their presence was
a nuisance. He would not submit to this slavery longer. He would
have given his Senatorship for a civilized house like Mrs. Lee's,
with a woman like Mrs. Lee at its head, and twenty thousand a year
for life. He smiled his only smile that evening when he thought how
rapidly she would rout every man Jack of his political following out
of her parlours, and how meekly they would submit to banishment
into a back-office with an oil-cloth carpet and two cane chairs. He
felt that Mrs. Lee was more necessary to him than the Presidency
itself; he could not go on without her; he needed human companionship; some Christian comfort for his old age; some avenue of com-
munication with that social world, which made his present
surroundings look cold and foul; some touch of that refinement of
mind and morals beside which his own seemed coarse. He felt unutterably lonely. He wished Mrs. Lee had asked him home to dinner; but Mrs. Lee had gone to bed with a headache. He should not
see her again for a week. Then his mind turned back upon their
morning at Mount Vernon, and bethinking himself of Mrs. Sam
Baker, he took a sheet of note-paper, and wrote a line to Wilson
Keen, Esq., at Georgetown, requesting him to call, if possible, the

next morning towards one o'clock at the Senator's rooms on a matter of business. Wilson Keen was chief of the Secret Service Bureau in the Treasury Department, and, as the depositary of all secrets, was often called upon for assistance which he was very good-natured in furnishing to senators, especially if they were likely to be Secretaries of the Treasury.

This note despatched, Mr. Ratcliffe fell back into his reflective mood, which led him apparently into still lower depths of discontent until, with a muttered oath, he swore he could "stand no more of this," and, suddenly rising, he informed his visitors that he was sorry to leave them, but he felt rather poorly and was going to bed; and to bed he went, while his guests departed, each as his business or desires might point him, some to drink whiskey and some to repose.

On Sunday morning Mr. Ratcliffe, as usual, went to church. He always attended morning service—at the Methodist Episcopal Church—not wholly on the ground of religious conviction, but because a large number of his constituents were church-going people and he would not willingly shock their principles so long as he needed their votes. In church, he kept his eyes closely fixed upon the clergyman, and at the end of the sermon he could say with truth that he had not heard a word of it, although the respectable minister was gratified by the attention his discourse had received from the Senator from Illinois, an attention all the more praiseworthy because of the engrossing public cares which must at that moment have distracted the Senator's mind. In this last idea, the minister was right. Mr. Ratcliffe's mind was greatly distracted by public cares, and one of his strongest reasons for going to church at all was that he might get an hour or two of undisturbed reflection. During the entire service he was absorbed in carrying on a series of imaginary conversations with the new President. He brought up in succession every form of proposition which the President might make to him; every trap which could be laid for him; every sort of treatment he might expect, so that he could not be taken by surprise, and his frank, simple nature could never be at a loss. One object, however, long escaped him. Supposing, what was more than probable, that the President's opposition to Ratcliffe's declared friends made it impossible to force any of them into office; it would then be necessary to try some new man, not obnoxious to the President, as a candidate for the Cabinet. Who should this be? Ratcliffe pondered long and deeply, searching out a man who combined the most powerful interests, with the fewest enmities. This subject was still uppermost at the moment when service ended. Ratcliffe pondered over it as he walked back to his rooms. Not until he reached his own door did he come to a conclusion: Carson would do; Carson of Pennsylvania; the President had probably never heard of him.

Mr. Wilson Keen was waiting the Senator's return, a heavy man with a square face, and good-natured, active blue eyes; a man of few words and those well-considered. The interview was brief. After apologising for breaking in upon Sunday with business, Mr. Ratcliffe excused himself on the ground that so little time was left before the close of the session. A bill now before one of his Committees, on which a report must soon be made, involved matters to which it was believed that the late Samuel Baker, formerly a well-known lobby-agent in Washington, held the only clue. He being dead, Mr. Ratcliffe wished to know whether he had left any papers behind him, and in whose hands these papers were, or whether any partner or associate of his was acquainted with his affairs.

Mr. Keen made a note of the request, merely remarking that he had been very well acquainted with Baker, and also a little with his wife, who was supposed to know his affairs as well as he knew them himself, and who was still in Washington. He thought he could bring the information in a day or two. As he then rose to go, Mr.

Ratcliffe added that entire secrecy was necessary, as the interests involved in obstructing the search were considerable, and it was not well to wake them up. Mr. Keen assented and went his way.

All this was natural enough and entirely proper, at least so far as appeared on the surface. Had Mr. Keen been so curious in other people's affairs as to look for the particular legislative measure which lay at the bottom of Mr. Ratcliffe's inquiries, he might have searched among the papers of Congress a very long time and found himself greatly puzzled at last. In fact there was no measure of the kind. The whole story was a fiction. Mr. Ratcliffe had scarcely thought of Baker since his death, until the day before, when he had seen his widow on the Mount Vernon steamer and had found her in relations with Carrington. Something in Carrington's habitual attitude and manner towards himself had long struck him as peculiar, and this connection with Mrs. Baker had suggested to the Senator the idea that it might be well to have an eye on both. Mrs. Baker was a silly woman, as he knew, and there were old transactions between Ratcliffe and Baker of which she might be informed, but which Ratcliffe had no wish to see brought within Mrs. Lee's ken. As for the fiction invented to set Keen in motion, it was an innocent one. It harmed nobody. Ratcliffe selected this particular method of inquiry because it was the easiest, safest, and most effectual. If he were always to wait until he could afford to tell the precise truth, business would very soon be at a standstill, and his career at an end.

This little matter disposed of, the Senator from Illinois passed his afternoon in calling upon some of his brother senators, and the first of those whom he honoured with a visit was Mr. Krebs, of Pennsylvania. There were many reasons which now made the co-operation of that high-minded statesman essential to Mr. Ratcliffe. The strongest of them was that the Pennsylvania delegation in Congress was well disciplined and could be used with peculiar advantage for purposes of "pressure." Ratcliffe's success in his contest with the new President depended on the amount of "pressure" he could employ. To keep himself in the background, and to fling over the head of the raw Chief Magistrate a web of intertwined influences, any one of which alone would be useless, but which taken together were not to be broken though; to revive the lost art of the Roman retiarius, who from a safe distance threw his net over his adversary, before attacking with the dagger; this was Ratcliffe's intention and towards this he had been directing all his manipulation for weeks past. How much bargaining and how many promises he found it necessary to make, was known to himself alone. About this time Mrs. Lee was a little surprised to find Mr. Gore speaking with entire confidence of having Ratcliffe's support in his application for the Spanish mission, for she had rather imagined that Gore was not a favourite with Ratcliffe. She noticed too that Schneidekoupon had come back again and spoke mysteriously of interviews with Ratcliffe; of attempts to unite the interests of New York and Pennsylvania; and his countenance took on a dark and dramatic expression as he proclaimed that no sacrifice of the principle of protection should be tolerated. Schneidekoupon disappeared as suddenly as he came, and from Sybil's innocent complaints of his spirits and temper, Mrs. Lee jumped to the conclusion that Mr. Ratcliffe, Mr. Clinton, and Mr. Krebs had for the moment combined to sit heavily upon poor Schneidekoupon, and to remove his disturbing influence from the scene, at least until other men should get what they wanted. These were merely the trifling incidents that fell within Mrs. Lee's observation. She felt an atmosphere of bargain and intrigue, but she could only imagine how far it extended. Even Carrington, when she spoke to him about it, only laughed and shook his head: "Those matters are private, my dear Mrs. Lee; you and I are not meant to know such things."

This Sunday afternoon Mr. Ratcliffe's object was to arrange the little manœuvre about Carson of Pennsylvania, which had disturbed him in church. His efforts were crowned with success. Krebs accepted Carson and promised to bring him forward at ten minutes' notice, should the emergency arise.

Ratcliffe was a great statesman. The smoothness of his manipulation was marvelous. No other man in politics, indeed no other man who had ever been in politics in this country, could—his admirers said—have brought together so many hostile interests and made so fantastic a combination. Some men went so far as to maintain that he would "rope in the President himself before the old man had time to swap knives with him." The beauty of his work consisted in the skill with which he evaded questions of principle. As he wisely said, the issue now involved was not one of principle but of power. The fate of that noble party to which they all belonged, and which had a record that could never be forgotten, depended on their letting principle alone. Their principle must be the want of principles. There were indeed individuals who said in reply that Ratcliffe had made promises which never could be carried out, and there were almost superhuman elements of discord in the combination, but as Ratcliffe shrewdly rejoined, he only wanted it to last a week, and he guessed his promises would hold it up for that time.

Such was the situation when on Monday afternoon the President-elect arrived in Washington, and the comedy began. The new President was, almost as much as Abraham Lincoln or Franklin Pierce, an unknown quantity in political mathematics. In the national convention of the party, nine months before, after some dozens of fruitless ballots in which Ratcliffe wanted but three votes of a majority, his opponents had done what he was now doing; they had laid aside their principles and set up for their candidate a plain Indiana farmer, whose political experience was limited to stump-speaking in his native State, and to one term as Governor. They had pitched upon him, not because they thought him competent, but because they hoped by doing so to detach Indiana from Ratcliffe's following, and they were so successful that within fifteen minutes Ratcliffe's friends were routed, and the Presidency had fallen upon this new political Buddha.

He had begun his career as a stone-cutter in a quarry, and was, not unreasonably, proud of the fact. During the campaign this incident had, of course, filled a large space in the public mind, or, more exactly, in the public eye. "The Stone-cutter of the Wabash," he was sometimes called; at others "the Hoosier Quarryman," but his favourite appellation was "Old Granite," although this last endearing name, owing to an unfortunate similarity of sound, was seized upon by his opponents, and distorted into "Old Granny." He had been painted on many thousand yards of cotton sheeting, either with a terrific sledge-hammer, smashing the skulls (which figured as paving-stones) of his political opponents, or splitting by gigantic blows a huge rock typical of the opposing party. His opponents in their turn had paraded illuminations representing the Quarryman in the garb of a State's-prison convict breaking the heads of Ratcliffe and other well-known political leaders with a very feeble hammer, or as "Old Granny" in pauper's rags, hopelessly repairing with the same heads the impossible roads which typified the ill-conditioned and miry ways of his party. But these violations of decency and good sense were universally reproved by the virtuous; and it was remarked with satisfaction that the purest and most highly cultivated newspaper editors on his side, without excepting those of Boston itself, agreed with one voice that the Stone-cutter was a noble type of man, perhaps the very noblest that had appeared to adorn this country since the incomparable Washington.

That he was honest, all admitted; that is to say, all who voted for him. This is a general characteristic of all new presidents. He himself took great pride in his home-spun honesty, which is a quality peculiar to nature's noblemen. Owing nothing, as he conceived, to politicians, but sympathising through every fibre of his unselfish nature with the impulses and aspirations of the people, he affirmed it to be his first duty to protect the people from those vultures, as he called them, those wolves in sheep's clothing, those harpies, those hyenas, the politicians; epithets which, as generally interpreted, meant Ratcliffe and Ratcliffe's friends. His cardinal principle in politics was hostility to Ratcliffe, yet he was not vindictive. He came to Washington determined to be the Father of his country; to gain a proud immortality——and a re-election.

Upon this gentleman Ratcliffe had let loose all the forms of "pressure" which could be set in motion either in or out of Washington. From the moment when he had left his humble cottage in Southern Indiana, he had been captured by Ratcliffe's friends, and smothered in demonstrations of affection. They had never allowed him to suggest the possibility of ill-feeling. They had assumed as a matter of course that the most cordial attachment existed between him and his party. On his arrival in Washington they systematically cut him off from contact with any influences but their own. This was not a very difficult thing to do, for great as he was, he liked to be told of his greatness, and they made him feel himself a colossus. Even the few personal friends in his company were manipulated with the utmost care, and their weaknesses put to use before they had been in Washington a single day.

Not that Ratcliffe had anything to do with all this underhand and grovelling intrigue. Mr. Ratcliffe was a man of dignity and self-respect, who left details to his subordinates. He waited calmly until the President, recovered from the fatigues of his journey, should begin to feel the effect of a Washington atmosphere. Then on Wednesday morning, Mr. Ratcliffe left his rooms an hour earlier than usual on his way to the Senate, and called at the President's Hotel: he was ushered into a large apartment in which the new Chief Magistrate was holding court, although at sight of Ratcliffe, the other visitors edged away or took their hats and left the room. The President proved to be a hard-featured man of sixty, with a hooked nose and thin, straight, iron-gray hair. His voice was rougher than his features and he received Ratcliffe awkwardly. He had suffered since his departure from Indiana. Out there it had seemed a mere flea-bite, as he expressed it, to brush Ratcliffe aside, but in Washington the thing was somehow different. Even his own Indiana friends looked grave when he talked of it, and shook their heads. They advised him to be cautious and gain time; to lead Ratcliffe on, and if possible to throw on him the responsibility of a quarrel. He was, therefore, like a brown bear undergoing the process of taming; very ill-tempered, very rough, and at the same time very much bewildered and a little frightened. Ratcliffe sat ten minutes with him, and obtained information in regard to pains which the President had suffered during the previous night, in consequence, as he believed, of an over-indulgence in fresh lobster, a luxury in which he had found a diversion from the cares of state. So soon as this matter was explained and condoled upon, Ratcliffe rose and took leave.

Every device known to politicians was now in full play against the Hoosier Quarryman. State delegations with contradictory requests were poured in upon him, among which that of Massachusetts presented as its only prayer the appointment of Mr. Gore to the Spanish mission. Difficulties were invented to embarrass and worry him. False leads were suggested, and false information carefully mingled with true. A wild dance was kept up under his eyes from daylight to midnight, until his brain reeled with the effort to follow it. Means were also found to convert one of his personal, confidential friends, who had come with him from Indiana and who had more brains or less principle than the others; from him every word of the President was brought directly to Ratcliffe's ear.

Early on Friday morning, Mr. Thomas Lord, a rival of the late Samuel Baker, and heir to his triumphs, appeared in Ratcliffe's rooms while the Senator was consuming his lonely egg and chop. Mr. Lord had been chosen to take general charge of the presidential party and to direct all matters connected with Ratcliffe's interests. Some people might consider this the work of a spy; he looked on it as a public duty. He reported that "Old Granny" had at last shown signs of weakness. Late the previous evening when, according to his custom, he was smoking his pipe in company with his kitchen-cabinet of followers, he had again fallen upon the subject of Ratcliffe, and with a volley of oaths had sworn that he would show him his place yet, and that he meant to offer him a seat in the Cabinet that would make him "sicker than a stuck hog." From this remark and some explanatory hints that followed, it seemed that the Quarryman had abandoned his scheme of putting Ratcliffe to immediate political death, and had now undertaken to invite him into a Cabinet which was to be specially constructed to thwart and humiliate him. The President, it appeared, warmly applauded the remark of one counsellor, that Ratcliffe was safer in the Cabinet than in the Senate, and that it would be easy to kick him out when the time came.

Ratcliffe smiled grimly as Mr. Lord, with much clever mimicry, described the President's peculiarities of language and manner, but he said nothing and waited for the event. The same evening came a note from the President's private secretary requesting his attendance, if possible, to-morrow, Saturday morning, at ten o'clock. The note was curt and cool. Ratcliffe merely sent back word that he would come, and felt a little regret that the President should not know enough etiquette to understand that this verbal answer was intended as a hint to improve his manners. He did come accordingly, and found the President looking blacker than before. This time there was no avoiding of tender subjects. The President meant to show Ratcliffe by the decision of his course, that he was master of the situation. He broke at once into the middle of the matter: "I sent for you," said he, "to consult with you about my Cabinet. Here is a list of the gentlemen I intend to invite into it. You will see that I have got you down for the Treasury. Will you look at the list and say what you think of it?"

Ratcliffe took the paper, but laid it at once on the table without looking at it. "I can have no objection," said he, "to any Cabinet you may appoint, provided I am not included in it. My wish is to remain where I am. There I can serve your administration better than in the Cabinet."

"Then you refuse?" growled the President.

"By no means. I only decline to offer any advice or even to hear the names of my proposed colleagues until it is decided that my services are necessary. If they are, I shall accept without caring with whom I serve."

The President glared at him with an uneasy look. What was to be done next? He wanted time to think, but Ratcliffe was there and must be disposed of. He involuntarily became more civil: "Mr. Ratcliffe, your refusal would knock everything on the head. I thought that matter was all fixed. What more can I do?"

But Ratcliffe had no mind to let the President out of his clutches so easily, and a long conversation followed, during which he forced his antagonist into the position of urging him to take the Treasury in order to prevent some undefined but portentous mischief in the Senate. All that could be agreed upon was that Ratcliffe should give a positive answer within two days, and on that agreement he took his leave.

As he passed through the corridor, a number of gentlemen were waiting for interviews with the President, and among them was the whole Pennsylvania delegation, "ready for biz," as Mr. Tom Lord remarked, with a wink. Ratcliffe drew Krebs aside and they exchanged a few words as he passed out. Ten minutes afterwards the delegation was admitted, and some of its members were a little surprised to hear their spokesman, Senator Krebs, press with extreme earnestness and in their names, the appointment of Josiah B. Carson to a place in the Cabinet, when they had been given to understand that they came to recommend Jared Caldwell as postmaster of Philadelphia. But Pennsylvania is a great and virtuous State, whose representatives have entire confidence in their chief. Not one of them so much as winked.

The dance of democracy round the President now began again with wilder energy. Ratcliffe launched his last bolts. His two-days' delay was a mere cover for bringing new influences to bear. He needed no delay. He wanted no time for reflection. The President had undertaken to put him on the horns of a dilemma; either to force him into a hostile and treacherous Cabinet, or to throw on him the blame of a refusal and a quarrel. He meant to embrace one of the horns and to impale the President on it, and he felt perfect confidence in his own success. He meant to accept the Treasury and he was ready to back himself with a heavy wager to get the government entirely into his own hands within six weeks. His contempt for the Hoosier Stone-cutter was unbounded, and his confidence in himself more absolute than ever.

Busy as he was, the Senator made his appearance the next evening at Mrs. Lee's, and finding her alone with Sybil, who was occupied with her own little devices, Ratcliffe told Madeleine the story of his week's experience. He did not dwell on his exploits. On the contrary he quite ignored those elaborate arrangements which had taken from the President his power of volition. His picture presented himself, solitary and unprotected, in the character of that honest beast who was invited to dine with the lion and saw that all the footmarks of his predecessors led into the lion's cave, and none away from it. He described in humorous detail his interviews with the Indiana lion, and the particulars of the surfeit of lobster as given in the President's dialect; he even repeated to her the story told him by Mr. Tom Lord, without omitting oaths or gestures; he told her how matters stood at the moment, and how the President had laid a trap for him which he could not escape; he must either enter a Cabinet constructed on purpose to thwart him and with the certainty of ignominious dismissal at the first opportunity, or he must refuse an offer of friendship which would throw on him the blame of a quarrel, and enable the President to charge all future difficulties to the account of Ratcliffe's "insatiable ambition." "And now, Mrs. Lee," he continued, with increasing seriousness of tone; "I want your advice; what shall I do?"

Even this half revelation of the meanness which distorted politics; this one-sided view of human nature in its naked deformity playing pranks with the interests of forty million people, disgusted and depressed Madeleine's mind. Ratcliffe spared her nothing except the exposure of his own moral sores. He carefully called her attention to every leprous taint upon his neighbours' persons, to every rag in their foul clothing, to every slimy and fetid pool that lay beside their path. It was his way of bringing his own qualities into relief. He meant that she should go hand in hand with him through the brimstone lake, and the more repulsive it seemed to her, the more overwhelming would his superiority become. He meant to destroy those doubts of his character which Carrington was so carefully fostering, to rouse her sympathy, to stimulate her feminine sense of self-sacrifice.

When he asked this question she looked up at him with an expression of indignant pride, as she spoke:

"I say again, Mr. Ratcliffe, what I said once before. Do whatever is most for the public good."

"And what *is* most for the public good?"

Madeleine half opened her mouth to reply, then hesitated, and stared silently into the fire before her. What was indeed most for the public good? Where did the public good enter at all into this maze of personal intrigue, this wilderness of stunted natures where no straight road was to be found, but only the tortuous and aimless tracks of beasts and things that crawl? Where was she to look for a principle to guide, an ideal to set up and to point at?

Ratcliffe resumed his appeal, and his manner was more serious than ever.

"I am hard pressed, Mrs. Lee. My enemies encompass me about.

They mean to ruin me. I honestly wish to do my duty. You once said that personal considerations should have no weight. Very well! throw them away! And now tell me what I should do."

For the first time, Mrs. Lee began to feel his power. He was simple, straightforward, earnest. His words moved her. How should she imagine that he was playing upon her sensitive nature precisely as he played upon the President's coarse one, and that this heavy western politician had the instincts of a wild Indian in their sharpness and quickness of perception; that he divined her character and read it as he read the faces and tones of thousands from day to day? She was uneasy under his eye. She began a sentence, hesitated in the middle, and broke down. She lost her command of thought, and sat dumb-founded. He had to draw her out of the confusion he had himself made.

"I see your meaning in your face. You say that I should accept the duty and disregard the consequences."

"I don't know," said Madeleine, hesitatingly; "Yes, I think that would be my feeling."

"And when I fall a sacrifice to that man's envy and intrigue, what will you think then, Mrs. Lee? Will you not join the rest of the world and say that I overreached myself, and walked into this trap with my eyes open, and for my own objects? Do you think I shall ever be thought better of, for getting caught here? I don't parade high moral views like our friend French. I won't cant about virtue. But I do claim that in my public life I have tried to do right. Will you do me the justice to think so?"

Madeleine still struggled to prevent herself from being drawn into indefinite promises of sympathy with this man. She would keep him at arm's length whatever her sympathies might be. She would not pledge herself to espouse his cause. She turned upon him with an effort, and said that her thoughts, now or at any time, were folly and nonsense, and that the consciousness of right-doing was the only reward any public man had a right to expect.

"And yet you are a hard critic, Mrs. Lee. If your thoughts are what you say, your words are not. You judge with the judgment of abstract principles, and you wield the bolts of divine justice. You look on and condemn, but you refuse to acquit. When I come to you on the verge of what is likely to be the fatal plunge of my life, and ask you only for some clue to the moral principle that ought to guide me, you look on and say that virtue is its own reward. And you do not even say where virtue lies."

"I confess my sins," said Madeleine, meekly and despondently; "life is more complicated than I thought."

"I shall be guided by your advice," said Ratcliffe; "I shall walk into that den of wild beasts, since you think I ought. But I shall hold you to your responsibility. You cannot refuse to see me through dangers you have helped to bring me into."

"No, no!" cried Madeleine, earnestly; "no responsibility. You ask more than I can give."

Ratcliffe looked at her a moment with a troubled and careworn face. His eyes seemed deep sunk in their dark circles, and his voice was pathetic in its intensity. "Duty is duty, for you as well as for me. I have a right to the help of all pure minds. You have no right to refuse it. How *can* you reject your own responsibility and hold me to mine?"

Almost as he spoke, he rose and took his departure, leaving her no time to do more than murmur again her ineffectual protest. After he was gone, Mrs. Lee sat long, with her eyes fixed on the fire, reflecting upon what he had said. Her mind was bewildered by the new suggestions which Ratcliffe had thrown out. What woman of thirty, with aspirations for the infinite, could resist an attack like this? What woman with a soul could see before her the most powerful public man of her time, appealing—with a face furrowed by anxieties, and a voice vibrating with only half-suppressed affection—to her for counsel and sympathy, without yielding some response? and what woman could have helped bowing her head to that rebuke of her over-confident judgment, coming as it did from one who in the same breath appealed to that judgment as final? Ratcliffe, too, had a curious instinct for human weaknesses. No magnetic needle was ever truer than his finger when he touched the vulnerable spot in an opponent's mind. Mrs. Lee was not to be reached by an appeal to religious sentiment, to ambition, or to affection. Any such appeal would have fallen flat on her ears and destroyed its own hopes. But she was a woman to the very last drop of her blood. She could not be induced to love Ratcliffe, but she might be deluded into sacrificing herself for him. She atoned for want of devotion to God, by devotion to man. She had a woman's natural tendency towards asceticism, self-extinction, self-abnegation. All through life she had made painful efforts to understand and follow out her duty. Ratcliffe knew her weak point when he attacked her from this side. Like all great orators and advocates, he was an actor; the more effective because of a certain dignified air that forbade familiarity. He had appealed to her sympathy, her sense of right and of duty, to her courage, her loyalty, her whole higher nature; and while he made this appeal he felt more than half convinced that he was all he pretended to be, and that he really had a right to her devotion. What wonder that she in her turn was more than half inclined to admit that right. She knew him now better than Carrington or Jacobi knew him. Surely a man who spoke as he spoke, had noble instincts and lofty aims? Was not his career a thousand times more important than hers? If he, in his isolation and his cares, needed her assistance, had she an excuse for refusing it? What was there in her aimless and useless life which made it so precious that she could not afford to fling it into the gutter, if need be, on the bare chance of enriching some fuller existence?

Chapter VIII

Of all titles ever assumed by prince or potentate, the proudest is that of the Roman pontiffs: "Servus servorum Dei"—"Servant of the servants of God." In former days it was not admitted that the devil's servants could by right have any share in government. They were to be shut out, punished, exiled, maimed, and burned. The devil has no servants now; only the people have servants. There may be some mistake about a doctrine which makes the wicked, when a majority, the mouthpiece of God against the virtuous, but the hopes of mankind are staked on it; and if the weak in faith sometimes quail when they see humanity floating in a shoreless ocean, on this plank, which experience and religion long since condemned as rotten, mistake or not, men have thus far floated better by its aid, than the popes ever did with their prettier principle; so that it will be a long time yet before society repents.

Whether the new President and his chief rival, Mr. Silas P. Ratcliffe, were or were not servants of the servants of God, is not material here. Servants they were to some one. No doubt many of those who call themselves servants of the people are no better than wolves in sheep's clothing, or asses in lions' skins. One may see scores of them any day in the Capitol when Congress is in session, making noisy demonstrations, or more usefully doing nothing. A wiser generation will employ them in manual labour; as it is, they serve only themselves. But there are two officers, at least, whose service is real—the President and his Secretary of the Treasury. The Hoosier Quarryman had not been a week in Washington before he was heartily home-sick for Indiana. No maid-of-all-work in a cheap boarding-house was ever more harassed. Everyone conspired against him. His enemies gave him no peace. All Washington was laughing at his blunders, and ribald sheets, published on a Sunday, took delight in printing the new Chief Magistrate's sayings and doings, chronicled with outrageous humour, and placed by malicious hands where the President could not but see them. He was sensitive to ridicule, and it mortified him to the heart to find that remarks and acts, which to him seemed sensible enough, should be capable of such perversion. Then he was overwhelmed with public business. It came upon him in a deluge, and he now, in his despair, no longer tried to control it. He let it pass over him like a wave. His mind was muddled by the innumerable visitors to whom he had to listen. But his greatest anxiety was the Inaugural Address which, distracted as he was, he could not finish, although in another week it must be delivered. He was nervous about his Cabinet; it seemed to him that he could do nothing until he had disposed of Ratcliffe. Already, thanks to the President's friends, Ratcliffe had become indispensable; still an enemy, of course, but one whose hands must be tied; a sort of Sampson, to be kept in bonds until the time came for putting him out of the way, but in the meanwhile, to be utilized. This point being settled, the President had in imagination begun to lean upon him; for the last few days he had postponed everything till next week, "when I get my Cabinet arranged;" which meant, when he got Ratcliffe's assistance; and he fell into a panic whenever he thought of the chance that Ratcliffe might refuse.

He was pacing his room impatiently on Monday morning, an hour before the time fixed for Ratcliffe's visit. His feelings still fluctuated violently, and if he recognized the necessity of using Ratcliffe, he was not the less determined to tie Ratcliffe's hands. He must be made to come into a Cabinet where every other voice would be against him. He must be prevented from having any patronage to dispose of. He must be induced to accept these conditions at the start. How present this to him in such a way as not to repel him at once? All this was needless, if the President had only known it, but he thought himself a profound statesman, and that his hand was guiding the destinies of America to his own re-election. When at length, on the stroke of ten o'clock, Ratcliffe entered the room, the President turned to him with nervous eagerness, and almost before offering his hand, said that he hoped Mr. Ratcliffe had come prepared to begin work at once. The Senator replied that, if such was the President's decided wish, he would offer no further opposition. Then the President drew himself up in the attitude of an American Cato, and delivered a prepared address, in which he said that he had chosen the members of his Cabinet with a careful regard to the public interests; that Mr. Ratcliffe was essential to the combination; that he expected no disagreement on principles, for there was but one principle which he should consider fundamental, namely, that there should be no removals from office except for cause; and that under these circumstances he counted upon Mr. Ratcliffe's assistance as a matter of patriotic duty.

To all this Ratcliffe assented without a word of objection, and the President, more convinced than ever of his own masterly statesmanship, breathed more freely than for a week past. Within ten minutes they were actively at work together, clearing away the mass of accumulated business. The relief of the Quarryman surprised himself. Ratcliffe lifted the weight of affairs from his shoulders with hardly an effort. He knew everybody and everything. He took most of the President's visitors at once into his own hands and dismissed them with great rapidity. He knew what they wanted; he knew what recommendations were strong and what were weak; who was to be treated with deference and who was to be sent away abruptly; where a blunt refusal was safe, and where a pledge was allowable. The President even trusted him with the unfinished manuscript of the Inaugural Address, which Ratcliffe returned to him the next day with such notes and suggestions as left nothing to be done beyond copying them out in a fair hand. With all this, he proved himself a very agreeable companion. He talked well and enlivened the work; he was not a hard taskmaster, and when he saw that the President was tired, he boldly asserted that there was no more business that could not as well wait a day, and so took the weary Stone-cutter out to drive for a couple of hours, and let him go peacefully to sleep in the carriage. They dined together and Ratcliffe took care to send for Tom Lord to amuse them, for Tom was a wit and a humourist, and kept the President in a laugh. Mr. Lord ordered the dinner and chose the wines. He could be coarse enough to suit even the President's palate, and Ratcliffe was not behindhand. When the new Secretary went away at ten o'clock that night, his chief, who was in high good humour with his dinner, his champagne, and his conversation, swore with some unnecessary granite oaths, that Ratcliffe was "a clever fellow anyhow," and he was glad "that job was fixed."

The truth was that Ratcliffe had now precisely ten days before the new Cabinet could be set in motion, and in these ten days he must establish his authority over the President so firmly that nothing could shake it. He was diligent in good works. Very soon the court began to feel his hand. If a business letter or a written memorial came in, the President found it easy to endorse: "Referred to the Secretary of the Treasury." If a visitor wanted anything for himself or another, the invariable reply came to be: "Just mention it to Mr. Ratcliffe;" or, "I guess Ratcliffe will see to that." Before long he even made jokes in a Catonian manner; jokes that were not peculiarly witty, but somewhat gruff and boorish, yet significant of a resigned and self-contented mind. One morning he ordered Ratcliffe to take an iron-clad ship of war and attack the Sioux in Montana, seeing that he was in charge of the army and navy and Indians at once, and Jack of all trades; and again he told a naval officer who wanted a court-martial that he had better get Ratcliffe to sit on him for he was a whole court-martial by himself. That Ratcliffe held his chief in no less contempt than before, was probable but not certain, for he kept silence on the subject before the world, and looked solemn whenever the President was mentioned.

Before three days were over, the President, with a little more than his usual abruptness, suddenly asked him what he knew about this fellow Carson, whom the Pennsylvanians were bothering him to put in his Cabinet. Ratcliffe was guarded: he scarcely knew the man; Mr. Carson was not in politics, he believed, but was pretty respectable—for a Pennsylvanian. The President returned to the subject several times; got out his list of Cabinet officers and figured industriously upon it with a rather perplexed face; called Ratcliffe to help him; and at last the "slate" was fairly broken, and Ratcliffe's eyes gleamed when the President caused his list of nominations to be sent to the Senate on the 5th March, and Josiah B. Carson, of Pennsylvania, was promptly confirmed as Secretary of the Interior.

But his eyes gleamed still more humorously when, a few days afterwards, the President gave him a long list of some two score names, and asked him to find places for them. He assented good-naturedly, with a remark that it might be necessary to make a few removals to provide for these cases.

"Oh, well," said the President, "I guess there's just about as many as that had ought to go out anyway. These are friends of mine; got to be looked after. Just stuff 'em in somewhere."

Even he felt a little awkward about it, and, to do him justice, this was the last that was heard about the fundamental rule of his administration. Removals were fast and furious, until all Indiana became easy in circumstances. And it was not to be denied that, by one means or another, Ratcliffe's friends did come into their fair share of the public money. Perhaps the President thought it best to wink at such use of the Treasury patronage for the present, or was already a little overawed by his Secretary.

Ratcliffe's work was done. The public had, with the help of some clever intrigue, driven its servants into the traces. Even an Indiana stone-cutter could be taught that his personal prejudices must yield to the public service. What mischief the selfishness, the ambition, or the ignorance of these men might do, was another matter. As the affair stood, the President was the victim of his own schemes. It remained to be seen whether, at some future day, Mr. Ratcliffe would think it worth his while to strangle his chief by some quiet Eastern intrigue, but the time had gone by when the President could make use of either the bow-string or the axe upon him.

All this passed while Mrs. Lee was quietly puzzling her poor little brain about her duty and her responsibility to Ratcliffe, who, meanwhile, rarely failed to find himself on Sunday evenings by her side in her parlour, where his rights were now so well established that no one presumed to contest his seat, unless it were old Jacobi, who from time to time reminded him that he was fallible and mortal. Occasionally, though not often, Mr. Ratcliffe came at other times, as when he persuaded Mrs. Lee to be present at the Inauguration, and to call on the President's wife. Madeleine and Sybil went to the Capitol and had the best places to see and hear the Inauguration, as well as a cold March wind would allow. Mrs. Lee found fault with the ceremony; it was of the earth, earthy, she said. An elderly western farmer, with silver spectacles, new and glossy evening clothes, bony features, and stiff, thin, gray hair, trying to address a large crowd of people, under the drawbacks of a piercing wind and a cold in his head, was not a hero. Sybil's mind was lost in wondering whether the President would not soon die of pneumonia. Even this experience, however, was happy when compared with that of the call upon the President's wife, after which Madeleine decided to leave the new dynasty alone in future. The lady, who was somewhat stout and coarse-featured, and whom Mrs. Lee declared she wouldn't engage as a cook, showed qualities which, seen under that fierce light which beats upon a throne, seemed ungracious. Her antipathy to Ratcliffe was more violent than her husband's, and was even more openly expressed, until the President was quite put out of countenance by it. She extended her hostility to every one who could be supposed to be Ratcliffe's friend, and the newspapers, as well as private gossip, had marked out Mrs. Lee as one who, by an alliance with Ratcliffe, was aiming at supplanting her own rule over the White House. Hence, when Mrs. Lightfoot Lee was announced, and the two sisters were ushered into the presidential parlour, she put on a coldly patronizing air, and in reply to Madeleine's hope that she found Washington agreeable, she intimated that there was much in Washington which struck her as awful wicked, especially the women; and, looking at Sybil, she spoke of the style of dress in this city which she said she meant to do what she could to put a stop to. She'd heard tell that people sent to Paris for their gowns, just as though America wasn't good enough to make one's clothes! Jacob (all Presidents' wives speak of their husbands by their first names) had promised her to get a law passed against it. In her town in Indiana, a young woman who was seen on the street in such clothes wouldn't be spoken to. At these remarks, made with an air and in a temper quite unmistakable, Madeleine became exasperated beyond measure, and said that "Washington would be pleased to see the President do something in regard to dress-reform—or any other reform;" and with this allusion to the President's ante–election reform speeches, Mrs. Lee turned her back and left the room, followed by Sybil in convulsions of suppressed laughter, which would not have been suppressed had she seen the face of their hostess as the door shut behind them, and the

energy with which she shook her head and said: "See if I don't reform you yet, you—jade!"

Mrs. Lee gave Ratcliffe a lively account of this interview, and he
laughed nearly as convulsively as Sybil over it, though he tried to
pacify her by saying that the President's most intimate friends
openly declared his wife to be insane, and that he himself was the
person most afraid of her. But Mrs. Lee declared that the President
was as bad as his wife; that an equally good President and President's wife could be picked up in any corner-grocery between the
Lakes and the Ohio; and that no inducement should ever make her
go near that coarse washerwoman again.

Ratcliffe did not attempt to change Mrs. Lee's opinion. Indeed
he knew better than any man how Presidents were made, and he
had his own opinions in regard to the process as well as the fabric
produced. Nothing Mrs. Lee could say now affected him. He threw
off his responsibility and she found it suddenly resting on her own
shoulders. When she spoke with indignation of the wholesale removals from office with which the new administration marked its
advent to power, he told her the story of the President's fundamental principle, and asked her what she would have him do. "He
meant to tie my hands," said Ratcliffe, "and to leave his own free,
and I accepted the condition. Can I resign now on such a ground as
this?" And Madeleine was obliged to agree that he could not. She
had no means of knowing how many removals he made in his own
interest, or how far he had outwitted the President at his own game.
He stood before her a victim and a patriot. Every step he had taken
had been taken with her approval. He was now in office to prevent
what evil he could, not to be responsible for the evil that was done;
and he honestly assured her that much worse men would come in
when he went out, as the President would certainly take good care
that he did go out when the moment arrived.

Mrs. Lee had the chance now to carry out her scheme in coming
to Washington, for she was already deep in the mire of politics and

could see with every advantage how the great machine floundered about, bespattering with mud even her own pure garments. Ratcliffe himself, since entering the Treasury, had begun to talk with a sneer of the way in which laws were made, and openly said that he wondered how government got on at all. Yet he declared still that this particular government was the highest expression of political thought. Mrs. Lee stared at him and wondered whether he knew what thought was. To her the government seemed to have less thought in it than one of Sybil's gowns, for if they, like the government, were monstrously costly, they were at least adapted to their purpose, the parts fitted together, and they were neither awkward nor unwieldy.

There was nothing very encouraging in all this, but it was better than New York. At least it gave her something to look at, and to think about. Even Lord Dunbeg preached practical philanthropy to her by the hour. Ratcliffe, too, was compelled to drag himself out of the rut of machine politics, and to justify his right of admission to her house. There Mr. French discoursed at great length, until the fourth of March sent him home to Connecticut; and he brought more than one intelligent member of Congress to Mrs. Lee's parlour. Underneath the scum floating on the surface of politics, Madeleine felt that there was a sort of healthy ocean current of honest purpose, which swept the scum before it, and kept the mass pure.

This was enough to draw her on. She reconciled herself to accepting the Ratcliffian morals, for she could see no choice. She herself had approved every step she had seen him take. She could not deny that there must be something wrong in a double standard of morality, but where was it? Mr. Ratcliffe seemed to her to be doing good work with as pure means as he had at hand. He ought to be encouraged, not reviled. What was she that she should stand in judgment?

Others watched her progress with less satisfaction. Mr. Nathan

Gore was one of these, for he came in one evening, looking much out of temper, and, sitting down by her side he said he had come to bid good-bye and to thank her for the kindness she had shown him; he was to leave Washington the next morning. She too expressed her warm regret, but added that she hoped he was only going in order to take his passage to Madrid.

He shook his head. "I am going to take my passage," said he, "but not to Madrid. The fates have cut that thread. The President does not want my services, and I can't blame him, for if our situations were reversed, I should certainly not want his. He has an Indiana friend, who, I am told, wanted to be postmaster at Indianapolis, but as this did not suit the politicians, he was bought off at the exorbitant price of the Spanish mission. But I should have no chance even if he were out of the way. The President does not approve of me. He objects to the cut of my overcoat which is unfortunately an English one. He also objects to the cut of my hair. I am afraid that his wife objects to me because I am so happy as to be thought a friend of yours."

Madeleine could only acknowledge that Mr. Gore's case was a bad one. "But after all," said she, "why should politicians be expected to love you literary gentlemen who write history. Other criminal classes are not expected to love their judges."

"No, but they have sense enough to fear them," replied Gore vindictively; "not one politician living has the brains or the art to defend his own cause. The ocean of history is foul with the carcases of such statesmen, dead and forgotten except when some historian fishes one of them up to gibbet it."

Mr. Gore was so much out of temper that after this piece of extravagance he was forced to pause a moment to recover himself. Then he went on:—

"You are perfectly right, and so is the President. I have no business to be meddling in politics. It is not my place. The next time you hear of me, I promise it shall not be as an office-seeker."

Then he rapidly changed the subject, saying that he hoped Mrs. Lee was soon going northward again, and that they might meet at Newport.

"I don't know," replied Madeleine; "the spring is pleasant here, and we shall stay till the warm weather, I think."

Mr. Gore looked grave. "And your politics!" said he; "are you satisfied with what you have seen?"

"I have got so far as to lose the distinction between right and wrong. Isn't that the first step in politics?"

Mr. Gore had no mind even for serious jesting. He broke out into a long lecture which sounded like a chapter of some future history: "But Mrs. Lee, is it possible that you don't see what a wrong path you are on. If you want to know what the world is really doing to any good purpose, pass a winter at Samarcand, at Timbuctoo, but not at Washington. Be a bank-clerk, or a journeyman printer, but not a Congressman. Here you will find nothing but wasted effort and clumsy intrigue."

"Do you think it a pity for me to learn that?" asked Madeleine when his long essay was ended.

"No!" replied Gore, hesitating; "not if you do learn it. But many people never get so far, or only when too late. I shall be glad to hear that you are mistress of it and have given up reforming politics. The Spaniards have a proverb that smells of the stable, but applies to people like you and me: The man who washes his donkey's head, loses time and soap."

Gore took his leave before Madeleine had time to grasp all the impudence of this last speech. Not until she was fairly in bed that night did it suddenly flash on her mind that Mr. Gore had dared to caricature her as wasting time and soap on Mr. Ratcliffe. At first she was violently angry and then she laughed in spite of herself; there was truth in the portrait. In secret, too, she was the less offended because she half thought that it had depended only on herself to make of Mr. Gore something more than a friend. If she had overheard his parting words to Carrington, she would have had still more reason to think that a little jealousy of Ratcliffe's success sharpened the barb of Gore's enmity.

"Take care of Ratcliffe!" was his farewell; "he is a clever dog. He has set his mark on Mrs. Lee. Look out that he doesn't walk off with her!"

A little startled by this sudden confidence, Carrington could only ask what he could do to prevent it.

"Cats that go ratting, don't wear gloves," replied Gore, who always carried a Spanish proverb in his pocket. Carrington, after painful reflection, could only guess that he wanted Ratcliffe's enemies to show their claws. But how?

Mrs. Lee not long afterwards spoke to Ratcliffe of her regret at Gore's disappointment and hinted at his disgust. Ratcliffe replied that he had done what he could for Gore, and had introduced him to the President, who, after seeing him, had sworn his usual granitic oath that he would sooner send his nigger farm-hand Jake to Spain than that man-milliner. "You know how I stand;" added Ratcliffe; "what more could I do?" And Mrs. Lee's implied reproach was silenced.

If Gore was little pleased with Ratcliffe's conduct, poor Schneidekoupon was still less so. He turned up again at Washington not long after the Inauguration and had a private interview with the Secretary of the Treasury. What passed at it was known only to themselves, but, whatever it was, Schneidekoupon's temper was none the better for it. From his conversations with Sybil, it seemed that there was some question about appointments in which his protectionist friends were interested, and he talked very openly about Ratcliffe's want of good faith, and how he had promised everything to everybody and had failed to keep a single pledge; if Schneidekoupon's advice had been taken, this wouldn't have happened. Mrs. Lee told Ratcliffe that Schneidekoupon seemed out of temper, and asked the reason. He only laughed and evaded the question, remarking that cattle of this kind were always complaining unless they were allowed to run the whole government; Schneidekoupon had nothing to grumble about; no one had ever made any promises to him. But nevertheless Schneidekoupon confided to Sybil his antipathy to Ratcliffe and solemnly begged her not to let Mrs. Lee fall into his hands, to which Sybil answered tartly that she only wished Mr. Schneidekoupon would tell her how to help it.

The reformer French had also been one of Ratcliffe's backers in the fight over the Treasury. He remained in Washington a few days after the Inauguration, and then disappeared, leaving cards with P.P.C. in the corner, at Mrs. Lee's door. Rumour said that he too was disappointed, but he kept his own counsel, and, if he really wanted the mission to Belgium, he contented himself with waiting for it. A respectable stage-coach proprietor from Oregon got the place.

As for Jacobi, who was not disappointed, and who had nothing to ask for, he was bitterest of all. He formally offered his congratulations to Ratcliffe on his appointment. This little scene occurred in Mrs. Lee's parlour. The old Baron, with his most suave manner, and his most Voltairean leer, said that in all his experience, and he had seen a great many court intrigues, he had never seen anything better managed than that about the Treasury. Ratcliffe was furiously angry, and told the Baron outright that foreign ministers who insulted the governments to which they were accredited ran a risk of being sent home.

"Ce serait toujours un pis aller," said Jacobi, seating himself with calmness in Ratcliffe's favourite chair by Mrs. Lee's side.

Madeleine, alarmed as she was, could not help interposing, and hastily asked whether that remark was translatable.

"Ah!" said the Baron; "I can do nothing with your language. You would only say that it was a choice of evils, to go, or to stay."

"We might translate it by saying: 'One may go farther and fare worse,'" rejoined Madeleine; and so the storm blew over for the time, and Ratcliffe sulkily let the subject drop. Nevertheless the two men never met in Mrs. Lee's parlour without her dreading a personal altercation. Little by little, what with Jacobi's sarcasms and Ratcliffe's roughness, they nearly ceased to speak, and glared at each other like quarrelsome dogs. Madeleine was driven to all kinds of expedients to keep the peace, yet at the same time she could not but be greatly amused by their behaviour, and as their hatred of each other only stimulated their devotion to her, she was content to hold an even balance between them.

Nor were these all the awkward consequences of Ratcliffe's attentions. Now that he was distinctly recognized as an intimate friend of Mrs. Lee's, and possibly her future husband, no one ventured any longer to attack him in her presence, but nevertheless she was conscious in a thousand ways that the atmosphere became more and more dense under the shadow of the Secretary of the Treasury. In spite of herself she sometimes felt uneasy, as though there were conspiracy in the air. One March afternoon she was sitting by her fire, with an English Review in her hand, trying to read the last Symposium on the sympathies of Eternal Punishment, when her servant brought in a card, and Mrs. Lee had barely time to read the name of Mrs. Samuel Baker when that lady followed the servant into the room, forcing the countersign in so effective style that for once Madeleine was fairly disconcerted. Her manner when thus intruded upon, was cool, but in this case, on Carrington's account, she tried to smile courteously and asked her visitor to sit down, which Mrs. Baker was doing without an invitation, very soon putting her hostess entirely at her ease. She was, when seen without her veil, a showy woman verging on forty, decidedly large, tall, over-dressed even in mourning, and with a complexion rather fresher than nature had made it. There was a geniality in her address, savouring of easy Washington ways, a fruitiness of smile, and a rich southern accent, that explained on the spot her success in the lobby. She looked about her with fine self-possession, and approved Mrs. Lee's surroundings with a cordiality so different from the northern stinginess of praise, that Madeleine was rather pleased than offended. Yet when her eye rested on the Corot, Madeleine's only pride, she was evidently perplexed, and resorted to eye-glasses, in order, as it seemed, to gain time for reflection. But she was not to be disconcerted even by Corot's masterpiece:

"How pretty! Japanese, isn't it? Sea-weeds seen through a fog. I went to an auction yesterday, and do you know I bought a tea-pot with a picture just like that."

Madeleine inquired with extreme interest about the auction, but after learning all that Mrs. Baker had to tell, she was on the point of being reduced to silence, when she bethought herself to mention Carrington. Mrs. Baker brightened up at once, if she could be said to brighten where there was no sign of dimness:

"Dear Mr. Carrington! Isn't he sweet? I think he's a delicious man. I don't know what I should do without him. Since poor Mr. Baker left me, we have been together all the time. You know my poor husband left directions that all his papers should be burned, and though I would not say so unless you were such a friend of Mr. Carrington's, I reckon it's just as well for some people that he did. I never could tell you what quantities of papers Mr. Carrington and I have put in the fire; and we read them all too."

Madeleine asked whether this was not dull work.

"Oh, dear, no! You see I knew all about it, and told Mr. Carrington the story of every paper as we went on. It was quite amusing, I assure you."

Mrs. Lee then boldly said she had got from Mr. Carrington an idea that Mrs. Baker was a very skilful diplomatist.

"Diplomatist!" echoed the widow with her genial laugh; "Well! it was as much that as anything, but there's not many diplomatists' wives in this city ever did as much work as I used to do. Why, I knew half the members of Congress intimately, and all of them by sight. I knew where they came from and what they liked best. I could get round the greater part of them, sooner or later."

Mrs. Lee asked what she did with all this knowledge. Mrs. Baker shook her pink-and-white countenance, and almost paralysed her opposite neighbour by a sort of Grande Duchesse wink:

"Oh, my dear! you are new here. If you had seen Washington in war-times and for a few years afterwards, you wouldn't ask that. We had more congressional business than all the other agents put together. Every one came to us then, to get his bill through, or his appropriation watched. We were hard at work all the time. You see, one can't keep the run of three hundred men without some trouble. My husband used to make lists of them in books with a history of each man and all he could learn about him, but I carried it all in my head."

"Do you mean that you could get them all to vote as you pleased?" asked Madeleine.

"Well! we got our bills through," replied Mrs. Baker.

"But how did you do it? did they take bribes?"

"Some of them did. Some of them liked suppers and cards and theatres and all sorts of things. Some of them could be led, and some had to be driven like Paddy's pig who thought he was going the other way. Some of them had wives who could talk to them, and some—hadn't," said Mrs. Baker, with a queer intonation in her abrupt ending.

"But surely," said Mrs. Lee, "many of them must have been above—I mean they must have had nothing to get hold of, so that you could manage them."

Mrs. Baker laughed cheerfully and remarked that they were very much of a muchness.

"But I can't understand how you did it," urged Madeleine; "now, how would you have gone to work to get a respectable senator's vote—a man like Mr. Ratcliffe, for instance?"

"Ratcliffe!" repeated Mrs. Baker with a sight elevation of voice that gave way to a patronising laugh. "Oh, my dear! don't mention names. I should get into trouble. Senator Ratcliffe was a good friend of my husband's. I guess Mr. Carrington could have told you that. But you see, what we generally wanted was all right enough. We had to know where our bills were, and jog people's elbows to get them reported in time. Sometimes we had to convince them that our bill was a proper one, and they ought to vote for it. Only now and then, when there was a great deal of money and the vote was close, we had to find out what votes were worth. It was mostly dining and talking, calling them out into the lobby or asking them to supper. I wish I could tell you things I have seen, but I don't dare. It wouldn't be safe. I've told you already more than I ever said to any one else; but then you are so intimate with Mr. Carrington, that I always think of you as an old friend."

Thus Mrs. Baker rippled on, while Mrs. Lee listened with more and more doubt and disgust. The woman was showy, handsome in a coarse style, and perfectly presentable. Mrs. Lee had seen Duchesses as vulgar. She knew more about the practical working of government than Mrs. Lee could ever expect or hope to know. Why then draw back from this interesting lobbyist with such babyish repulsion?

When, after a long, and, as she declared, a most charming call, Mrs. Baker wended her way elsewhere and Madeleine had given the strictest order that she should never be admitted again, Carrington entered, and Madeleine showed him Mrs. Baker's card and gave a lively account of the interview.

"What shall I do with the woman?" she asked; "must I return her card?" But Carrington declined to offer advice on this interesting point. "And she says that Mr. Ratcliffe was a friend of her husband's and that you could tell me about that."

"Did she say so?" remarked Carrington vaguely.

"Yes! and that she knew every one's weak points and could get all their votes."

Carrington expressed no surprise, and so evidently preferred to change the subject, that Mrs. Lee desisted and said no more.

But she determined to try the same experiment on Mr. Ratcliffe, and chose the very next chance that offered. In her most indifferent manner she remarked that Mrs. Sam Baker had called upon her and had initiated her into the mysteries of the lobby till she had become quite ambitious to start on that career.

"She said you were a friend of her husband's," added Madeleine softly.

Ratcliffe's face betrayed no sign.

"If you believe what those people tell you," said he drily, "you will be wiser than the Queen of Sheba."

Chapter IX

Whenever a man reaches the top of the political ladder, his enemies unite to pull him down. His friends become critical and exacting. Among the many dangers of this sort which now threatened Ratcliffe, there was one that, had he known it, might have made him more uneasy than any of those which were the work of senators and congressmen. Carrington entered into an alliance, offensive and defensive, with Sybil. It came about in this wise. Sybil was fond of riding, and occasionally, when Carrington could spare the time, he went as her guide and protector in these country excursions; for every Virginian, however out at elbows, has a horse, as he has shoes or a shirt. In a thoughtless moment Carrington had been drawn into a promise that he would take Sybil to Arlington. The promise was one that he did not hurry to keep, for there were reasons which made a visit to Arlington anything but a pleasure to him; but Sybil would listen to no excuses, and so it came about that, one lovely March morning, when the shrubs and the trees in the square before the house were just beginning, under the warmer sun, to show signs of their coming wantonness, Sybil stood at the open window waiting for him, while her new Kentucky horse before the door showed what he thought of the delay by curving his neck, tossing his head, and pawing the pavement. Carrington was late and kept her waiting so long, that the mignonette and geraniums, which adorned the window, suffered for his slowness, and the curtain tassels showed signs of wilful damage. Nevertheless he arrived at length, and they set out together, choosing the streets least enlivened by horse-cars and provision-carts, until they had crept through the great metropolis of Georgetown and come upon the bridge which crosses the noble river just where its bold banks open out to clasp the city of Washington in their easy embrace. Then reaching the Virginia side they cantered gaily up the laurel-margined road, with glimpses of woody defiles, each carrying its trickling stream and rich in promise of summer flowers, while from point to point they caught glorious glimpses of the distant city and river. They passed the small military station on the heights, still dignified by the name of fort, though Sybil silently wondered how a fort was possible without fortifications, and complained that there was nothing more warlike than a "nursery of telegraph poles." The day was blue and gold; everything smiled and sparkled in the crisp freshness of the morning. Sybil was in bounding spirits, and not at all pleased to find that her companion became moody and abstracted as they went on. "Poor Mr. Carrington!" thought she to herself; "he is so nice; but when he puts on that solemn air, one might as well go to sleep. I am quite certain no nice woman will ever marry him if he looks like that;" and her practical mind ran off among all the girls of her acquaintance, in search of one who would put up with Carrington's melancholy face. She knew his devotion to her sister, but had long ago rejected this as a hopeless chance. There was a simplicity about Sybil's way of dealing with life, which had its own charm. She never troubled herself about the impossible or the unthinkable. She had feelings, and was rather quick in her sympathies and sorrows, but she was equally quick in getting over them, and she expected other people to do likewise. Madeleine dissected her own feelings and was always wondering whether they were real or not; she had a habit of taking off her mental clothing, as she might take off a dress, and looking at it as though it belonged to some one else, and as though sensations were manufactured like clothes. This seems to be one of the easier ways of deadening sorrow, as though the mind could teach itself to lop off its feelers. Sybil particularly disliked this self-inspection. In the first place she did not understand it, and in the second her mind was all feelers, and amputation was death. She could no more analyse a feeling than doubt its existence, both which were habits of her sister.

How was Sybil to know what was passing in Carrington's mind? He was thinking of nothing in which she supposed herself interested. He was troubled with memories of civil war and of associations still earlier, belonging to an age already vanishing or vanished; but what could she know about civil war who had been almost an infant at the time? At this moment, she happened to be interested in the battle of Waterloo, for she was reading "Vanity Fair," and had cried as she ought for poor little Emmy, when her husband, George Osborne, lay dead on the field there, with a bullet through his heart. But how was she to know that here, only a few rods before her, lay scores and hundreds of George Osbornes, or his betters, and in their graves the love and hope of many Emmys, not creatures of the imagination, but flesh and blood, like herself? To her, there was no more in those associations which made Carrington groan in the silence of his thoughts, than if he had been old Kaspar, and she the little Wilhelmine. What was a skull more or less to her? What concern had she in the famous victory?

Yet even Sybil was startled as she rode through the gate and found herself suddenly met by the long white ranks of head-stones, stretching up and down the hill-sides by thousands, in order of battle; as though Cadmus had reversed his myth, and had sown living men, to come up dragons' teeth. She drew in her horse with a shiver and a sudden impulse to cry. Here was something new to her. This was war—wounds, disease, death. She dropped her voice and with a look almost as serious as Carrington's, asked what all these graves meant. When Carrington told her, she began for the first time to catch some dim notion why his face was not quite as gay as her own. Even now this idea was not very precise, for he said little about himself, but at least she grappled with the fact that he had actually, year after year, carried arms against these men who lay at her feet and who had given their lives for her cause. It suddenly occurred to her as a new thought that perhaps he himself might have killed one of them with his own hand. There was a strange shock in this idea. She felt that Carrington was further from her. He gained dignity in his rebel isolation. She wanted to ask him how he could have been a traitor, and she did not dare. Carrington a traitor! Carrington killing her friends! The idea was too large to grasp. She fell back on the simpler task of wondering how he had looked in his rebel uniform.

They rode slowly round to the door of the house and dismounted, after he had with some difficulty found a man to hold their horses. From the heavy brick porch they looked across the superb river to the raw and incoherent ugliness of the city, idealised into dreamy beauty by the atmosphere, and the soft background of purple hills behind. Opposite them, with its crude "thus saith the law" stamped on white dome and fortress-like walls, rose the Capitol. Carrington stood with her a short time while they looked at the view; then said he would rather not go into the house himself, and sat down on the steps while she strolled alone through the rooms. These were bare and gaunt, so that she, with her feminine sense of fitness, of course considered what she would do to make them habitable. She had a neat fancy for furniture, and distributed her tones and half tones and bits of colour freely about the walls and ceilings, with a high-backed chair here, a spindle-legged sofa there, and a claw-footed table in the centre, until her eye was caught by a very dirty deal desk, on which stood an open book, with an inkstand and some pens. On the leaf she read the last entry: "Eli M. Grow and lady, Thermopyle Centre." Not even the graves outside had brought the horrors of war so near. What a scourge it was! This respectable family turned out of such a lovely house, and all the pretty old furniture swept away before a horde of coarse invaders "with ladies." Did the hosts of Attila write their names on visiting books in the temple of Vesta and the house of Sallust? What a new terror they would have added to the name of the scourge of God! Sybil returned to the portico and sat down by Carrington on the steps.

"How awfully sad it is!" said she; "I suppose the house was prettily furnished when the Lees lived here? Did you ever see it then?"

Sybil was not very profound, but she had sympathy, and at this moment Carrington felt sorely in need of comfort. He wanted some one to share his feelings, and he turned towards her hungry for companionship.

"The Lees were old family friends of mine," said he. "I used to stay here when I was a boy, even as late as the spring of 1861. The last time I sat here, it was with them. We were wild about disunion and talked of nothing else. I have been trying to recall what was said then. We never thought there would be war, and as for coercion, it was nonsense. Coercion, indeed! The idea was ridiculous. I thought so, too, though I was a Union man and did not want the State to go out. But though I felt sure that Virginia must suffer, I never thought we could be beaten. Yet now I am sitting here a pardoned rebel, and the poor Lees are driven away and their place is a grave-yard."

Sybil became at once absorbed in the Lees and asked many questions, all which Carrington gladly answered. He told her how he had admired and followed General Lee through the war. "We thought he was to be our Washington, you know; and perhaps he had some such idea himself;" and then, when Sybil wanted to hear about the battles and the fighting, he drew a rough map on the gravel path to show her how the two lines had run, only a few miles away; then he told her how he had carried his musket day after day over all this country, and where he had seen his battles. Sybil had everything to learn; the story came to her with all the animation of real life, for here under her eyes were the graves of her own champions, and by her side was a rebel who had stood under our fire at Malvern Hill and at South Mountain, and who was telling her how men looked and what they thought in face of death. She listened with breathless interest, and at last summoned courage to ask in an awestruck tone whether Carrington had ever killed anyone himself. She was relieved, although a little disappointed, when he said that he believed not; he hoped not; though no private who has discharged a musket in battle can be quite sure where the bullet went. "I never tried to kill any one," said he, "though they tried to kill me incessantly." Then Sybil begged to know how they had tried to kill him, and he told her one or two of those experiences, such as most soldiers have had, when he had been fired upon and the balls had torn his clothes or drawn blood. Poor Sybil was quite overcome, and found a deadly fascination in the horror. As they sat together on the steps with the glorious view spread before them, her attention was so closely fixed on his story that she saw neither the view nor even the carriages of tourists who drove up, looked about, and departed, envying Carrington his occupation with the lovely girl. She was in imagination rushing with him down the valley of Virginia on the heels of our flying army, or gloomily toiling back to the Potomac after the bloody days at Gettysburg, or watching the last grand *debâcle* on the road from Richmond to Appomattox. They would have sat there till sunset if Carrington had not at length insisted that they must go, and then she rose slowly with a deep sigh and undisguised regret.

As they rode away, Carrington, whose thoughts were not devoted to his companion so entirely as they should have been, ventured to say that he wished her sister had come with them, but he found that his hint was not well received.

Sybil emphatically rejected the idea: "I'm very glad she didn't come. If she had, you would have talked with her all the time, and I should have been left to amuse myself. You would have been discussing things, and I hate discussions. She would have been hunting for first principles, and you would have been running about, trying to catch some for her. Besides, she is coming herself some Sunday with that tiresome Mr. Ratcliffe. I don't see what she finds in that man to amuse her. Her taste is getting to be demoralised in Washington. Do you know, Mr. Carrington, I'm not clever or serious, like Madeleine, and I can't read laws, and hate politics, but I've more common sense than she has, and she makes me cross with her. I understand now why young widows are dangerous, and why they're burned at their husband's funerals in India. Not that I want to have Madeleine burned, for she's a dear, good creature, and I love her better than anything in the world; but she will certainly do herself some dreadful mischief one of these days; she has the most extravagant notions about self-sacrifice and duty; if she hadn't luckily thought of taking charge of me, she would have done some awful thing long ago, and if I could only be a little wicked, she would be quite happy all the rest of her life in reforming me; but now she has got hold of that Mr. Ratcliffe, and he is trying to make her think she can reform him, and if he does, it's all up with us. Madeleine will just go and break her heart over that odious, great, coarse brute, who only wants her money."

Sybil delivered this little oration with a degree of energy that went to Carrington's heart. She did not often make such sustained efforts, and it was clear that on this subject she had exhausted her whole mind. Carrington was delighted, and urged her on. "I dislike

Mr. Ratcliffe as much as you do;—more perhaps. So does every one who knows much about him. But we shall only make the matter worse if we interfere. What can we do?"

"That is just what I tell everybody," resumed Sybil. "There is Victoria Dare always telling me I ought to do something; and Mr. Schneidekoupon too; just as though I could do anything. Madeleine has done nothing but get into mischief here. Half the people think her worldly and ambitious. Only last night that spiteful old woman, Mrs. Clinton, said to me: 'Your sister is quite spoiled by Washington. She is more wild for power than any human being I ever saw.' I was dreadfully angry and told her she was quite mistaken—Madeleine was not the least spoiled. But I couldn't say that she was not fond of power, for she is; but not in the way Mrs. Clinton meant. You should have seen her the other evening when Mr. Ratcliffe said about some matter of public business that he would do whatever she thought right; she spoke up quite sharply for her, with a scornful little laugh, and said that he had better do what *he* thought right. He looked for a moment almost angry, and muttered something about women's being incomprehensible. He is always trying to tempt her with power. She might have had long ago all the power he could give her, but I can see, and he sees too, that she always keeps him at arm's length. He doesn't like it, but he expects one of these days to find a bribe that will answer. I wish we had never come to Washington. New York is so much nicer and the people there are much more amusing; they dance ever so much better and send one flowers all the time, and then they never talk about first principles. Maude had her hospitals and paupers and training school, and got along very well. It was so safe. But when I say so to her, she only smiles in a patronising kind of way, and tells me that I shall have as much of Newport as I want; just as though I were a child, and not a woman of twenty-five. Poor Maude! I can't stay with her if she marries Mr. Ratcliffe, and it would break my heart to leave her with that man. Do you think he would beat her?

Does he drink? I would almost rather be beaten a little, if I cared for a man, than be taken out to Peonia. Oh, Mr. Carrington! you are our only hope. She, will listen to you. Don't let her marry that dreadful politician."

To all this pathetic appeal, some parts of which were as little calculated to please Carrington as Ratcliffe himself, Carrington answered that he was ready to do all in his power but that Sybil must tell him when and how to act.

"Then, it's a bargain," said she; "whenever I want you, I shall call on you for help, and you shall prevent the marriage."

"Alliance offensive and defensive," said he, laughing; "war to the knife on Ratcliffe. We will have his scalp if necessary, but I rather think he will soon commit hari-kari himself if we leave him alone."

"Madeleine will like him all the better if he does anything Japanese," replied Sybil, with great seriousness; "I wish there was more Japanese bric-à-brac here, or any kind of old pots and pans to talk about. A little art would be good for her. What a strange place this is, and how people do stand on their heads in it! Nobody thinks like any one else. Victoria Dare says she is trying on principle not to be good, because she wants to keep some new excitements for the next world. I'm sure she practices as she preaches. Did you see her at Mrs. Clinton's last night. She behaved more outrageously than ever. She sat on the stairs all through supper, looking like a demure yellow cat with two bouquets in her paws—and I know Lord Dunbeg sent one of them;—and she actually let Mr. French feed her with ice-cream from a spoon. She says she was showing Lord Dunbeg a phase, and that he is going to put it into his article on American Manners and Customs in the *Quarterly,* but I don't think it's nice, do you, Mr. Carrington? I wish Madeleine had her to take care of. She would have enough to do then, I can tell her."

And so, gently prattling, Miss Sybil returned to the city, her alliance with Carrington completed; and it was a singular fact that she never again called him dull. There was henceforward a look of more positive pleasure and cordiality on her face when he made his appearance wherever she might be; and the next time he suggested a horseback excursion she instantly agreed to go, although aware that she had promised a younger gentleman of the diplomatic body to be at home that same afternoon, and the good fellow swore polyglot oaths on being turned away from her door.

Mr. Ratcliffe knew nothing of this conspiracy against his peace and prospects. Even if he had known it, he might only have laughed, and pursued his own path without a second thought. Yet it was certain that he did not think Carrington's enmity a thing to be overlooked, and from the moment of his obtaining a clue to its cause, he had begun to take precautions against it. Even in the middle of the contest for the Treasury, he had found time to listen to Mr. Wilson Keen's report on the affairs of the late Samuel Baker. Mr. Keen came to him with a copy of Baker's will and with memoranda of remarks made by the unsuspecting Mrs. Baker; "from which it appears," said he, "that Baker, having no time to put his affairs in order, left special directions that his executors should carefully destroy all papers that might be likely to compromise individuals."

"What is the executor's name?" interrupted Ratcliffe.

"The executor's name is—John Carrington," said Keen, methodically referring to his copy of the will.

Ratcliffe's face was impassive, but the inevitable, "I knew it," almost sprang to his lips. He was rather pleased at the instinct which had led him so directly to the right trail.

Keen went on to say that from Mrs. Baker's conversation it was certain that the testator's directions had been carried out, and that the great bulk of these papers had been burned.

"Then it will be useless to press the inquiry further," said Ratcliffe; "I am much obliged to you for your assistance," and he turned the conversation to the condition of Mr. Keen's bureau in the Treasury department.

The next time Ratcliffe saw Mrs. Lee, after his appointment to the Treasury was confirmed, he asked her whether she did not think Carrington very well suited for public service, and when she warmly assented, he said it had occurred to him to offer the place of Solicitor of the Treasury to Mr. Carrington, for although the actual salary might not be very much more than he earned by his private practice, the incidental advantages to a Washington lawyer were considerable; and to the Secretary it was especially necessary to have a solicitor in whom he could place entire confidence. Mrs. Lee was pleased by this motion of Ratcliffe's, the more because she had supposed that Ratcliffe had no liking for Carrington. She doubted whether Carrington would accept the place, but she hoped that it might modify his dislike for Ratcliffe, and she agreed to sound him on the subject. There was something a little compromising in thus allowing herself to appear as the dispenser of Mr. Ratcliffe's patronage, but she dismissed this objection on the ground that Carrington's interests were involved, and that it was for him to judge whether he should take the place or not. Perhaps the world would not be so charitable if the appointment were made. What then? Mrs. Lee asked herself the question and did not feel quite at ease.

So far as Carrington was concerned, she might have dismissed her doubts. There was not a chance of his taking the place, as very soon appeared. When she spoke to him on the subject, and repeated what Ratcliffe had said, his face flushed, and he sat for some moments in silence. He never thought very rapidly, but now the ideas seemed to come so fast as to bewilder his mind. The situation flashed before his eyes like electric sparks. His first impression was that Ratcliffe wanted to buy him; to tie his tongue; to make him run, like a fastened dog, under the waggon of the Secretary of the Treasury. His second notion was that Ratcliffe wanted to put Mrs. Lee under obligations, in order to win her regard; and, again, that he wanted to raise himself in her esteem by posing as a friend of honest administration and unassisted virtue. Then suddenly it occurred to him that the scheme was to make him appear jealous and vindictive; to put him in an attitude where any reason he might give for declining would bear a look of meanness, and tend to separate him from Mrs. Lee. Carrington was so absorbed by these thoughts, and his mind worked so slowly, that he failed to hear one or two remarks addressed to him by Mrs. Lee, who became a little alarmed, under the impression that he was unexpectedly paralyzed.

When at length he heard her and attempted to frame an answer, his embarrassment increased. He could only stammer that he was sorry to be obliged to decline, but this office was one he could not undertake.

If Madeleine felt a little relieved by this decision, she did not show it. From her manner one might have supposed it to be her fondest wish that Carrington should be Solicitor of the Treasury. She cross-questioned him with obstinacy. Was not the offer a good one?—and he was obliged to confess that it was. Were the duties such as he could not perform? Not at all! there was nothing in the duties which alarmed him. Did he object to it because of his southern prejudices against the administration? Oh, no! he had no political feeling to stand in his way. What, then, could be his reason for refusing?

Carrington resorted again to silence, until Mrs. Lee, a little impatiently, asked whether it was possible that his personal dislike to Ratcliffe could blind him so far as to make him reject so fair a proposal. Carrington, finding himself more and more uncomfortable, rose restlessly from his chair and paced the room. He felt that Ratcliffe had fairly out-generaled him, and he was at his wits' end to know what card he could play that would not lead directly into Ratcliffe's trump suit. To refuse such an offer was hard enough at best, for a man who wanted money and professional advancement as he did, but to injure himself and help Ratcliffe by this refusal, was abominably hard. Nevertheless, he was obliged to admit that he would rather not take a position so directly under Ratcliffe's control. Madeleine said no more, but he thought she looked annoyed, and he felt himself in an intolerably painful situation. He was not certain that she herself might not have had some share in proposing the plan, and that his refusal might not have some mortifying consequences for her. What must she think of him, then? At this very moment he would have given his right arm for a word of real affection from Mrs. Lee. He adored her. He would willingly enough have damned himself for her. There was no sacrifice he would not have made to bring her nearer to him. In his upright, quiet, simple kind of way, he immolated himself before her. For months his heart had ached with this hopeless passion. He recognized that it was hopeless. He knew that she would never love him, and, to do her justice, she never had given him reason to suppose that it was in her power to love him, or any man. And here he stood, obliged to appear ungrateful and prejudiced, mean and vindictive, in her eyes. He took his seat again, looking so unutterably dejected, his patient face so tragically mournful, that Madeleine, after a while, began to see the absurd side of the matter, and presently burst into a laugh.

"Please do not look so frightfully miserable!" said she; "I did not mean to make you unhappy. After all, what does it matter? You have a perfect right to refuse, and, for my part, I have not the least wish to see you accept."

On this, Carrington brightened, and declared that if she thought him right in declining, he cared for nothing else. It was only the idea of hurting her feelings that weighed on his mind. But in saying this, he spoke in a tone that implied a deeper feeling, and made Mrs. Lee again look grave and sigh.

"Ah, Mr. Carrington," she said, "this world will not run as we want. Do you suppose the time will ever come when every one will be good and happy and do just what they ought? I thought this offer might possibly take one anxiety off your shoulders. I am sorry now that I let myself be led into making it."

Carrington could not answer her. He dared not trust his voice. He rose to go, and as she held out her hand, he suddenly raised it to his lips, and so left her. She sat for a moment with tears in her eyes after he was gone. She thought she knew all that was in his mind, and with a woman's readiness to explain every act of men by their consuming passions for her own sex, she took it as a matter of course that jealousy was the whole cause of Carrington's hostility to Ratcliffe, and she pardoned it with charming alacrity. "Ten years ago, I could have loved him," she thought to herself, and then, while she was half smiling at the idea, suddenly another thought flashed upon her, and she threw her hand up before her face as though some one had struck her a blow. Carrington had reopened the old wound.

When Ratcliffe came to see her again, which he did very shortly afterwards, glad of so good an excuse, she told him of Carrington's refusal, adding only that he seemed unwilling to accept any position that had a political character. Ratcliffe showed no sign of displeasure; he only said, in a benignant tone, that he was sorry to be unable to do something for so good a friend of hers; thus establishing, at all events, his claim on her gratitude. As for Carrington, the offer which Ratcliffe had made was not intended to be accepted, and Carrington could not have more embarrassed the secretary than by closing with it. Ratcliffe's object had been to settle for his own satisfaction the question of Carrington's hostility, for he knew the man well enough to feel sure that in any event he would act a perfectly straightforward part. If he accepted, he would at least be true to his chief. If he refused, as Ratcliffe expected, it would be a proof that some means must be found of getting him out of the way. In any case the offer was a new thread in the net that Mr. Ratcliffe flattered himself he was rapidly winding about the affections and ambitions of Mrs. Lee. Yet he had reasons of his own for thinking that Carrington, more easily than any other man, could cut the meshes of this net if he chose to do so, and therefore that it would be wiser to postpone action until Carrington were disposed of.

Without a moment's delay he made inquiries as to all the vacant or eligible offices in the gift of the government outside his own department. Very few of these would answer his purpose. He wanted some temporary law business that would for a time take its holder away to a distance, say to Australia or Central Asia, the further the better; it must be highly paid, and it must be given in such a way as not to excite suspicion that Ratcliffe was concerned in the matter. Such an office was not easily found. There is little law business in Central Asia, and at this moment there was not enough to require a special agent in Australia. Carrington could hardly be induced to lead an expedition to the sources of the Nile in search of business merely to please Mr. Ratcliffe, nor could the State Department offer encouragement to a hope that government would pay the expenses of such an expedition. The best that Ratcliffe could do was to select the place of counsel to the Mexican claims-commission which was soon to meet in the city of Mexico, and which would require about six months' absence. By a little management he could contrive to get the counsel sent away in advance of the commission, in order to work up a part of the case on the spot. Ratcliffe acknowledged that Mexico was too near, but he drily remarked to himself that if Carrington could get back in time to dislodge him after he had once got a firm hold on Mrs. Lee, he would never try to run another caucus.

The point once settled in his own mind, Ratcliffe, with his usual rapidity of action, carried his scheme into effect. In this there was little difficulty. He dropped in at the office of the Secretary of State within eight-and-forty hours after his last conversation with Mrs. Lee. During these early days of every new administration, the absorbing business of government relates principally to appointments. The Secretary of the Treasury was always ready to oblige his colleagues in the Cabinet by taking care of their friends to any reasonable extent. The Secretary of State was not less courteous. The moment he understood that Mr. Ratcliffe had a strong wish to secure the appointment of a certain person as counsel to the Mexican claims-commission, the Secretary of State professed readiness to gratify him, and when he heard who the proposed person was, the suggestion was hailed with pleasure, for Carrington was well known and much liked at the Department, and was indeed an excellent man for the place. Ratcliffe hardly needed to promise an equivalent. The business was arranged in ten minutes.

"I only need say," added Ratcliffe, "that if my agency in the affair is known, Mr. Carrington will certainly refuse the place, for he is one of your old-fashioned Virginia planters, proud as Lucifer, and willing to accept nothing by way of favour. I will speak to your Assistant Secretary about it, and the recommendation shall appear to come from him."

The very next day Carrington received a private note from his old friend, the Assistant Secretary of State, who was overjoyed to do him a kindness. The note asked him to call at the Department at his earliest convenience. He went, and the Assistant Secretary announced that he had recommended Carrington's appointment as counsel to the Mexican claims-commission, and that the Secretary had approved the recommendation. "We want a Southern man, a lawyer with a little knowledge of international law, one who can go at once, and, above all, an honest man. You fit the description to a hair; so pack your trunk as soon as you like."

Carrington was startled. Coming as it did, this offer was not only unobjectionable, but tempting. It was hard for him even to imagine a reason for hesitation. From the first he felt that he must go, and yet to go was the very last thing he wanted to do. That he should suspect Ratcliffe to be at the bottom of this scheme of banishment was a matter of course, and he instantly asked whether any influence had been used in his favour; but the Assistant Secretary so stoutly averred that the appointment was made on his recommendation alone, as to block all further inquiry. Technically this assertion was exact, and it made Carrington feel that it would be base ingratitude on his part not to accept a favour so handsomely offered.

Yet he could not make up his mind to acceptance. He begged four and twenty hours' delay, in order, as he said, to see whether he could arrange his affairs for a six months' absence, although he knew there would be no difficulty in his doing so. He went away and sat in his office alone, gloomily wondering what he could do, although from the first he saw that the situation was only too clear, and there could not be the least dark corner of a doubt to crawl into. Six months ago he would have jumped at this offer. What had happened within six months to make it seem a disaster?

Mrs. Lee! There was the whole story. To go away now was to give up Mrs. Lee, and probably to give her up to Ratcliffe. Carrington gnashed his teeth when he thought how skilfully Ratcliffe was playing his cards. The longer he reflected, the more certain he felt that Ratcliffe was at the bottom of this scheme to get rid of him; and yet, as he studied the situation, it occurred to him that after all it was possible for Ratcliffe to make a blunder. This Illinois politician was clever, and understood men; but a knowledge of men is a very different thing from a knowledge of women. Carrington himself had no great experience in the article of women, but he thought he knew more than Ratcliffe, who was evidently relying most on his usual theory of political corruption as applied to feminine weaknesses, and who was only puzzled at finding how high a price Mrs. Lee set on herself. If Ratcliffe were really at the bottom of the scheme for separating Carrington from her, it could only be because he thought that six months, or even six weeks, would be enough to answer his purpose. And on reaching this point in his reflections, Carrington suddenly rose, lit a cigar, and walked up and down his room steadily for the next hour, with the air of a general arranging a plan of campaign, or a lawyer anticipating his opponent's line of argument. On one point his mind was made up. He would accept. If Ratcliffe really had a hand in this move, he should be gratified. If he had laid a trap, he should be caught in it. And when the evening came, Carrington took his hat and walked off to call upon Mrs. Lee.

He found the sisters alone and quietly engaged in their occupations. Madeleine was dramatically mending an open-work silk stocking, a delicate and difficult task which required her whole mind. Sybil was at the piano as usual, and for the first time since he had known her, she rose when he came in, and, taking her work-basket, sat down to share in the conversation. She meant to take her place as a woman, henceforward. She was tired of playing girl. Mr. Carrington should see that she was not a fool.

Carrington plunged at once into his subject, and announced the offer made to him, at which Madeleine expressed delight, and asked many questions. What was the pay? How soon must he go? How long should he be away? Was there danger from the climate? and finally she added, with a smile, "What am I to say to Mr. Ratcliffe if you accept this offer after refusing his?" As for Sybil, she made one reproachful exclamation: "Oh, Mr. Carrington!" and sank back into silence and consternation. Her first experiment at taking a stand of her own in the world was not encouraging. She felt betrayed.

Nor was Carrington gay. However modest a man may be, only an idiot can forget himself entirely in pursuing the moon and the stars. In the bottom of his soul, he had a lingering hope that when he told his story, Madeleine might look up with a change of expression, a glance of unpremeditated regard, a little suffusion of the eyes, a little trembling of the voice. To see himself relegated to Mexico with such cheerful alacrity by the woman he loved was not the experience he would have chosen. He could not help feeling that his hopes were disposed of, and he watched her with a painful sinking of the heart, which did not lead to lightness of conversation. Madeleine herself felt that her expressions needed to be qualified, and she tried to correct her mistake. What should she do without a tutor? she said. He must let her have a list of books to read while he was away: they were themselves going north in the middle of May, and Carrington would be back by the time they returned in December. After all, they should see as little of him during the summer if he were in Virginia as if he were in Mexico.

Carrington gloomily confessed that he was very unwilling to go; that he wished the idea had never been suggested; that he should be perfectly happy if for any reason the scheme broke down; but he gave no explanation of his feeling, and Madeleine had too much tact to press for one. She contented herself by arguing against it, and talking as vivaciously as she could. Her heart really bled for him as she saw his face grow more and more pathetic in its quiet expression of disappointment. But what could she say or do? He sat till after ten o'clock; he could not tear himself away. He felt that this was the end of his pleasure in life; he dreaded the solitude of his thoughts. Mrs. Lee's resources began to show signs of exhaustion. Long pauses intervened between her remarks; and at length Carrington, with a superhuman effort, apologized for inflicting himself upon her so unmercifully. If she knew, he said, how he dreaded being alone, she would forgive him. Then he rose to go, and, in taking leave, asked Sybil if she was inclined to ride the next day; if so, he was at her service. Sybil's face brightened as she accepted the invitation.

Mrs. Lee, a day or two afterwards, did mention Carrington's appointment to Mr. Ratcliffe, and she told Carrington that the Secretary certainly looked hurt and mortified, but showed it only by almost instantly changing the subject.

CHAPTER X

The next morning Carrington called at the Department and announced his acceptance of the post. He was told that his instructions would be ready in about a fortnight, and that he would be expected to start as soon as he received them; in the meanwhile, he must devote himself to the study of a mass of papers in the Department. There was no trifling allowable here. Carrington had to set himself vigorously to work.

This did not, however, prevent him from keeping his appointment with Sybil, and at four o'clock they started together, passing out into the quiet shadows of Rock Creek, and seeking still lanes through the woods where their horses walked side by side, and they themselves could talk without the risk of criticism from curious eyes. It was the afternoon of one of those sultry and lowering spring days when life germinates rapidly, but as yet gives no sign, except perhaps some new leaf or flower pushing its soft head up against the dead leaves that have sheltered it. The two riders had something of the same sensation, as though the leafless woods and the laurel thickets, the warm, moist air and the low clouds, were a protection and a soft shelter. Somewhat to Carrington's surprise, he found that it was pleasant to have Sybil's company. He felt towards her as to a sister—a favourite sister.

She at once attacked him for abandoning her and breaking his treaty so lately made, and he tried to gain her sympathy by saying that if she knew how much he was troubled, she would forgive him. Then when Sybil asked whether he really must go and leave her without any friend whom she could speak to, his feelings got the better of him: he could not resist the temptation to confide all his troubles in her, since there was no one else in whom he could confide. He told her plainly that he was in love with her sister.

"You say that love is nonsense, Miss Ross. I tell you it is no such thing. For weeks and months it is a steady physical pain, an ache about the heart, never leaving one, by night or by day; a long strain on one's nerves like toothache or rheumatism, not intolerable at any one instant, but exhausting by its steady drain on the strength. It is a disease to be borne with patience, like any other nervous complaint, and to be treated with counter-irritants. My trip to Mexico will be good for it, but that is not the reason why I must go."

Then he told her all his private circumstances; the ruin which the war had brought on him and his family; how, of his two brothers, one had survived the war only to die at home, a mere wreck of disease, privation, and wounds; the other had been shot by his side, and bled slowly to death in his arms during the awful carnage in the Wilderness; how his mother and two sisters were struggling for a bare subsistence on a wretched Virginian farm, and how all his exertions barely kept them from beggary.

"You have no conception of the poverty to which our southern women are reduced since the war," said he; "they are many of them literally without clothes or bread." The fee he should earn by going to Mexico would double his income this year. Could he refuse? Had he a right to refuse? And poor Carrington added, with a groan, that if he alone were in question, he would sooner be shot than go.

Sybil listened with tears in her eyes. She never before had seen a man show suffering. The misery she had known in life had been more or less veiled to her and softened by falling on older and friendly shoulders. She now got for the first time a clear view of Carrington, apart from the quiet exterior in which the man was hidden. She felt quite sure, by a sudden flash of feminine inspiration, that the curious look of patient endurance on his face was the work of a single night when he had held his brother in his arms, and knew that the blood was draining drop by drop from his side, in the dense, tangled woods, beyond the reach of help, hour after hour, till the voice failed and the limbs grew stiff and cold. When he had finished his story, she was afraid to speak. She did not know how to show her sympathy, and she could not bear to seem unsympathetic. In her embarrassment she fairly broke down and could only dry her eyes in silence.

Having once got this weight of confidence off his mind, Carrington felt comparatively gay and was ready to make the best of things. He laughed at himself to drive away the tears of his pretty companion, and obliged her to take a solemn pledge never to betray him. "Of course your sister knows it all," he said; "but she must never know that I told you, and I never would tell any one but you."

Sybil promised faithfully to keep his confidence to herself, and she went on to defend her sister.

"You must not blame Madeleine," said she; "if you knew as well as I do what she has been through, you would not think her cold. You do know how suddenly her husband died, after only one day's illness, and what a nice fellow he was. She was very fond of him, and his death seemed to stun her. We hardly knew what to make of it, she was so quiet and natural. Then just a week later her little child died of diphtheria, suffering horribly, and she wild with despair because she could not relieve it. After that, she was almost insane; indeed, I have always thought she was quite insane for a time. I know she was excessively violent and wanted to kill herself, and I never heard any one rave as she did about religion and resignation and God. After a few weeks she became quiet and stupid and went about like a machine; and at last she got over it, but has never been what she was before. You know she was a rather fast New York girl before she married, and cared no more about politics and philanthropy than I do. It was a very late thing, all this stuff. But she is not really hard, though she may seem so. It is all on the surface. I always know when she is thinking about her husband or child, because her face gets rigid; she looks then as she used to look after her child died, as though she didn't care what became of her and she would just as lieve kill herself as not. I don't think she will ever let herself love any one again. She has a horror of it. She is much more likely to go in for ambition, or duty, or self-sacrifice."

They rode on for a while in silence, Carrington perplexed by the problem how two harmless people such as Madeleine and he could have been made by a beneficent Providence the sport of such cruel tortures; and Sybil equally interested in thinking what sort of a brother-in-law Carrington would make; on the whole, she thought she liked him better as he was. The silence was only broken by Carrington's bringing the conversation back to its starting-point: "Something must be done to keep your sister out of Ratcliffe's power. I have thought about it till I am tired. Can you make no suggestion?"

No! Sybil was helpless and dreadfully alarmed. Mr. Ratcliffe came to the house as often as he could, and seemed to tell Madeleine everything that was going on in politics, and ask her advice, and Madeleine did not discourage him. "I do believe she likes it, and thinks she can do some good by it. I don't dare speak to her about it. She thinks me a child still, and treats me as though I were fifteen. What can I do?"

Carrington said he had thought of speaking to Mrs. Lee himself, but he did not know what to say, and if he offended her, he might drive her directly into Ratcliffe's arms. But Sybil thought she would not be offended if he went to work in the right way. "She will stand more from you than from any one else. Tell her openly that you— that you love her," said Sybil with a burst of desperate courage; "she can't take offence at that; and then you can say almost anything."

Carrington looked at Sybil with more admiration than he had ever expected to feel for her, and began to think that he might do worse than to put himself under her orders. After all, she had some practical sense, and, what was more to the point, she was handsomer than ever, as she sat erect on her horse, the rich colour rushing up under the warm skin, at the impropriety of her speech. "You are certainly right," said he; "after all, I have nothing to lose. Whether she marries Ratcliffe or not, she will never marry me, I suppose."

This speech was a cowardly attempt to beg encouragement from Sybil, and met with the fate it deserved, for Sybil, highly flattered at Carrington's implied praise, and bold as a lioness now that it was Carrington's fingers, and not her own, that were to go into the fire, gave him on the spot a feminine view of the situation that did not encourage his hopes. She plainly said that men seemed to take leave of their senses as soon as women were concerned; for her part, she could not understand what there was in any woman to make such a fuss about; she thought most women were horrid; men were ever so much nicer; "and as for Madeleine, whom all of you are ready to cut each other's throats about, she's a dear, good sister, as good as gold, and I love her with all my heart, but you wouldn't like her, any of you, if you married her; she has always had her own way, and she could not help taking it; she never could learn to take yours; both of you would be unhappy in a week; and as for that old Mr. Ratcliffe, she would make his life a burden—and I hope she will," concluded Sybil with a spiteful little explosion of hatred.

Carrington could not help being amused by Sybil's way of dealing with affairs of the heart. Emboldened by encouragement, she went on to attack him pitilessly for going down on his knees before her sister, "just as though you were not as good as she is," and openly avowed that, if she were a man, she would at least have some pride. Men like this kind of punishment. Carrington did not attempt to defend himself; he even courted Sybil's attack. They both enjoyed their ride through the bare woods, by the rippling spring streams, under the languid breath of the moist south wind. It was a small idyll, all the more pleasant because there was gloom before and behind it. Sybil's irrepressible gaiety made Carrington doubt whether, after all, life need be so serious a matter. She had animal spirits in plenty, and it needed an effort for her to keep them down, while Carrington's spirits were nearly exhausted after twenty years of strain, and he required a greater effort to hold himself up. There was every reason why he should be grateful to Sybil for lending to him from her superfluity. He enjoyed being laughed at by her. Suppose Madeleine Lee did refuse to marry him! What of it? "Pooh!" said Sybil; "you men are all just alike. How can you be so silly? Madeleine and you would be intolerable together. Do find some one who won't be solemn!"

They laid out their little plot against Madeleine and elaborated it carefully, both as to what Carrington should say and how he should say it, for Sybil asserted that men were too stupid to be trusted even in making a declaration of love, and must be taught, like little children to say their prayers. Carrington enjoyed being taught how to make a declaration of love. He did not ask where Sybil had learned so much about men's stupidity. He thought perhaps Schneidekoupon could have thrown light on the subject. At all events, they were so busily occupied with their schemes and lessons, that they did not reach home till Madeleine had become anxious lest they had met with some accident. The long dusk had become darkness before she heard the clatter of hoofs on the asphalt pavement, and she went down to the door to scold them for their delay. Sybil only laughed at her, and said it was all Mr. Carrington's fault: he had lost his way, and she had been forced to find it for him.

Ten days more passed before their plan was carried into effect. April had come. Carrington's work was completed and he was ready to start on his journey. Then at last he appeared one evening at Mrs. Lee's at the very moment when Sybil, as chance would have it, was going out to pass an hour or two with her friend Victoria Dare a few doors away. Carrington felt a little ashamed as she went. This kind of conspiracy behind Mrs. Lee's back was not to his taste.

He resolutely sat down, and plunged at once into his subject. He was almost ready to go, he said; he had nearly completed his work in the Department, and he was assured that his instructions and papers would be ready in two days more; he might not have another chance to see Mrs. Lee so quietly again, and he wanted to take his leave now, for this was what lay most heavily on his mind; he should have gone willingly and gladly if it had not been for uneasiness about her; and yet he had till now been afraid to speak openly on the subject. Here he paused for a moment as though to invite some reply.

Madeleine laid down her work with a look of regret though not of annoyance, and said frankly and instantly that he had been too good a friend to allow of her taking offence at anything he could say; she would not pretend to misunderstand him. "My affairs," she added with a shade of bitterness, "seem to have become public property, and I would rather have some voice in discussing them myself than to know they are discussed behind my back."

This was a sharp thrust at the very outset, but Carrington turned it aside and went quietly on:

"You are frank and loyal, as you always are. I will be so too. I can't help being so. For months I have had no other pleasure than in being near you. For the first time in my life I have known what it is to forget my own affairs in loving a woman who seems to me without a fault, and for one solitary word from whom I would give all I have in life, and perhaps life itself."

Madeleine flushed and bent towards him with an earnestness of manner that repeated itself in her tone:

"Mr. Carrington, I am the best friend you have on earth. One of these days you will thank me with your whole soul for refusing to listen to you now. You do not know how much misery I am saving you. I have no heart to give. You want a young, fresh life to help yours; a gay, lively temperament to enliven your despondency; some one still young enough to absorb herself in you and make all her existence yours. I could not do it. I can give you nothing. I have done my best to persuade myself that some day I might begin life again with the old hopes and feelings, but it is no use. The fire is burned out. If you married me, you would destroy yourself. You would wake up some day, and find the universe dust and ashes."

Carrington listened in silence. He made no attempt to interrupt or to contradict her. Only at the end he said with a little bitterness: "My own life is worth so much to the world and to me, that I suppose it would be wrong to risk it on such a venture; but I would risk it, nevertheless, if you gave me the chance. Do you think me wicked for tempting Providence? I do not mean to annoy you with entreaties. I have a little pride left, and a great deal of respect for you. Yet I think, in spite of all you have said or can say, that one disappointed life may be as able to find happiness and repose in another, as to get them by sucking the young life-blood of a fresh soul."

To this speech, which was unusually figurative for Carrington, Mrs. Lee could find no ready answer. She could only reply that Carrington's life was worth quite as much as his neighbour's, and that it was worth so much to her, if not to himself, that she would not let him wreck it.

Carrington went on: "Forgive my talking in this way. I do not mean to complain. I shall always love you just as much, whether you care for me or not, because you are the only woman I have ever met, or am ever likely to meet, who seems to me perfect."

If this was Sybil's teaching, she had made the best of her time. Carrington's tone and words pierced through all Mrs. Lee's armour as though they were pointed with the most ingenious cruelty, and designed to torture her. She felt hard and small before him. Life for life, his had been, and was now, far less bright than hers, yet he was her superior. He sat there, a true man, carrying his burden calmly, quietly, without complaint, ready to face the next shock of life with the same endurance he had shown against the rest. And he thought her perfect! She felt humiliated that any brave man should say to her face that he thought her perfect! She! Perfect! In her contrition she was half ready to go down at his feet and confess her sins; her hysterical dread of sorrow and suffering, her narrow sympathies, her feeble faith, her miserable selfishness, her abject cowardice. Every nerve in her body tingled with shame when she thought what a miserable fraud she was; what a mass of pretensions unfounded, of deceit ingrained. She was ready to hide her face in her hands. She was disgusted, outraged with her own image as she saw it, contrasted with Carrington's single word: Perfect!

Nor was this the worst. Carrington was not the first man who had thought her perfect. To hear this word suddenly used again, which had never been uttered to her before except by lips now dead and gone, made her brain reel. She seemed to hear her husband once more telling her that she was perfect. Yet against this torture, she had a better defence. She had long since hardened herself to bear these recollections, and they steadied and strengthened her. She had been called perfect before now, and what had come of it? Two graves, and a broken life! She drew herself up with a face now grown quite pale and rigid. In reply to Carrington, she said not a word, but only shook her head slightly without looking at him.

He went on: "After all, it is not my own happiness I am thinking of, but yours. I never was vain enough to think that I was worth your love, or that I could ever win it. Your happiness is another thing. I care so much for that as to make me dread going away, for fear that you may yet find yourself entangled in this wretched political life here, when, perhaps if I stayed, I might be of some use."

"Do you really think, then, that I am going to fall a victim to Mr. Ratcliffe?" asked Madeleine, with a cold smile.

"Why not?" replied Carrington, in a similar tone. "He can put forward a strong claim to your sympathy and help, if not to your love. He can offer you a great field of usefulness which you want. He has been very faithful to you. Are you quite sure that even now you can refuse him without his complaining that you have trifled with him?"

"And are you quite sure," added Mrs. Lee, evasively, "that you have not been judging him much too harshly? I think I know him better than you. He has many good qualities, and some high ones. What harm can he do me? Supposing even that he did succeed in persuading me that my life could be best used in helping his, why should I be afraid of it?"

"You and I," said Carrington, "are wide apart in our estimates of Mr. Ratcliffe. To you, of course, he shows his best side. He is on his good behaviour, and knows that any false step will ruin him. I see in him only a coarse, selfish, unprincipled politician, who would either drag you down to his own level, or, what is more likely, would very soon disgust you and make your life a wretched self-immolation before his vulgar ambition, or compel you to leave him. In either case you would be the victim. You cannot afford to make another false start in life. Reject me! I have not a word to say against it. But be on your guard against giving your existence up to him."

"Why do you think so ill of Mr. Ratcliffe?" asked Madeleine; "he always speaks highly of you. Do you know anything against him that the world does not?"

"His public acts are enough to satisfy me," replied Carrington, evading a part of the question. "You know that I have never had but one opinion about him."

There was a pause in the conversation. Both parties felt that as yet no good had come of it. At length Madeleine asked, "What would you have me do? Is it a pledge you want that I will under no circumstances marry Mr. Ratcliffe?"

"Certainly not," was the answer; "you know me better than to think I would ask that. I only want you to take time and keep out of his influence until your mind is fairly made up. A year hence I feel certain that you will think of him as I do."

"Then you will allow me to marry him if I find that you are mistaken," said Mrs. Lee, with a marked tone of sarcasm.

Carrington looked annoyed, but he answered quietly, "What I fear is his influence here and now. What I would like to see you do is this: go north a month earlier than you intended, and without giving him time to act. If I were sure you were safely in Newport, I should feel no anxiety."

"You seem to have as bad an opinion of Washington as Mr. Gore," said Madeleine, with a contemptuous smile. "He gave me the same advice, though he was afraid to tell me why. I am not a child. I am thirty years old, and have seen something of the world. I am not afraid, like Mr. Gore, of Washington malaria, or, like you, of Mr. Ratcliffe's influence. If I fall a victim I shall deserve my fate, and certainly I shall have no cause to complain of my friends. They have given me advice enough for a lifetime."

Carrington's face darkened with a deeper shade of regret. The turn which the conversation had taken was precisely what he had expected, and both Sybil and he had agreed that Madeleine would probably answer just in this way. Nevertheless, he could not but feel acutely the harm he was doing to his own interests, and it was only by a sheer effort of the will that he forced himself to a last and more earnest attack.

"I know it is an impertinence," he said; "I wish it were in my power to show how much it costs me to offend you. This is the first time you ever had occasion to be offended. If I were to yield to the fear of your anger and were to hold my tongue now, and by any chance you were to wreck your life on this rock, I should never forgive myself the cowardice. I should always think I might have done something to prevent it. This is probably the last time I shall have the chance to talk openly with you, and I implore you to listen to me. I want nothing for myself. If I knew I should never see you again, I would still say the same thing. Leave Washington! Leave it now!—at once!—without giving more than twenty-four hours' notice! Leave it without letting Mr. Ratcliffe see you again in private! Come back next winter if you please, and then accept him if you think proper. I only pray you to think long about it and decide when you are not here."

Madeleine's eyes flashed, and she threw aside her embroidery with an impatient gesture: "No! Mr. Carrington! I will not be dictated to! I will carry out my own plans! I do not mean to marry Mr. Ratcliffe. If I had meant it, I should have done it before now. But I will not run away from him or from myself. It would be unladylike, undignified, cowardly."

Carrington could say no more. He had come to the end of his lesson. A long silence ensued and then he rose to go. "Are you angry with me?" said she in a softer tone.

"I ought to ask that question," said he. "Can you forgive me? I am afraid not. No man can say to a woman what I have said to you, and be quite forgiven. You will never think of me again as you would have done if I had not spoken. I knew that before I did it. As for me, I can only go on with my old life. It is not gay, and will not be the gayer for our talk to-night."

Madeleine relented a little: "Friendships like ours are not so easily broken," she said. "Do not do me another injustice. You will see me again before you go?"

He assented and bade good-night. Mrs. Lee, weary and disturbed in mind, hastened to her room. "When Miss Sybil comes in, tell her that I am not very well, and have gone to bed," were her instructions to her maid, and Sybil thought she knew the cause of this headache.

But before Carrington's departure he had one more ride with Sybil, and reported to her the result of the interview, at which both of them confessed themselves much depressed. Carrington expressed some hope that Madeleine meant, after a sort, to give a kind of pledge by saying that she had no intention of marrying Mr. Ratcliffe, but Sybil shook her head emphatically: "How can a woman tell whether she is going to accept a man until she is asked?" said she with entire confidence, as though she were stating the simplest fact in the world. Carrington looked puzzled, and ventured to ask whether women did not generally make up their minds beforehand on such an interesting point; but Sybil overwhelmed him with contempt: "What good will they do by making up their minds, I should like to know? of course they would go and do the opposite. Sensible women don't pretend to make up their minds, Mr. Carrington. But you men are so stupid, and you can't understand in the least."

Carrington gave it up, and went back to his stale question: Could Sybil suggest any other resource? and Sybil sadly confessed that she could not. So far as she could see they must trust to luck, and she thought it was cruel for Mr. Carrington to go away and leave her alone without help. He had promised to prevent the marriage.

"One thing more I mean to do," said Carrington: "and here everything will depend on your courage and nerve. You may depend upon it that Mr. Ratcliffe will offer himself before you go north. He does not suspect you of making trouble, and he will not think about you in any way if you let him alone and keep quiet. When he does offer himself you will know it; at least your sister will tell you if she has accepted him. If she refuses him point blank, you will have nothing to do but to keep her steady. If you see her hesitating, you must break in at any cost, and use all your influence to stop her. Be bold, then, and do your best. If everything fails and she still clings to him, I must play my last card, or rather you must play it for me. I shall leave with you a sealed letter which you are to give her if everything else fails. Do it before she sees Ratcliffe a second time. See that she reads it and, if necessary, make her read it, no matter when or where. No one else must know that it exists, and you must take as much care of it as though it were a diamond. You are not to know what is in it; it must be a complete secret. Do you under-stand?"

Sybil thought she did, but her heart sank. "When shall you give me this letter?" she asked.

"The evening before I start, when I come to bid good-bye; probably next Sunday. This letter is our last hope. If, after reading that, she does not give him up, you will have to pack your trunk, my dear Sybil, and find a new home, for you can never live with them."

He had never before called her by her first name, and it pleased her to hear it now, though she generally had a strong objection to such familiarities. "Oh, I wish you were not going!" she exclaimed tearfully. "What shall I do when you are gone?"

At this pitiful appeal, Carrington felt a sudden pang. He found that he was not so old as he had thought. Certainly he had grown to like her frank honesty and sound common sense, and he had at length discovered that she was handsome, with a very pretty figure. Was it not something like a flirtation he had been carrying on with this young person for the last month? A glimmering of suspicion crossed his mind, though he got rid of it as quickly as possible. For a man of his age and sobriety to be in love with two sisters at once was impossible; still more impossible that Sybil should care for him.

As for her, however, there was no doubt about the matter. She had grown to depend upon him, and she did it with all the blind confidence of youth. To lose him was a serious disaster. She had never before felt the sensation, and she thought it most disagreeable. Her youthful diplomatists and admirers could not at all fill Carrington's place. They danced and chirruped cheerfully on the hollow crust of society, but they were wholly useless when one suddenly fell through and found oneself struggling in the darkness and dangers beneath. Young women, too, are apt to be flattered by the confidences of older men; they have a keen palate for whatever savours of experience and adventure. For the first time in her life, Sybil had found a man who gave some play to her imagination; one who had been a rebel, and had grown used to the shocks of fate, so as to walk with calmness into the face of death, and to command or obey with equal indifference. She felt that he would tell her what to do when the earthquake came, and would be at hand to consult, which is in a woman's eyes the great object of men's existence, when trouble comes. She suddenly conceived that Washington would be intolerable without him, and that she should never get the courage to fight Mr. Ratcliffe alone, or, if she did, she should make some fatal mistake. They finished their ride very soberly. She began to show a new interest in all that concerned him, and asked many questions about his sisters and their plantation. She wanted to ask him whether she could not do something to help them, but this seemed too awkward. On his part he made her promise to write him faithfully all that took place, and this request pleased her, though she knew his interest was all on her sister's account.

The following Sunday evening when he came to bid good-bye, it was still worse. There was no chance for private talk. Ratcliffe was there, and several diplomatists, including old Jacobi, who had eyes like a cat and saw every motion of one's face. Victoria Dare was on the sofa, chattering with Lord Dunbeg; Sybil would rather have had any ordinary illness, even to the extent of a light case of scarlet fever or small-pox than let her know what was the matter. Carrington found means to get Sybil into another room for a moment and to give her the letter he had promised. Then he bade her good-bye, and in doing so he reminded her of her promise to write, pressing her hand and looking into her eyes with an earnestness that made her heart beat faster, although she said to herself that his interest was all about her sister; as it was—mostly. The thought did not raise her spirits, but she went through with her performance like a heroine. Perhaps she was a little pleased to see that he parted from Madeleine with much less apparent feeling. One would have said that they were two good friends who had no troublesome sentiment to worry them. But then every eye in the room was watching this farewell, and speculating about it. Ratcliffe looked on with particular interest and was a little perplexed to account for this too fraternal cordiality. Could he have made a miscalculation? or was there something behind? He himself insisted upon shaking hands genially with Carrington and wished him a pleasant journey and a successful one.

That night, for the first time since she was a child, Sybil actually cried a little after she went to bed, although it is true that her sentiment did not keep her awake. She felt lonely and weighed down by a great responsibility. For a day or two afterwards she was nervous and restless. She would not ride, or make calls, or see guests. She tried to sing a little, and found it tiresome. She went out and sat for hours in the Square, where the spring sun was shining warm and bright on the prancing horse of the great Andrew Jackson. She was a little cross, too, and absent, and spoke so often about Carrington that at last Madeleine was struck by sudden suspicion, and began to watch her with anxious care.

Tuesday night, after this had gone on for two days, Sybil was in Madeleine's room, where she often stayed to talk while her sister was at her toilet. This evening she threw herself listlessly on the couch, and within five minutes again quoted Carrington. Madeleine turned from the glass before which she was sitting, and looked her steadily in the face.

"Sybil," said she, "this is the twenty-fourth time you have mentioned Mr. Carrington since we sat down to dinner. I have waited for the round number to decide whether I should take any notice of it or not? what does it mean, my child? Do you care for Mr. Carrington?"

"Oh, Maude!" exclaimed Sybil reproachfully, flushing so violently that, even by that dim light, her sister could not but see it.

Mrs. Lee rose and, crossing the room, sat down by Sybil who was lying on the couch and turned her face away. Madeleine put her arms round her neck and kissed her.

"My poor—poor child!" said she pityingly. "I never dreamed of this! What a fool I have been! How could I have been so thoughtless! Tell me!" she added, with a little hesitation; "has he—does he care for you?"

"No! no!" cried Sybil, fairly breaking down into a burst of tears; "no! he loves you! nobody but you! he never gave a thought to me. I don't care for him so very much," she continued, drying her tears; "only it seems so lonely now he is gone."

Mrs. Lee remained on the couch, with her arm round her sister's neck, silent, gazing into vacancy, the picture of perplexity and consternation. The situation was getting beyond her control.

CHAPTER XI

In the middle of April a sudden social excitement started the indolent city of Washington to its feet. The Grand-Duke and Duchess of Saxe-Baden-Hombourg arrived in America on a tour of pleasure, and in due course came on to pay their respects to the Chief Magistrate of the Union. The newspapers hastened to inform their readers that the Grand-Duchess was a royal princess of England, and, in the want of any other social event, every one who had any sense of what was due to his or her own dignity, hastened to show this august couple the respect which all republicans who have a large income derived from business, feel for English royalty. New York gave a dinner, at which the most insignificant person present was worth at least a million dollars, and where the gentlemen who sat by the Princess entertained her for an hour or two by a calculation of the aggregate capital represented. New York also gave a ball at which the Princess appeared in an ill-fitting black silk dress with mock lace and jet ornaments, among several hundred toilets that proclaimed the refined republican simplicity of their owners at a cost of various hundred thousand dollars. After these hospitalities the Grand-ducal pair came on to Washington, where they became guests of Lord Skye, or, more properly, Lord Skye became their guest, for he seemed to consider that he handed the Legation over to them, and he told Mrs. Lee, with true British bluntness of speech, that they were a great bore and he wished they had stayed in Saxe-Baden-Hombourg, or wherever they belonged, but as they were here, he must be their lackey. Mrs. Lee was amused and a little astonished at the candour with which he talked about them, and she was instructed and improved by his dry account of the Princess, who, it seemed, made herself disagreeable by her airs of royalty; who had suffered dreadfully from the voyage; and who detested America and everything American; but who was, not without some show of reason, jealous of her husband, and endured endless sufferings, though with a very bad grace, rather than lose sight of him.

Not only was Lord Skye obliged to turn the Legation into an hotel, but in the full enthusiasm of his loyalty he felt himself called upon to give a ball. It was, he said, the easiest way of paying off all his debts at once, and if the Princess was good for nothing else, she could be utilized as a show by way of "promoting the harmony of the two great nations." In other words, Lord Skye meant to exhibit the Princess for his own diplomatic benefit, and he did so. One would have thought that at this season, when Congress had adjourned, Washington would hardly have afforded society enough to fill a ball-room, but this, instead of being a drawback, was an advantage. It permitted the British Minister to issue invitations without limit. He asked not only the President and his Cabinet, and the judges, and the army, and the navy, and all the residents of Washington who had any claim to consideration, but also all the senators, all the representatives in Congress, all the governors of States with their staffs, if they had any, all eminent citizens and their families throughout the Union and Canada, and finally every private individual, from the North Pole to the Isthmus of Panama, who had ever shown him a civility or was able to control interest enough to ask for a card. The result was that Baltimore promised to come in a body, and Philadelphia was equally well-disposed; New York provided several scores of guests, and Boston sent the governor and a delegation; even the well-known millionaire who represented California in the United States Senate was irritated because, his invitation having been timed to arrive just one day too late, he was prevented from bringing his family across the continent with a choice party in a director's car, to enjoy the smiles of royalty in the halls of the British lion. It is astonishing what efforts freemen will make in a just cause.

Lord Skye himself treated the whole affair with easy contempt. One afternoon he strolled into Mrs. Lee's parlour and begged her to give him a cup of tea. He said he had got rid of his menagerie for a few hours by shunting it off upon the German Legation, and he was by way of wanting a little human society. Sybil, who was a great favourite with him, entreated to be told all about the ball, but he insisted that he knew no more than she did. A man from New York had taken possession of the Legation, but what he would do with it was not within the foresight of the wisest; from the talk of the young members of his Legation, Lord Skye gathered that the entire city was to be roofed in and forty millions of people expected, but his own concern in the affair was limited to the flowers he hoped to receive.

"All young and beautiful women," said he to Sybil, "are to send me flowers. I prefer Jacqueminot roses, but will accept any handsome variety, provided they are not wired. It is diplomatic etiquette that each lady who sends me flowers shall reserve at least one dance for me. You will please inscribe this at once upon your tablets, Miss Ross."

To Madeleine this ball was a godsend, for it came just in time to divert Sybil's mind from its troubles. A week had now passed since that revelation of Sybil's heart which had come like an earthquake upon Mrs. Lee. Since then Sybil had been nervous and irritable, all the more because she was conscious of being watched. She was in secret ashamed of her own conduct, and inclined to be angry with Carrington, as though he were responsible for her foolishness; but she could not talk with Madeleine on the subject without discussing Mr. Ratcliffe, and Carrington had expressly forbidden her to attack Mr. Ratcliffe until it was clear that Ratcliffe had laid himself open to attack. This reticence deceived poor Mrs. Lee, who saw in her sister's moods only that unrequited attachment for which she held herself solely to blame. Her gross negligence in allowing Sybil to be improperly exposed to such a risk weighed heavily on her mind. With a saint's capacity for self-torment, Madeleine wielded the scourge over her own back until the blood came. She saw the roses rapidly fading from Sybil's cheeks, and by the help of an active imagination she discovered a hectic look and symptoms of a cough. She became fairly morbid on the subject, and fretted herself into a fever, upon which Sybil sent, on her own responsibility, for the medical man, and Madeleine was obliged to dose herself with quinine. In fact, there was much more reason for anxiety about her than for her anxiety about Sybil, who, barring a little youthful nervousness in the face of responsibility, was as healthy and comfortable a young woman as could be shown in America, and whose sentiment never cost her five minutes' sleep, although her appetite may have become a shade more exacting than before. Madeleine was quick to notice this, and surprised her cook by making daily and almost hourly demands for new and impossible dishes, which she exhausted a library of cookery-books to discover.

Lord Skye's ball and Sybil's interest in it were a great relief to Madeleine's mind, and she now turned her whole soul to frivolity. Never, since she was seventeen, had she thought or talked so much about a ball, as now about this ball to the Grand-Duchess. She wore out her own brain in the effort to amuse Sybil. She took her to call on the Princess; she would have taken her to call on the Grand Lama had he come to Washington. She instigated her to order and send to Lord Skye a mass of the handsomest roses New York could afford. She set her at work on her dress several days before there was any occasion for it, and this famous costume had to be taken out, examined, criticised, and discussed with unending interest. She talked about the dress, and the Princess, and the ball, till her tongue clove to the roof of her mouth, and her brain refused to act. From morning till night, for one entire week, she ate, drank, breathed, and dreamt of the ball. Everything that love could suggest or labour carry out, she did, to amuse and occupy her sister.

She knew that all this was only temporary and palliative, and that more radical measures must be taken to secure Sybil's happiness. On this subject she thought in secret until both head and heart ached. One thing and one thing only was clear: if Sybil loved Carrington, she should have him. How Madeleine expected to bring about this change of heart in Carrington, was known only to herself. She regarded men as creatures made for women to dispose of, and capable of being transferred like checks, or baggage-labels, from one woman to another, as desired. The only condition was that he should first be completely disabused of the notion that he could dispose of himself. Mrs. Lee never doubted that she could make Carrington fall in love with Sybil provided she could place herself beyond his reach. At all events, come what might, even though she had to accept the desperate alternative offered by Mr. Ratcliffe, nothing should be allowed to interfere with Sybil's happiness. And thus it was, that, for the first time, Mrs. Lee began to ask herself whether it was not better to find the solution of her perplexities in marriage.

Would she ever have been brought to this point without the violent pressure of her sister's supposed interests? This is one of those questions which wise men will not ask, because it is one which the wisest man or woman cannot answer. Upon this theme, an army of ingenious authors have exhausted their ingenuity in entertaining the public, and their works are to be found at every book-stall.

They have decided that any woman will, under the right conditions, marry any man at any time, provided her "higher nature" is properly appealed to. Only with regret can a writer forbear to moralize on this subject. "Beauty and the Beast," "Bluebeard," "Auld Robin Gray," have the double charm to authors of being very pleasant to read, and still easier to dilute with sentiment. But at least ten thousand modern writers, with Lord Macaulay at their head, have so ravaged and despoiled the region of fairy-stories and fables, that an allusion even to the "Arabian Nights" is no longer decent. The capacity of women to make unsuitable marriages must be considered as the corner-stone of society.

Meanwhile the ball had, in truth, very nearly driven all thought of Carrington out of Sybil's mind. The city filled again. The streets swarmed with fashionable young men and women from the provinces of New York, Philadelphia, and Boston, who gave Sybil abundance of occupation. She received bulletins of the progress of affairs. The President and his wife had consented to be present, out of their high respect for Her Majesty the Queen and their desire to see and to be seen. All the Cabinet would accompany the Chief Magistrate. The diplomatic corps would appear in uniform; so, too, the officers of the army and navy; the Governor-General of Canada was coming, with a staff. Lord Skye remarked that the Governor-General was a flat.

The day of the ball was a day of anxiety to Sybil, although not on account of Mr. Ratcliffe or of Mr. Carrington, who were of trifling consequence compared with the serious problem now before her. The responsibility of dressing both her sister and herself fell upon Sybil, who was the real author of all Mrs. Lee's millinery triumphs when they now occurred, except that Madeleine managed to put character into whatever she wore, which Sybil repudiated on her own account. On this day Sybil had reasons for special excitement. All winter two new dresses, one especially a triumph of Mr.

Worth's art, had lain in state upstairs, and Sybil had waited in vain for an occasion that should warrant the splendour of these garments.

One afternoon in early June of the preceding summer, Mr. Worth had received a letter on the part of the reigning favourite of the King of Dahomey, directing him to create for her a ball-dress that should annihilate and utterly destroy with jealousy and despair the hearts of her seventy-five rivals; she was young and beautiful; expense was not a consideration. Such were the words of her chamberlain. All that night, the great genius of the nineteenth century tossed wakefully on his bed revolving the problem in his mind. Visions of flesh-coloured tints shot with blood-red perturbed his brain, but he fought against and dismissed them; that combination would be commonplace in Dahomey. When the first rays of sunlight showed him the reflection of his careworn face in the plate-glass mirrored ceiling, he rose and, with an impulse of despair, flung open the casements. There before his blood-shot eyes lay the pure, still, new-born, radiant June morning. With a cry of inspiration the great man leaned out of the casement and rapidly caught the details of his new conception. Before ten o'clock he was again at his bureau in Paris. An imperious order brought to his private room every silk, satin, and gauze within the range of pale pink, pale crocus, pale green, silver and azure. Then came chromatic scales of colour; combinations meant to vulgarise the rainbow; sinfonies and fugues; the twittering of birds and the great peace of dewy nature; maidenhood in her awakening innocence; "The Dawn in June." The Master rested content.

A week later came an order from Sybil, including "an entirely original ball-dress,—unlike any other sent to America." Mr. Worth pondered, hesitated; recalled Sybil's figure; the original pose of her head; glanced anxiously at the map, and speculated whether the *New York Herald* had a special correspondent at Dahomey; and at last, with a generosity peculiar to great souls, he duplicated for "Miss S. Ross, New York, U.S. America," the order for "L'Aube, Mois de Juin."

The Schneidekoupons and Mr. French, who had reappeared in Washington, came to dine with Mrs. Lee on the evening of the ball, and Julia Schneidekoupon sought in vain to discover what Sybil was going to wear. "Be happy, my dear, in your ignorance!" said Sybil; "the pangs of envy will rankle soon enough." An hour later her room, except the fire-place, where a wood fire was gently smouldering, became an altar of sacrifice to the Deity of Dawn in June. Her bed, her low couch, her little tables, her chintz arm-chairs, were covered with portions of the divinity, down to slippers and handkerchief, gloves and bunches of fresh roses. When at length, after a long effort, the work was complete, Mrs. Lee took a last critical look at the result, and enjoyed a glow of satisfaction. Young, happy, sparkling with consciousness of youth and beauty, Sybil stood, Hebe Anadyomene, rising from the foam of soft creplisse which swept back beneath the long train of pale, tender, pink silk, fainting into breadths of delicate primrose, relieved here and there by facings of June green—or was it the blue of early morning?—or both? suggesting unutterable freshness. A modest hint from her maid that "the girls," as women-servants call each other in American households, would like to offer their share of incense at the shrine, was amiably met, and they were allowed a glimpse of the divinity before she was enveloped in wraps. An admiring group, huddled in the doorway, murmured approval, from the leading "girl," who was the cook, a coloured widow of some sixty winters, whose admiration was irrepressible, down to a New England spinster whose Anabaptist conscience wrestled with her instincts, and who, although disapproving of "French folks," paid in her heart that secret homage to their gowns and bonnets which her sterner lips refused. The applause of this audience has, from generation to generation, cheered the hearts of myriads of young women starting out on their little adventures, while the domestic laurels flourish green and fresh for one half hour, until they wither at the threshold of the ball-room.

Mrs. Lee toiled long and earnestly over her sister's toilet, for had not she herself in her own day been the best-dressed girl in New York?—at least, she held that opinion, and her old instincts came to life again whenever Sybil was to be prepared for any great occasion. Madeleine kissed her sister affectionately, and gave her unusual praise when the "Dawn in June" was complete. Sybil was at this moment the ideal of blooming youth, and Mrs. Lee almost dared to hope that her heart was not permanently broken, and that she might yet survive until Carrington could be brought back. Her own toilet was a much shorter affair, but Sybil was impatient long before it was concluded; the carriage was waiting, and she was obliged to disappoint her household by coming down enveloped in her long opera-cloak, and hurrying away.

When at length the sisters entered the reception-room at the British Legation, Lord Skye rebuked them for not having come early to receive with him. His Lordship, with a huge riband across his breast, and a star on his coat, condescended to express himself vigorously on the subject of the "Dawn in June." Schneidekoupon, who was proud of his easy use of the latest artistic jargon, looked with respect at Mrs. Lee's silver-gray satin and its Venetian lace, the arrangement of which had been conscientiously stolen from a picture in the Louvre, and he murmured audibly, "Nocturne in silver-gray!"—then, turning to Sybil—"and you? Of course! I see! A song without words!" Mr. French came up and, in his most fascinating tones, exclaimed, "Why, Mrs. Lee, you look real handsome tonight!" Jacobi, after a close scrutiny, said that he took the liberty of an old man in telling them that they were both dressed absolutely without fault. Even the Grand-Duke was struck by Sybil, and made

Lord Skye introduce him, after which ceremony he terrified her by asking the pleasure of a waltz. She disappeared from Madeleine's view, not to be brought back again until Dawn met dawn.

The ball was, as the newspapers declared, a brilliant success. Every one who knows the city of Washington will recollect that, among some scores of magnificent residences which our own and foreign governments have built for the comfort of cabinet officers, judges, diplomatists, vice-presidents, speakers, and senators, the British Legation is by far the most impressive. Combining in one harmonious whole the proportions of the Pitti Palace with the decoration of the Casa d'Oro and the dome of an Eastern mosque, this architectural triumph offers extraordinary resources for society. Further description is unnecessary, since anyone may easily refer back to the New York newspapers of the following morning, where accurate plans of the house on the ground floor, will be found; while the illustrated newspapers of the same week contain excellent sketches of the most pleasing scenic effects, as well as of the ball-room and of the Princess smiling graciously from her throne. The lady just behind the Princess on her left, is Mrs. Lee, a poor likeness, but easily distinguishable from the fact that the artist, for his own objects, has made her rather shorter, and the Princess rather taller, than was strictly correct, just as he has given the Princess a gracious smile, which was quite different from her actual expression. In short, the artist is compelled to exhibit the world rather as we would wish it to be, than as it was, or is, or, indeed, is like shortly to become. The strangest part of his picture is, however, the fact that he actually did see Mrs. Lee where he has put her, at the Princess's elbow, which was almost the last place in the room where any one who knew Mrs. Lee would have looked for her. The explanation of this curious accident shall be given immediately, since the facts are not mentioned in the public reports of the ball, which only said that, "close behind her Royal Highness the Grand-Duchess, stood our charming and aristocratic countrywoman, Mrs. Lightfoot

Lee, who has made so great a sensation in Washington this winter, and whose name public rumour has connected with that of the Secretary of the Treasury. To her the Princess appeared to address most of her conversation."

The show was a very pretty one, and on a pleasant April evening there were many places less agreeable to be in than this. Much ground outside had been roofed over, to make a ball-room, large as an opera-house, with a daïs and a sofa in the centre of one long side, and another daïs with a second sofa immediately opposite to it in the centre of the other long side. Each daïs had a canopy of red velvet, one bearing the Lion and the Unicorn, the other the American Eagle. The Royal Standard was displayed above the Unicorn; the Stars-and-Stripes, not quite so effectively, waved above the Eagle. The Princess, being no longer quite a child, found gas trying to her complexion, and compelled Lord Skye to illuminate her beauty by one hundred thousand wax candles, more or less, which were arranged to be becoming about the Grand-ducal throne, and to be showy and unbecoming about the opposite institution across the way.

The exact facts were these. It had happened that the Grand-Duchess, having been necessarily brought into contact with the President, and particularly with his wife, during the past week, had conceived for the latter an antipathy hardly to be expressed in words. Her fixed determination was at any cost to keep the Presidential party at a distance, and it was only after a stormy scene that the Grand-Duke and Lord Skye succeeded in extorting her consent that the President should take her to supper. Further than this she would not go. She would not speak to "that woman," as she called the President's wife, nor be in her neighbourhood. She would rather stay in her own room all the evening, and she did not care in the least what the Queen would think of it, for she was no subject of the Queen's. The case was a hard one for Lord Skye, who was perplexed to know, from this point of view, why he was entertaining the Princess at all; but, with the help of the Grand-Duke and Lord Dunbeg, who was very active and smiled deprecation with some success, he found a way out of it; and this was the reason why there were two thrones in the ball-room, and why the British throne was lighted with such careful reference to the Princess's complexion. Lord Skye immolated himself in the usual effort of British and American Ministers, to keep the two great powers apart. He and the Grand-Duke and Lord Dunbeg acted as buffers with watchful diligence, dexterity, and success. As one resource, Lord Skye had bethought himself of Mrs. Lee, and he told the Princess the story of Mrs. Lee's relations with the President's wife, a story which was no secret in Washington, for, apart from Madeleine's own account, society was left in no doubt of the light in which Mrs. Lee was regarded by the mistress of the White House, whom Washington ladies were now in the habit of drawing out on the subject of Mrs. Lee, and who always rose to the bait with fresh vivacity, to the amusement and delight of Victoria Dare and other mischief-makers.

"She will not trouble you so long as you can keep Mrs. Lee in your neighbourhood," said Lord Skye, and the Princess accordingly seized upon Mrs. Lee and brandished her, as though she were a charm against the evil eye, in the face of the President's party. She made Mrs. Lee take a place just behind her as though she were a lady-in-waiting. She even graciously permitted her to sit down, so near that their chairs touched. Whenever "that woman" was within sight, which was most of the time, the Princess directed her conversation entirely to Mrs. Lee and took care to make it evident. Even before the Presidential party had arrived, Madeleine had fallen into the Princess's grasp, and when the Princess went forward to receive the President and his wife, which she did with a bow of stately and distant dignity, she dragged Madeleine closely by her side. Mrs. Lee bowed too; she could not well help it; but was cut dead for her pains, with a glare of contempt and hatred. Lord

Skye, who was acting as cavalier to the President's wife, was panic-stricken, and hastened to march his democratic potentate away, under pretence of showing her the decorations. He placed her at last on her own throne, where he and the Grand-Duke relieved each other in standing guard at intervals throughout the evening. When the Princess followed with the President, she compelled her husband to take Mrs. Lee on his arm and conduct her to the British throne, with no other object than to exasperate the President's wife, who, from her elevated platform, looked down upon the cortège with a scowl.

In all this affair Mrs. Lee was the principal sufferer. No one could relieve her, and she was literally penned in as she sat. The Princess kept up an incessant fire of small conversation, principally complaint and fault-finding, which no one dared to interrupt. Mrs. Lee was painfully bored, and after a time even the absurdity of the thing ceased to amuse her. She had, too, the ill-luck to make one or two remarks which appealed to some hidden sense of humour in the Princess, who laughed and, in the style of royal personages, gave her to understand that she would like more amusement of the same sort. Of all things in life, Mrs. Lee held this kind of court-service in contempt, for she was something more than republican—a little communistic at heart, and her only serious complaint of the President and his wife was that they undertook to have a court and to ape monarchy. She had no notion of admitting social superiority in any one, President or Prince, and to be suddenly converted into a lady-in-waiting to a small German Grand-Duchess, was a terrible blow. But what was to be done? Lord Skye had drafted her into the service and she could not decently refuse to help him when he came to her side and told her, with his usual calm directness, what his difficulties were, and how he counted upon her to help him out.

The same play went on at supper, where there was a royal-presidential table, which held about two dozen guests, and the two great ladies presiding, as far apart as they could be placed. The Grand-Duke and Lord Skye, on either side of the President's wife, did their duty like men, and were rewarded by receiving from her much information about the domestic arrangements of the White House. The President, however, who sat next the Princess at the opposite end, was evidently depressed, owing partly to the fact that the Princess, in defiance of all etiquette, had compelled Lord Dunbeg to take Mrs. Lee to supper and to place her directly next the President. Madeleine tried to escape, but was stopped by the Princess, who addressed her across the President and in a decided tone asked her to sit precisely there. Mrs. Lee looked timidly at her neighbour, who made no sign, but ate his supper in silence only broken by an occasional reply to a rare remark. Mrs. Lee pitied him, and wondered what his wife would say when they reached home. She caught Ratcliffe's eye down the table, watching her with a smile; she tried to talk fluently with Dunbeg; but not until supper was long over and two o'clock was at hand; not until the Presidential party, under all the proper formalities, had taken their leave of the Grand-ducal party; not until Lord Skye had escorted them to their carriage and returned to say that they were gone, did the Princess loose her hold upon Mrs. Lee and allow her to slip away into obscurity.

Meanwhile the ball had gone on after the manner of balls. As Madeleine sat in her enforced grandeur she could watch all that passed. She had seen Sybil whirling about with one man after another, amid a swarm of dancers, enjoying herself to the utmost and occasionally giving a nod and a smile to her sister as their eyes met. There, too, was Victoria Dare, who never appeared flurried even when waltzing with Lord Dunbeg, whose education as a dancer had been neglected. The fact was now fully recognized that Victoria was carrying on a systematic flirtation with Dunbeg, and had undertaken as her latest duty the task of teaching him to waltz. His struggles and her calmness in assisting them commanded respect.

On the opposite side of the room, by the republican throne, Mrs. Lee had watched Mr. Ratcliffe standing by the President, who appeared unwilling to let him out of arm's length and who seemed to make to him most of his few remarks. Schneidekoupon and his sister were mixed in the throng, dancing as though England had never countenanced the heresy of free-trade. On the whole, Mrs. Lee was satisfied. If her own sufferings were great, they were not without reward. She studied all the women in the ball-room, and if there was one prettier than Sybil, Madeleine's eyes could not discover her. If there was a more perfect dress, Madeleine knew nothing of dressing. On these points she felt the confidence of conviction. Her calm would have been complete, had she felt quite sure that none of Sybil's gaiety was superficial and that it would not be followed by reaction. She watched nervously to see whether her face changed its gay expression, and once she thought it became depressed, but this was when the Grand-Duke came up to claim his waltz, and the look rapidly passed away when they got upon the floor and his Highness began to wheel round the room with a precision and momentum that would have done honour to a regiment of Life Guards. He seemed pleased with his experiment, for he was seen again and again careering over the floor with Sybil until Mrs. Lee herself became nervous, for the Princess frowned.

After her release Madeleine lingered awhile in the ball-room to speak with her sister and to receive congratulations. For half an hour she was a greater belle than Sybil. A crowd of men clustered about her, amused at the part she had played in the evening's entertainment and full of compliments upon her promotion at Court. Lord Skye himself found time to offer her his thanks in a more serious tone than he generally affected. "You have suffered much," said he, "and I am grateful." Madeleine laughed as she answered that her sufferings had seemed nothing to her while she watched his. But at last she became weary of the noise and glare of the ball-room, and, accepting the arm of her excellent friend Count Popoff, she strolled with him back to the house. There at last she sat down on a sofa in a quiet window-recess where the light was less strong and where a convenient laurel spread its leaves in front so as to make a bower through which she could see the passers-by without being seen by them except with an effort. Had she been a younger woman, this would have been the spot for a flirtation, but Mrs. Lee never flirted, and the idea of her flirting with Popoff would have seemed ludicrous to all mankind.

He did not sit down, but was leaning against the angle of the wall, talking with her, when suddenly Mr. Ratcliffe appeared and took the seat by her side with such deliberation and apparent sense of property that Popoff incontinently turned and fled. No one knew where the Secretary came from, or how he learned that she was there. He made no explanation and she took care to ask for none. She gave him a highly-coloured account of her evening's service as lady-in-waiting, which he matched by that of his own trials as gentleman-usher to the President, who, it seemed, had clung desperately to his old enemy in the absence of any other rock to clutch at.

Ratcliffe looked the character of Prime Minister sufficiently well at this moment. He would have held his own, at a pinch, in any Court, not merely in Europe but in India or China, where dignity is still expected of gentlemen. Excepting for a certain coarse and animal expression about the mouth, and an indefinable coldness in the eye, he was a handsome man and still in his prime. Every one remarked how much he was improved since entering the Cabinet. He had dropped his senatorial manner. His clothes were no longer congressional, but those of a respectable man, neat and decent. His shirts no longer protruded in the wrong places, nor were his shirt-collars frayed or soiled. His hair did not stray over his eyes, ears, and coat, like that of a Scotch terrier, but had got itself cut. Having overheard Mrs. Lee express on one occasion her opinion of people who did not take a cold bath every morning, he had thought it best to adopt this reform, although he would not have had it generally known, for it savoured of caste. He made an effort not to be dictatorial and to forget that he had been the Prairie Giant, the bully of the Senate. In short, what with Mrs. Lee's influence and what with his emancipation from the Senate chamber with its code of bad manners and worse morals, Mr. Ratcliffe was fast becoming a respectable member of society whom a man who had never been in prison or in politics might safely acknowledge as a friend.

Mr. Ratcliffe was now evidently bent upon being heard. After chatting for a time with some humour on the President's successes as a man of fashion, he changed the subject to the merits of the President as a statesman, and little by little as he spoke he became serious and his voice sank into low and confidential tones. He plainly said that the President's incapacity had now become notorious among his followers; that it was only with difficulty his Cabinet and friends could prevent him from making a fool of himself fifty times a day; that all the party leaders who had occasion to deal with him were so thoroughly disgusted that the Cabinet had to pass its time in trying to pacify them; while this state of things lasted, Ratcliffe's own influence must be paramount; he had good reason to know that if the Presidential election were to take place this year, nothing could prevent his nomination and election; even at three years' distance the chances in his favour were at least two to one; and after this exordium he went on in a low tone with increasing earnestness, while Mrs. Lee sat motionless as the statue of Agrippina, her eyes fixed on the ground:

"I am not one of those who are happy in political life. I am a politician because I cannot help myself; it is the trade I am fittest for, and ambition is my resource to make it tolerable. In politics we cannot keep our hands clean. I have done many things in my political career that are not defensible. To act with entire honesty and self-respect, one should always live in a pure atmosphere, and the atmosphere of politics is impure. Domestic life is the salvation of many public men, but I have for many years been deprived of it. I have now come to that point where increasing responsibilities and temptations make me require help. I must have it. You alone can give it to me. You are kind, thoughtful, conscientious, high-minded, cultivated, fitted better than any woman I ever saw, for public duties. Your place is there. You belong among those who exercise an influence beyond their time. I only ask you to take the place which is yours."

This desperate appeal to Mrs. Lee's ambition was a calculated part of Ratcliffe's scheme. He was well aware that he had marked high game, and that in proportion to this height must be the power of his lure. Nor was he embarrassed because Mrs. Lee sat still and pale with her eyes fixed on the ground and her hands twisted together in her lap. The eagle that soars highest must be longer in descending to the ground than the sparrow or the partridge. Mrs. Lee had a thousand things to think about in this brief time, and yet she found that she could not think at all; a succession of mere images and fragments of thought passed rapidly over her mind, and her will exercised no control upon their order or their nature. One of these fleeting reflections was that in all the offers of marriage she had ever heard, this was the most unsentimental and businesslike. As for his appeal to her ambition, it fell quite dead upon her ear, but a woman must be more than a heroine who can listen to flattery so evidently sincere, from a man who is pre-eminent among men, without being affected by it. To her, however, the great and overpowering fact was that she found herself unable to retreat or escape; her tactics were disconcerted, her temporary barriers beaten down. The offer was made. What should she do with it?

She had thought for months on this subject without being able to form a decision; what hope was there that she should be able to decide now, in a ball-room, at a minute's notice? When, as occasionally happens, the conflicting sentiments, prejudices, and passions of a lifetime are compressed into a single instant, they sometimes overcharge the mind and it refuses to work. Mrs. Lee sat still and let things take their course; a dangerous expedient, as thousands of women have learned, for it leaves them at the mercy of the strong will, bent upon mastery.

The music from the ball-room did not stop. Crowds of persons passed by their retreat. Some glanced in, and not one of these felt a doubt what was going on there. An unmistakeable atmosphere of mystery and intensity surrounded the pair. Ratcliffe's eyes were fixed upon Mrs. Lee, and hers on the ground. Neither seemed to speak or to stir. Old Baron Jacobi, who never failed to see everything, saw this as he went by, and ejaculated a foreign oath of frightful import. Victoria Dare saw it and was devoured by curiosity to such a point as to be hardly capable of containing herself.

After a silence which seemed interminable, Ratcliffe went on: "I do not speak of my own feelings because I know that unless compelled by a strong sense of duty, you will not be decided by any devotion of mine. But I honestly say that I have learned to depend on you to a degree I can hardly express; and when I think of what I should be without you, life seems to me so intolerably dark that I am ready to make any sacrifice, to accept any conditions that will keep you by my side."

Meanwhile Victoria Dare, although deeply interested in what Dunbeg was telling her, had met Sybil and had stopped a single second to whisper in her ear: "You had better look after your sister, in the window, behind the laurel with Mr. Ratcliffe!" Sybil was on Lord Skye's arm, enjoying herself amazingly, though the night was far gone, but when she caught Victoria's words, the expression of her face wholly changed. All the anxieties and terrors of the last fortnight, came back upon it. She dragged Lord Skye across the hall and looked in upon her sister. One glance was enough. Desperately frightened but afraid to hesitate, she went directly up to Madeleine who was still sitting like a statue, listening to Ratcliffe's last words. As she hurriedly entered, Mrs. Lee, looking up, caught sight of her pale face, and started from her seat.

"Are you ill, Sybil?" she exclaimed; "is anything the matter?"

"A little—fatigued," gasped Sybil; "I thought you might be ready to go home."

"I am," cried Madeleine; "I am quite ready. Good evening, Mr. Ratcliffe. I will see you to-morrow. Lord Skye, shall I take leave of the Princess?"

"The Princess retired half an hour ago," replied Lord Skye, who saw the situation and was quite ready to help Sybil; "let me take you to the dressing-room and order your carriage."

Mr. Ratcliffe found himself suddenly left alone, while Mrs. Lee hurried away, torn by fresh anxieties. They had reached the dressing-room and were nearly ready to go home, when Victoria Dare suddenly dashed in upon them, with an animation of manner very unusual in her, and, seizing Sybil by the hand, drew her into an adjoining room and shut the door.

"Can you keep a secret?" said she abruptly.

"What!" said Sybil, looking at her with open-mouthed interest; "you don't mean—are you really—tell me, quick!"

"Yes!" said Victoria relapsing into composure; "I am engaged!"

"To Lord Dunbeg?"

Victoria nodded, and Sybil, whose nerves were strung to the highest pitch by excitement, flattery, fatigue, perplexity, and terror, burst into a paroxysm of laughter, that startled even the calm Miss Dare.

"Poor Lord Dunbeg! don't be hard on him, Victoria!" she gasped when at last she found breath; "do you really mean to pass the rest of your life in Ireland? Oh, how much you will teach them!"

"You forget, my dear," said Victoria, who had placidly enthroned herself on the foot of a bed, "that I am not a pauper. I am told that Dunbeg Castle is a romantic summer residence, and in the dull season we shall of course go to London or somewhere. I shall be civil to you when you come over. Don't you think a coronet will look well on me?"

Sybil burst again into laughter so irrepressible and prolonged that it puzzled even poor Dunbeg, who was impatiently pacing the corridor outside. It alarmed Madeleine, who suddenly opened the door. Sybil recovered herself, and, her eyes streaming with tears, presented Victoria to her sister:

"Madeleine, allow me to introduce you to the Countess Dunbeg!"

But Mrs. Lee was much too anxious to feel any interest in Lady Dunbeg. A sudden fear struck her that Sybil was going into hysterics because Victoria's engagement recalled her own disappointment. She hurried her sister away to the carriage.

Chapter XII

They drove home in silence, Mrs. Lee disturbed with anxieties and doubts, partly caused by her sister, partly by Mr. Ratcliffe; Sybil divided between amusement at Victoria's conquest, and alarm at her own boldness in meddling with her sister's affairs. Desperation, however, was stronger than fear. She made up her mind that further suspense was not to be endured; she would fight her battle now before another hour was lost; surely no time could be better. A few moments brought them to their door. Mrs. Lee had told her maid not to wait for them, and they were alone. The fire was still alive on Madeleine's hearth, and she threw more wood upon it. Then she insisted that Sybil must go to bed at once. But Sybil refused; she felt quite well, she said, and not in the least sleepy; she had a great deal to talk about, and wanted to get it off her mind. Nevertheless, her feminine regard for the "Dawn in June" led her to postpone what she had to say until with Madeleine's help she had laid the triumph of the ball carefully aside; then, putting on her dressing-gown, and hastily plunging Carrington's letter into her breast, like a concealed weapon, she hurried back to Madeleine's room and established herself in a chair before the fire. There, after a moment's pause, the two women began their long-deferred trial of strength, in which the match was so nearly equal as to make the result doubtful; for, if Madeleine were much the cleverer, Sybil in this case knew much better what she wanted, and had a clear idea how she meant to gain it, while Madeleine, unsuspicious of attack, had no plan of defence at all.

"Madeleine," began Sybil, solemnly, and with a violent palpitation of the heart, "I want you to tell me something."

"What is it, my child?" said Mrs. Lee, puzzled, and yet half ready to see that there must be some connection between her sister's coming question and the sudden illness at the ball, which had disappeared as suddenly as it came.

"Do you mean to marry Mr. Ratcliffe?"

Poor Mrs. Lee was quite disconcerted by the directness of the attack. This fatal question met her at every turn. Hardly had she succeeded in escaping from it at the ball scarcely an hour ago, by a stroke of good fortune for which she now began to see she was indebted to Sybil, and here it was again presented to her face like a pistol. The whole town, then, was asking it. Ratcliffe's offer must have been seen by half Washington, and her reply was awaited by an immense audience, as though she were a political returning-board. Her disgust was intense, and her first answer to Sybil was a quick inquiry:

"Why do you ask such a question? have you heard anything,—has anyone talked about it to you?"

"No!" replied Sybil; "but I must know; I can see for myself without being told, that Mr. Ratcliffe is trying to make you marry him. I don't ask out of curiosity; this is something that concerns me nearly as much as it does you yourself. Please tell me! don't treat me like a child any longer! let me know what you are thinking about! I am so tired of being left in the dark! You have no idea how much this thing weighs on me. Oh, Maude, I shall never be happy again until you trust me about this."

Mrs. Lee felt a little pang of conscience, and seemed suddenly to become conscious of a new coil, tightening about her, in this wretched complication. Unable to see her way, ignorant of her sister's motives, urged on by the idea that Sybil's happiness was involved, she was now charged with want of feeling, and called upon for a direct answer to a plain question. How could she aver that she did not mean to marry Mr. Ratcliffe? to say this would be to shut the door on all the objects she had at heart. If a direct answer must be given, it was better to say "Yes!" and have it over; better to leap blindly and see what came of it. Mrs. Lee, therefore, with an internal gasp, but with no visible sign of excitement, said, as though she were in a dream:

"Well, Sybil, I *will* tell you. I would have told you long ago if I had known myself. Yes! I have made up my mind to marry Mr. Ratcliffe!"

Sybil sprang to her feet with a cry: "And have you told him so?" she asked.

"No! you came and interrupted us just as we were speaking. I was glad you did come, for it gives me a little time to think. But I am decided now. I shall tell him to-morrow."

This was not said with the air of one whose heart beat warmly at the thought of confessing her love. Mrs. Lee spoke mechanically, and almost with an effort. Sybil flung herself with all her energy upon her sister; violently excited, and eager to make herself heard, without waiting for arguments, she broke out into a torrent of entreaties:

"Oh, don't, don't, don't! Oh, please, please, don't, my dearest, dearest Maude! unless you want to break my heart, don't marry that man! You can't love him! You can never be happy with him! he will take you away to Peonia, and you will die there! I shall never see you again! He will make you unhappy; he will beat you, I know he will! Oh, if you care for me at all, don't marry him! Send him away! don't see him again! let us go ourselves, now, in the morning train, before he comes back. I'm all ready; I'll pack everything for you; we'll go to Newport; to Europe—anywhere, to be out of his reach!"

With this passionate appeal, Sybil threw herself on her knees by her sister's side, and, clasping her arms round Madeleine's waist, sobbed as though her heart were already broken. Had Carrington seen her then he must have admitted that she had carried out his instructions to the letter. She was quite honest, too, in it all. She meant what she said, and her tears were real tears that had been pent up for weeks. Unluckily, her logic was feeble. Her idea of Mr. Ratcliffe's character was vague, and biased by mere theories of what a Prairie Giant of Peonia should be in his domestic relations. Her idea of Peonia, too, was indistinct. She was haunted by a vision of her sister, sitting on a horse-hair sofa before an air-tight iron stove in a small room with high, bare white walls, a chromo-lithograph on each, and at her side a marble-topped table surmounted by a glass vase containing funereal dried grasses; the only literature, Frank Leslie's periodical and the *New York Ledger,* with a strong smell of cooking everywhere prevalent. Here she saw Madeleine receiving visitors, the wives of neighbours and constituents, who told her the Peonia news.

Notwithstanding her ignorant and unreasonable prejudice against western men and women, western towns and prairies, and, in short, everything western, down to western politics and western politicians, whom she perversely asserted to be the lowest of all western products, there was still some common sense in Sybil's idea. When that inevitable hour struck for Mr. Ratcliffe, which strikes sooner or later for all politicians, and an ungrateful country permitted him to pine among his friends in Illinois, what did he propose to do with his wife? Did he seriously suppose that she, who was bored to death by New York, and had been able to find no permanent pleasure in

Europe, would live quietly in the romantic village of Peonia? If not, did Mr. Ratcliffe imagine that they could find happiness in the enjoyment of each other's society, and of Mrs. Lee's income, in the excitements of Washington? In the ardour of his pursuit, Mr. Ratcliffe had accepted in advance any conditions which Mrs. Lee might impose, but if he really imagined that happiness and content lay on the purple rim of this sunset, he had more confidence in women and in money than a wider experience was ever likely to justify.

Whatever might be Mr. Ratcliffe's schemes for dealing with these obstacles they could hardly be such as would satisfy Sybil, who, if inaccurate in her theories about Prairie Giants, yet understood women, and especially her sister, much better than Mr. Ratcliffe ever could do. Here she was safe, and it would have been better had she said no more, for Mrs. Lee, though staggered for a moment by her sister's vehemence, was reassured by what seemed the absurdity of her fears. Madeleine rebelled against this hysterical violence of opposition, and became more fixed in her decision. She scolded her sister in good, set terms—

"Sybil, Sybil! you must not be so violent. Behave like a woman, and not like a spoiled child!"

Mrs. Lee, like most persons who have to deal with spoiled or unspoiled children, resorted to severity, not so much because it was the proper way of dealing with them, as because she knew not what else to do. She was thoroughly uncomfortable and weary. She was not satisfied with herself or with her own motives. Doubt encompassed her on all sides, and her worst opponent was that sister whose happiness had turned the scale against her own judgment.

Nevertheless her tactics answered their object of checking Sybil's vehemence. Her sobs came to an end, and she presently rose with a quieter air.

"Madeleine," said she, "do you really want to marry Mr. Ratcliffe?"

"What else can I do, my dear Sybil? I want to do whatever is for the best. I thought you might be pleased."

"You thought I might be pleased?" cried Sybil in astonishment. "What a strange idea! If you had ever spoken to me about it I should have told you that I hate him, and can't understand how you can abide him. But I would rather marry him myself than see you marry him. I know that you will kill yourself with unhappiness when you have done it. Oh, Maude, please tell me that you won't!" And Sybil began gently sobbing again, while she caressed her sister.

Mrs. Lee was infinitely distressed. To act against the wishes of her nearest friends was hard enough, but to appear harsh and unfeeling to the one being whose happiness she had at heart, was intolerable. Yet no sensible woman, after saying that she meant to marry a man like Mr. Ratcliffe, could throw him over merely because another woman chose to behave like a spoiled child. Sybil was more childish than Madeleine herself had supposed. She could not even see where her own interest lay. She knew no more about Mr. Ratcliffe and the West than if he were the giant of a fairy-story, and lived at the top of a bean-stalk. She must be treated as a child; with gentleness, affection, forbearance, but with firmness and decision. She must be refused what she asked, for her own good.

Thus it came about that at last Mrs. Lee spoke, with an appearance of decision far from representing her internal tremor.

"Sybil, dear, I have made up my mind to marry Mr. Ratcliffe because there is no other way of making every one happy. You need not be afraid of him. He is kind and generous. Besides, I can take care of myself; and I will take care of you too. Now let us not discuss it any more. It is broad daylight, and we are both tired out."

Sybil grew at once perfectly calm, and standing before her sister, as though their *rôles* were henceforward to be reversed, said:

"You have really made up your mind, then? Nothing I can say will change it?"

Mrs. Lee, looking at her with more surprise than ever, could not force herself to speak; but she shook her head slowly and decidedly.

"Then," said Sybil, "there is only one thing more I can do. You must read this!" and she drew out Carrington's letter, which she held before Madeleine's face.

"Not now, Sybil!" remonstrated Mrs. Lee, dreading another long struggle. "I will read it after we have had some rest. Go to bed now!"

"I do not leave this room, nor will I ever go to bed until you have read that letter," answered Sybil, seating herself again before the fire with the resolution of Queen Elizabeth; "not if I sit here till you are married. I promised Mr. Carrington that you should read it instantly; it's all I can do now."

With a sigh, Mrs. Lee drew up the window-curtain, and in the gray morning light sat down to break the seal and read the following letter:—

"Washington, 2nd April.

"My dear Mrs. Lee,

"This letter will only come into your hands in case there should be a necessity for your knowing its contents. Nothing short of necessity would excuse my writing it. I have to ask your pardon for intruding again upon your private affairs. In this case, if I did not intrude, you would have cause for serious complaint against me.

"You asked me the other day whether I knew anything against Mr. Ratcliffe which the world did not know, to account for my low opinion of his character. I evaded your question then. I was bound by professional rules not to disclose facts that came to me under a pledge of confidence. I am going to violate these rules now, only because I owe you a duty which seems to me to override all others.

"I do know facts in regard to Mr. Ratcliffe, which have seemed to me to warrant a very low opinion of his character, and to mark him as unfit to be, I will not say your husband, but even your acquaintance.

"You know that I am executor to Samuel Baker's will. You know who Samuel Baker was. You have seen his wife. She has told you herself that I assisted her in the examination and destruction of all her husband's private papers according to his special death-bed request. One of the first facts I learned from these papers and her explanations, was the following.

"Just eight years ago, the great 'Inter-Oceanic Mail Steamship Company,' wished to extend its service round the world, and, in order to do so, it applied to Congress for a heavy subsidy. The management of this affair was put into the hands of Mr. Baker, and all his private letters to the President of the Company, in press copies, as well as the President's replies, came into my possession. Baker's letters were, of course, written in a sort of cypher, several kinds of which he was in the habit of using. He left among his papers a key to this cypher, but Mrs. Baker could have explained it without that help.

"It appeared from this correspondence that the bill was carried successfully through the House, and, on reaching the Senate, was referred to the appropriate Committee. Its ultimate passage was very doubtful; the end of the session was close at hand; the Senate was very evenly divided, and the Chairman of the Committee was decidedly hostile.

"The Chairman of that Committee was Senator Ratcliffe, always mentioned by Mr. Baker in cypher, and with every precaution. If you care, however, to verify the fact, and to trace the history of the Subsidy Bill through all its stages, together with Mr. Ratcliffe's report, remarks, and votes upon it, you have only to look into the journals and debates for that year.

"At last Mr. Baker wrote that Senator Ratcliffe had put the bill in his pocket, and unless some means could be found of overcoming his opposition, there would be no report, and the bill would never come to a vote. All ordinary kinds of argument and influence had been employed upon him, and were exhausted. In this exigency Baker suggested that the Company should give him authority to see what money would do, but he added that it would be worse than useless to deal with small sums. Unless at least one hundred thousand dollars could be employed, it was better to leave the thing alone.

"The next mail authorized him to use any required amount of

money not exceeding one hundred and fifty thousand dollars. Two days later he wrote that the bill was reported, and would pass the Senate within forty-eight hours; and he congratulated the Company on the fact that he had used only one hundred thousand dollars out of its last credit.

"The bill was actually reported, passed, and became law as he foretold, and the Company has enjoyed its subsidy ever since. Mrs. Baker also informed me that to her knowledge her husband gave the sum mentioned, in United States Coupon Bonds, to Senator Ratcliffe.

"This transaction, taken in connection with the tortuousness of his public course, explains the distrust I have always expressed for him. You will, however, understand that all these papers have been destroyed. Mrs. Baker could never be induced to hazard her own comfort by revealing the facts to the public. The officers of the Company in their own interests would never betray the transaction, and their books were undoubtedly so kept as to show no trace of it. If I made this charge against Mr. Ratcliffe, I should be the only sufferer. He would deny and laugh at it. I could prove nothing. I am therefore more directly interested that he is in keeping silence.

"In trusting this secret to you, I rely firmly upon your mentioning it to no one else—not even to your sister. You are at liberty, if you wish, to show this letter to one person only—to Mr. Ratcliffe himself. That done, you will, I beg, burn it immediately.

"With the warmest good wishes, I am,
"Ever most truly yours,
"John Carrington."

When Mrs. Lee had finished reading this letter, she remained for some time quite silent, looking out into the square below. The morning had come, and the sky was bright with the fresh April sunlight. She threw open her window, and drew in the soft spring air. She needed all the purity and quiet that nature could give, for her whole soul was in revolt, wounded, mortified, exasperated. Against the sentiment of all her friends she had insisted upon believing in this man; she had wrought herself up to the point of accepting him for her husband; a man who, if law were the same thing as justice, ought to be in a felon's cell; a man who could take money to betray his trust. Her anger at first swept away all bounds. She was impatient for the moment when she should see him again, and tear off his mask. For once she would express all the loathing she felt for the whole pack of political hounds. She would see whether the animal was made like other beings; whether he had a sense of honour; a single clean spot in his mind.

Then it occurred to her that after all there might be a mistake; perhaps Mr. Ratcliffe could explain the charge away. But this thought only laid bare another smarting wound in her pride. Not only did she believe the charge, but she believed that Mr. Ratcliffe would defend his act. She had been willing to marry a man whom she thought capable of such a crime, and now she shuddered at the idea that this charge might have been brought against her husband, and that she could not dismiss it with instant incredulity, with indignant contempt. How had this happened? how had she got into so foul a complication? When she left New York, she had meant to be a mere spectator in Washington. Had it entered her head that she could be drawn into any project of a second marriage, she never would have come at all, for she was proud of her loyalty to her husband's memory, and second marriages were her abhorrence. In her restlessness and solitude, she had forgotten this; she had only asked whether any life was worth living for a woman who had neither husband nor children. Was the family all that life had to offer? could she find no interest outside the household? And so, led by this will-of-the-wisp, she had, with her eyes open, walked into the quagmire of politics, in spite of remonstrance, in spite of conscience.

She rose and paced the room, while Sybil lay on the couch, watching her with eyes half shut. She grew more and more angry with herself, and as her self-reproach increased, her anger against Ratcliffe faded away. She had no right to be angry with Ratcliffe.

He had never deceived her. He had always openly enough avowed that he knew no code of morals in politics; that if virtue did not answer his purpose he used vice. How could she blame him for acts which he had repeatedly defended in her presence and with her tacit assent, on principles that warranted this or any other villainy?

The worst was that this discovery had come on her as a blow, not as a reprieve from execution. At this thought she became furious with herself. She had not known the recesses of her own heart. She had honestly supposed that Sybil's interests and Sybil's happiness were forcing her to an act of self-sacrifice; and now she saw that in the depths of her soul very different motives had been at work: ambition, thirst for power, restless eagerness to meddle in what did not concern her, blind longing to escape from the torture of watching other women with full lives and satisfied instincts, while her own life was hungry and sad. For a time she had actually, unconscious as she was of the delusion, hugged a hope that a new field of usefulness was open to her; that great opportunities for doing good were to supply the aching emptiness of that good which had been taken away; and that here at last was an object for which there would be almost a pleasure in squandering the rest of existence even if she knew in advance that the experiment would fail. Life was emptier than ever now that this dream was over. Yet the worst was not in that disappointment, but in the discovery of her own weakness and self-deception.

Worn out by long-continued anxiety, excitement and sleeplessness, she was unfit to struggle with the creatures of her own imagination. Such a strain could only end in a nervous crisis, and at length it came:

"Oh, what a vile thing life is!" she cried, throwing up her arms with a gesture of helpless rage and despair. "Oh, how I wish I were dead! how I wish the universe were annihilated!" and she flung herself down by Sybil's side in a frenzy of tears.

Sybil, who had watched all this exhibition in silence, waited quietly for the excitement to pass. There was little to say. She could only soothe. After the paroxysm had exhausted itself, Madeleine lay quiet for a time, until other thoughts began to disturb her. From reproaching herself about Ratcliffe she went on to reproach herself about Sybil, who really looked worn and pale, as though almost overcome by fatigue.

"Sybil," said she, "you must go to bed at once. You are tired out. It was very wrong in me to let you sit up so late. Go now, and get some sleep."

"I am not going to bed till you do, Maude!" replied Sybil, with quiet obstinacy.

"Go, dear! it is all settled. I shall not marry Mr. Ratcliffe. You need not be anxious about it any more."

"Are you very unhappy?"

"Only very angry with myself. I ought to have taken Mr. Carrington's advice sooner."

"Oh, Maude!" exclaimed Sybil, with a sudden explosion of energy; "I wish you had taken *him*!"

This remark roused Mrs. Lee to new interest: "Why, Sybil," said she, "surely you are not in earnest?"

"Indeed, I am," replied Sybil, very decidedly. "I know you think I am in love with Mr. Carrington myself; but I'm not. I would a great deal rather have him for a brother-in-law, and he is so much the nicest man you know, and you could help his sisters."

Mrs. Lee hesitated a moment, for she was not quite certain whether it was wise to probe a healing wound, but she was anxious to clear this last weight from her mind, and she dashed recklessly forward:

"Are you sure you are telling the truth, Sybil? Why, then, did you say that you cared for him? and why have you been so miserable ever since he went away?"

"Why? I should think it was plain enough why! Because I thought, as every one else did, that you were going to marry Mr.

Ratcliffe; and because if you married Mr. Ratcliffe, I must go and live alone; and because you treated me like a child, and never took me into your confidence at all; and because Mr. Carrington was the only person I had to advise me, and after he went away, I was left all alone to fight Mr. Ratcliffe and you both together, without a human soul to help me in case I made a mistake. You would have been a great deal more miserable than I if you had been in my place."

Madeleine looked at her for a moment in doubt. Would this last? did Sybil herself know the depth of her own wound? But what could Mrs. Lee do now? Perhaps Sybil did deceive herself a little. When this excitement had passed away, perhaps Carrington's image might recur to her mind a little too often for her own comfort. The future must take care of itself. Mrs. Lee drew her sister closer to her, and said:

"Sybil, I have made a horrible mistake, and you must forgive me."

CHAPTER XIII

Not until afternoon did Mrs. Lee reappear. How much she had slept she did not say, and she hardly looked like one whose slumbers had been long or sweet; but if she had slept little, she had made up for the loss by thinking much, and, while she thought, the storm which had raged so fiercely in her breast, more and more subsided into calm. If there was not sunshine yet, there was at least stillness. As she lay, hour after hour, waiting for the sleep that did not come, she had at first the keen mortification of reflecting how easily she had been led by mere vanity into imagining that she could be of use in the world. She even smiled in her solitude at the picture she drew of herself, reforming Ratcliffe, and Krebs, and Schuyler Clinton. The ease with which Ratcliffe alone had twisted her about his finger, now that she saw it, made her writhe, and the thought of what he might have done, had she married him, and of the endless succession of moral somersaults she would have had to turn, chilled her with mortal terror. She had barely escaped being dragged under the wheels of the machine, and so coming to an untimely end. When she thought of this, she felt a mad passion to revenge herself on the whole race of politicians, with Ratcliffe at their head; she passed hours in framing bitter speeches to be made to his face. Then as she grew calmer, Ratcliffe's sins took on a milder hue; life, after all, had not been entirely blackened by his arts; there was even some good in her experience, sharp though it were. Had she not come to Washington in search of men who cast a shadow, and was not Ratcliffe's shadow strong enough to satisfy her? Had she not penetrated the deepest recesses of politics, and learned how easily the mere possession of power could convert the shadow of a hobby-horse existing only in the brain of a foolish country farmer, into a lurid nightmare that convulsed the sleep of nations? The antics of Presidents and Senators had been amusing—so amusing that she had nearly been persuaded to take part in them. She had saved herself in time. She had got to the bottom of this business of democratic government, and found out that it was nothing more than government of any other kind. She might have known it by her own common sense, but now that experience had proved it, she was glad to quit the masquerade; to return to the true democracy of life, her paupers and her prisons, her schools and her hospitals. As for Mr. Ratcliffe, she felt no difficulty in dealing with him. Let Mr. Ratcliffe, and his brother giants, wander on their own political prairie, and hunt for offices, or other profitable game, as they would. Their objects were not her objects, and to join their company was not her ambition. She was no longer very angry with Mr. Ratcliffe. She had no wish to insult him, or to quarrel with him. What he had done as a politician, he had done according to his own moral code, and it was not her business to judge him; to protect herself was the only right she claimed. She thought she could easily hold him at arm's length, and although, if Carrington had written the truth, they could never again be friends, there need be no difficulty in their remaining acquaintances. If this view of her duty was narrow, it was at least proof that she had learned something from

Mr. Ratcliffe; perhaps it was also proof that she had yet to learn Mr. Ratcliffe himself.

Two o'clock had struck before Mrs. Lee came down from her chamber, and Sybil had not yet made her appearance. Madeleine rang her bell and gave orders that, if Mr. Ratcliffe called she would see him, but she was at home to no one else. Then she sat down to write letters and to prepare for her journey to New York, for she must now hasten her departure in order to escape the gossip and criticism which she saw hanging like an avalanche over her head. When Sybil at length came down, looking much fresher than her sister, they passed an hour together arranging this and other small matters, so that both of them were again in the best of spirits, and Sybil's face was wreathed in smiles.

A number of visitors came to the door that day, some of them prompted by friendliness and some by sheer curiosity, for Mrs. Lee's abrupt disappearance from the ball had excited remark. Against all these her door was firmly closed. On the other hand, as the afternoon went on, she sent Sybil away, so that she might have the field entirely to herself; and Sybil, relieved of all her alarms, sallied out to interrupt Dunbeg's latest interview with his Countess, and to amuse herself with Victoria's last "phase."

Towards four o'clock the tall form of Mr. Ratcliffe was seen to issue from the Treasury Department and to descend the broad steps of its western front. Turning deliberately towards the Square, the Secretary of the Treasury crossed the Avenue and stopping at Mrs. Lee's door, rang the bell. He was immediately admitted. Mrs. Lee was alone in her parlour and rose rather gravely as he entered, but welcomed him as cordially as she could. She wanted to put an end to his hopes at once and to do it decisively, but without hurting his feelings.

"Mr. Ratcliffe," said she, when he was seated; "I am sure you will be better pleased by my speaking instantly and frankly. I could not reply to you last night. I will do so now without delay. What you wish is impossible. I would rather not even discuss it. Let us leave it here and return to our old relations."

She could not force herself to express any sense of gratitude for his affection, or of regret at being obliged to meet it with so little return. To treat him with tolerable civility was all she thought required of her. Ratcliffe felt the change of manner. He had been prepared for a struggle, but not to be met with so blunt a rebuff at the start. His look became serious and he hesitated a moment before speaking, but when he spoke at last, it was with a manner as firm and decided as that of Mrs. Lee herself.

"I cannot accept such an answer. I will not say that I have a right to explanation,—I have no rights which you are bound to respect,—but from you I conceive that I may at least ask the favour of one, and that you will not refuse it. Are you willing to tell me your reasons for this abrupt and harsh decision?"

"I do not dispute your right of explanation, Mr. Ratcliffe. You have the right, if you choose to use it, and I am ready to give you every explanation in my power; but I hope you will not insist on my doing so. If I seemed to speak abruptly and harshly, it was merely to spare you the greater annoyance of doubt. Since I am forced to give you pain, was it not fairer and more respectful to you to speak at once? We have been friends. I am very soon going away. I sincerely want to avoid saying or doing anything that would change our relations."

Ratcliffe, however, paid no attention to these words, and gave them no answer. He was much too old a debater to be misled by such trifles, when he needed all his faculties to pin his opponent to the wall. He asked:—

"Is your decision a new one?"

"It is a very old one, Mr. Ratcliffe, which I had let myself lose sight of, for a time. A night's reflection has brought me back to it."

"May I ask why you have returned to it? surely you would not have hesitated without strong reasons."

"I will tell you frankly. If, by appearing to hesitate, I have misled you, I am honestly sorry for it. I did not mean to do it. My hesitation was owing to the doubt whether my life might not really be best used in aiding you. My decision was owing to the certainty that we are not fitted for each other. Our lives run in separate grooves. We are both too old to change them."

Ratcliffe shook his head with an air of relief. "Your reasons, Mrs. Lee, are not sound. There is no such divergence in our lives. On the contrary I can give to yours the field it needs, and that it can get in no other way; while you can give to mine everything it now wants. If these are your only reasons I am sure of being able to remove them."

Madeleine looked as though she were not altogether pleased at this idea, and became a little dogmatic. "It is no use our arguing on this subject, Mr. Ratcliffe. You and I take very different views of life. I cannot accept yours, and you could not practise on mine."

"Show me," said Ratcliffe, "a single example of such a divergence, and I will accept your decision without another word."

Mrs. Lee hesitated and looked at him for an instant as though to be quite sure that he was in earnest. There was an effrontery about this challenge which surprised her, and if she did not check it on the spot, there was no saying how much trouble it might give her. Then unlocking the drawer of the writing-desk at her elbow, she took out Carrington's letter and handed it to Mr. Ratcliffe.

"Here is such an example which has come to my knowledge very lately. I meant to show it to you in any case, but I would rather have waited."

Ratcliffe took the letter which she handed to him, opened it deliberately, looked at the signature, and read. He showed no sign of surprise or disturbance. No one would have imagined that he had, from the moment he saw Carrington's name, as precise a knowledge of what was in this letter as though he had written it himself. His first sensation was only one of anger that his projects had miscarried. How this had happened he could not at once understand, for the idea that Sybil could have a hand in it did not occur to him. He had made up his mind that Sybil was a silly, frivolous girl, who counted for nothing in her sister's actions. He had fallen into the usual masculine blunder of mixing up smartness of intelligence with strength of character. Sybil, without being a metaphysician, willed anything which she willed at all with more energy than her sister did, who was worn out with the effort of life. Mr. Ratcliffe missed this point, and was left to wonder who it was that had crossed his path, and how Carrington had managed to be present and absent, to get a good office in Mexico and to baulk his schemes in Washington, at the same time. He had not given Carrington credit for so much cleverness.

He was violently irritated at the check. Another day, he thought, would have made him safe on this side; and possibly he was right. Had he once succeeded in getting ever so slight a hold on Mrs. Lee he would have told her this story with his own colouring, and from his own point of view, and he fully believed he could do this in such a way as to rouse her sympathy. Now that her mind was prejudiced, the task would be much more difficult; yet he did not despair, for it was his theory that Mrs. Lee, in the depths of her soul, wanted to be at the head of the White House as much as he wanted to be there himself, and that her apparent coyness was mere feminine indecision in the face of temptation. His thoughts now turned upon the best means of giving again the upper hand to her ambition. He wanted to drive Carrington a second time from the field.

Thus it was that, having read the letter once in order to learn what was in it, he turned back, and slowly read it again in order to gain time. Then he replaced it in its envelope, and returned it to Mrs. Lee, who, with equal calmness, as though her interest in it were at an end, tossed it negligently into the fire, where it was reduced to ashes under Ratcliffe's eyes.

He watched it burn for a moment, and then turning to her, said, with his usual composure, "I meant to have told you of that affair myself. I am sorry that Mr. Carrington has thought proper to forestall me. No doubt he has his own motives for taking my character in charge."

"Then it is true!" said Mrs. Lee, a little more quickly than she had meant to speak.

"True in its leading facts; untrue in some of its details, and in the impression it creates. During the Presidential election which took place eight years ago last autumn, there was, as you may remember, a violent contest and a very close vote. We believed (though I was not so prominent in the party then as now), that the result of that election would be almost as important to the nation as the result of the war itself. Our defeat meant that the government must pass into the blood-stained hands of rebels, men whose designs were more than doubtful, and who could not, even if their designs had been good, restrain the violence of their followers. In consequence we strained every nerve. Money was freely spent, even to an amount much in excess of our resources. How it was employed, I will not say. I do not even know, for I held myself aloof from these details, which fell to the National Central Committee of which I was not a member. The great point was that a very large sum had been borrowed on pledged securities, and must be repaid. The members of the National Committee and certain senators held discussions on the subject, in which I shared. The end was that towards the close of the session the head of the committee, accompanied by two senators, came to me and told me that I must abandon my opposition to the Steamship Subsidy. They made no open avowal of their reasons, and I did not press for one. Their declaration, as the responsible heads of the organization, that certain action on my part was essential to the interests of the party, satisfied me. I did not consider myself at liberty to persist in a mere private opinion in regard to a measure about which I recognized the extreme likelihood of my being in error. I accordingly reported the bill, and voted for it, as did a large majority of the party. Mrs. Baker is mistaken in saying that the money was paid to me. If it was paid at all, of which I have no knowledge except from this letter, it was paid to the representative of the National Committee. I received no money. I had nothing to do with the money further than as I might draw my own conclusions in regard to the subsequent payment of the campaign debt."

Mrs. Lee listened to all this with intense interest. Not until this moment had she really felt as though she had got to the heart of politics, so that she could, like a physician with his stethoscope, measure the organic disease. Now at last she knew why the pulse beat with such unhealthy irregularity, and why men felt an anxiety which they could not or would not explain. Her interest in the disease overcame her disgust at the foulness of the revelation. To say that the discovery gave her actual pleasure would be doing her injustice; but the excitement of the moment swept away every other sensation. She did not even think of herself. Not until afterwards did she fairly grasp the absurdity of Ratcliffe's wish that in the face of such a story as this, she should still have vanity enough to undertake the reform of politics. And with his aid too! The audacity of the man would have seemed sublime if she had felt sure that he knew the difference between good and evil, between a lie and the truth; but the more she saw of him, the surer she was that his courage was mere moral paralysis, and that he talked about virtue and vice as a man who is colour-blind talks about red and green; he did not see them as she saw them; if left to choose for himself he would have nothing to guide him. Was it politics that had caused this atrophy of the moral senses by disuse? Meanwhile, here she sat face to face with a moral lunatic, who had not even enough sense of humour to see the absurdity of his own request, that she should go out to the shore of this ocean of corruption, and repeat the ancient *rôle* of King Canute, or Dame Partington with her mop and her pail. What was to be done with such an animal?

The bystander who looked on at this scene with a wider knowledge of facts, might have found entertainment in another view of the subject, that is to say, in the guilelessness of Madeleine Lee. With all her warnings she was yet a mere baby-in-arms in the face of the great politician. She accepted his story as true, and she thought it as bad as possible; but had Mr. Ratcliffe's associates now been present to hear his version of it, they would have looked at each other with a smile of professional pride, and would have roundly sworn that he was, beyond a doubt, the ablest man this country had ever produced, and next to certain of being President. They would not, however, have told their own side of the story if they could have helped it, but in talking it over among themselves they might have assumed the facts to have been nearly as follows: that Ratcliffe had dragged them into an enormous expenditure to carry his own State, and with it his own re-election to the Senate; that they had tried to hold him responsible, and he had tried to shirk the responsibility; that there had been warm discussions on the subject; that he himself had privately suggested recourse to Baker, had shaped his conduct accordingly, and had compelled them, in order to save their own credit, to receive the money.

Even if Mrs. Lee had heard this part of the story, though it might have sharpened her indignation against Mr. Ratcliffe, it would not have altered her opinions. As it was, she had heard enough, and with a great effort to control her expression of disgust, she sank back in her chair as Ratcliffe concluded. Finding that she did not speak, he went on:

"I do not undertake to defend this affair. It is the act of my public life which I most regret—not the doing, but the necessity of doing. I do not differ from you in opinion on that point. I cannot acknowledge that there is here any real divergence between us."

"I am afraid," said Mrs. Lee, "that I cannot agree with you."

This brief remark, the very brevity of which carried a barb of sarcasm, escaped from Madeleine's lips before she had fairly intended it. Ratcliffe felt the sting, and it started him from his studied calmness of manner. Rising from his chair he stood on the hearth-rug before Mrs. Lee, and broke out upon her with an oration in that old senatorial voice and style which was least calculated to enlist her sympathies:

"Mrs. Lee," said he, with harsh emphasis and dogmatic tone, "there are conflicting duties in all the transactions of life, except the simplest. However we may act, do what we may, we must violate some moral obligation. All that can be asked of us is that we should guide ourselves by what we think the highest. At the time this affair occurred, I was a Senator of the United States. I was also a trusted member of a great political party which I looked upon as identical with the nation. In both capacities I owed duties to my constituents, to the government, to the people. I might interpret these duties narrowly or broadly. I might say: Perish the government, perish the Union, perish this people, rather than that I should soil my hands! Or I might say, as I did, and as I would say again: Be my fate what it may, this glorious Union, the last hope of suffering humanity, shall be preserved."

Here he paused, and seeing that Mrs. Lee, after looking for a time at him, was now regarding the fire, lost in meditation over the strange vagaries of the senatorial mind, he resumed, in another line of argument. He rightly judged that there must be some moral defect in his last remarks, although he could not see it, which made persistence in that direction useless.

"You ought not to blame me—you cannot blame me justly. It is to your sense of justice I appeal. Have I ever concealed from you my opinions on this subject? Have I not on the contrary always avowed them? Did I not here, on this very spot, when challenged once before by this same Carrington, take credit for an act less defensible than this? Did I not tell you then that I had even violated the sanctity of a great popular election and reversed its result? That was my sole act! In comparison with it, this is a trifle! Who is injured by a steamship company subscribing one or ten hundred thousand dollars to a campaign fund? Whose rights are affected by it? Perhaps its stock holders receive one dollar a share in dividends less than they otherwise would. If they do not complain, who else can do so? But in that election I deprived a million people of rights which belonged to them as absolutely as their houses! You could not say that I had done wrong. Not a word of blame or criticism have you ever uttered to me on that account. If there was an offence, you condoned it! You certainly led me to suppose that you saw none. Why are you now so severe upon the smaller crime?"

This shot struck hard. Mrs. Lee visibly shrank under it, and lost her composure. This was the same reproach she had made against herself, and to which she had been able to find no reply. With some agitation she exclaimed:

"Mr. Ratcliffe, pray do *me* justice! I have tried not to be severe. I have said nothing in the way of attack or blame. I acknowledge that it is not my place to stand in judgment over your acts. I have more reason to blame myself than you, and God knows I have blamed myself bitterly."

The tears stood in her eyes as she said these last words, and her voice trembled. Ratcliffe saw that he had gained an advantage, and, sitting down nearer to her, he dropped his voice and urged his suit still more energetically:

"You did me justice then; why not do it now? You were convinced then that I did the best I could. I have always done so. On the other hand I have never pretended that all my acts could be justified by abstract morality. Where, then, is the divergence between us?"

Mrs. Lee did not undertake to answer this last argument: she only returned to her old ground. "Mr. Ratcliffe," she said, "I do not want to argue this question. I have no doubt that you can overcome me in argument. Perhaps on my side this is a matter of feeling rather than of reason, but the truth is only too evident to me that I am not fitted for politics. I should be a drag upon you. Let me be the judge of my own weakness! Do not insist upon pressing me, further!"

She was ashamed of herself for this appeal to a man whom she could not respect, as though she were a suppliant at his mercy, but she feared the reproach of having deceived him, and she tried pitiably to escape it. Ratcliffe was only encouraged by her weakness.

"I *must* insist upon pressing it, Mrs. Lee," replied he, and he became yet more earnest as he went on; "my future is too deeply involved in your decision to allow of my accepting your answer as final. I need your aid. There is nothing I will not do to obtain it. Do you require affection? mine for you is boundless. I am ready to prove it by a life of devotion. Do you doubt my sincerity? test it in whatever way you please. Do you fear being dragged down to the level of ordinary politicians? so far as concerns myself, my great wish is to have your help in purifying politics. What higher ambition can there be than to serve one's country for such an end? Your sense of duty is too keen not to feel that the noblest objects which can inspire any woman, combine to point out your course."

Mrs. Lee was excessively uncomfortable, although not in the least shaken. She began to see that she must take a stronger tone if she meant to bring this importunity to an end, and she answered:—

"I do not doubt your affection or your sincerity, Mr. Ratcliffe. It is myself I doubt. You have been kind enough to give me much of your confidence this winter, and if I do not yet know about politics all that is to be known, I have learned enough to prove that I could do nothing sillier than to suppose myself competent to reform anything. If I pretended to think so, I should be a mere worldly, ambitious woman, such as people think me. The idea of my purifying politics is absurd. I am sorry to speak so strongly, but I mean it. I do not cling very closely to life, and do not value my own very highly, but I will not tangle it in such a way; I will not share the profits of vice; I am not willing to be made a receiver of stolen goods, or to be put in a position where I am perpetually obliged to maintain that immorality is a virtue!"

As she went on she became more and more animated and her words took a sharper edge than she had intended. Ratcliffe felt it, and showed his annoyance. His face grew dark and his eyes looked out at her with their ugliest expression. He even opened his mouth for an angry retort, but controlled himself with an effort, and presently resumed his argument.

"I had hoped," he began more solemnly than ever, "that I should find in you a lofty courage which would disregard such risks. If all true men and women were to take the tone you have taken, our government would soon perish. If you consent to share my career, I do not deny that you may find less satisfaction than I hope, but you will lead a mere death in life if you place yourself like a saint on a solitary column. I plead what I believe to be your own cause in pleading mine. Do not sacrifice your life!"

Mrs. Lee was in despair. She could not reply what was on her lips, that to marry a murderer or a thief was not a sure way of diminishing crime. She had already said something so much like this that she shrank from speaking more plainly. So she fell back on her old theme.

"We must at all events, Mr. Ratcliffe, use our judgments according to our own consciences. I can only repeat now what I said at first. I am sorry to seem insensible to your expressions towards me, but I cannot do what you wish. Let us maintain our old relations if you will, but do not press me further on this subject."

Ratcliffe grew more and more sombre as he became aware that defeat was staring him in the face. He was tenacious of purpose, and he had never in his life abandoned an object which he had so much at heart as this. He would not abandon it. For the moment, so completely had the fascination of Mrs. Lee got the control of him, he would rather have abandoned the Presidency itself than her. He really loved her as earnestly as it was in his nature to love anything. To her obstinacy he would oppose an obstinacy greater still; but in the meanwhile his attack was disconcerted, and he was at a loss what next to do. Was it not possible to change his ground; to offer inducements that would appeal even more strongly to feminine ambition and love of display than the Presidency itself? He began again:—

"Is there no form of pledge I can give you? no sacrifice I can make? You dislike politics. Shall I leave political life? I will do anything rather than lose you. I can probably control the appointment of Minister to England. The President would rather have me there than here. Suppose I were to abandon politics and take the English mission. Would that sacrifice not affect you? You might pass four years in London where there would be no politics, and where your social position would be the best in the world; and this would lead to the Presidency almost as surely as the other." Then suddenly, seeing that he was making no headway, he threw off his studied calmness and broke out in an appeal of almost equally studied violence. "Mrs. Lee! Madeleine! I cannot live without you. The sound of your voice—the touch of your hand—even the rustle of your dress—are like wine to me. For God's sake, do not throw me over!"

He meant to crush opposition by force. More and more vehement as he spoke he actually bent over and tried to seize her hand. She drew it back as though he were a reptile. She was exasperated by this obstinate disregard of her forbearance, this gross attempt to bribe her with office, this flagrant abandonment of even a pretence of public virtue; the mere thought of his touch on her person was more repulsive than a loathsome disease. Bent upon teaching him a lesson he would never forget, she spoke out abruptly, and with evident signs of contempt in her voice and manner:

"Mr. Ratcliffe, I am not to be bought. No rank, no dignity, no consideration, no conceivable expedient would induce me to change my mind. Let us have no more of this!"

Ratcliffe had already been more than once, during this conversation, on the verge of losing his temper. Naturally dictatorial and violent, only long training and severe experience had taught him self-control, and when he gave way to passion his bursts of fury were still tremendous. Mrs. Lee's evident personal disgust, even more than her last sharp rebuke, passed the bounds of his patience. As he stood before her, even she, high-spirited as she was, and not in a calm frame of mind, felt a momentary shock at seeing how his face flushed, his eyes gleamed, and his hands trembled with rage.

"Ah!" exclaimed he, turning upon her with a harshness, almost a savageness, of manner that startled her still more; "I might have known what to expect! Mrs. Clinton warned me early. She said then that I should find you a heartless coquette!"

"Mr. Ratcliffe!" exclaimed Madeleine, rising from her chair, and speaking in a warning voice almost as passionate as his own.

"A heartless coquette!" he repeated, still more harshly than before; "she said you would do just this! that you meant to deceive me! that you lived on flattery! that you could never be anything but a coquette, and that if you married me, I should repent it all my life. I believe her now!"

Mrs. Lee's temper, too, was naturally a high one. At this moment she, too, was flaming with anger, and wild with a passionate impulse to annihilate this man. Conscious that the mastery was in her own hands, she could the more easily control her voice, and with an expression of unutterable contempt she spoke her last words to him, words which had been ringing all day in her ears:

"Mr. Ratcliffe! I have listened to you with a great deal more patience and respect than you deserve. For one long hour I have degraded myself by discussing with you the question whether I should marry a man who by his own confession has betrayed the highest trusts that could be placed in him, who has taken money for his votes as a Senator, and who is now in public office by means of a successful fraud of his own, when in justice he should be in a State's prison. I will have no more of this. Understand, once for all, that there is an impassable gulf between your life and mine. I do not doubt that you will make yourself President, but whatever or wherever you are, never speak to me or recognize me again!"

He glared a moment into her face with a sort of blind rage, and seemed about to say more, when she swept past him, and before he realized it, he was alone.

Overmastered by passion, but conscious that he was powerless, Ratcliffe, after a moment's hesitation, left the room and the house. He let himself out, shutting the front door behind him, and as he stood on the pavement old Baron Jacobi, who had special reasons for wishing to know how Mrs. Lee had recovered from the fatigue and excitements of the ball, came up to the spot. A single glance at Ratcliffe showed him that something had gone wrong in the career of that great man, whose fortunes he always followed with so bitter a sneer of contempt. Impelled by the spirit of evil always at his elbow, the Baron seized this moment to sound the depth of his friend's wound. They met at the door so closely that recognition was inevitable, and Jacobi, with his worst smile, held out his hand, saying at the same moment with diabolic malignity:

"I hope I may offer my felicitations to your Excellency!"

Ratcliffe was glad to find some victim on whom he could vent his rage. He had a long score of humiliations to repay this man, whose last insult was beyond all endurance. With an oath he dashed Jacobi's hand aside, and, grasping his shoulder, thrust him out of the path. The Baron, among whose weaknesses the want of high temper and personal courage was not recorded, had no mind to tolerate such an insult from such a man. Even while Ratcliffe's hand was still on his shoulder he had raised his cane, and before the Secretary saw what was coming, the old man had struck him with all his force full in the face. For a moment Ratcliffe staggered back and grew pale, but the shock sobered him. He hesitated a single instant whether to crush his assailant with a blow, but he felt that for one of his youth and strength, to attack an infirm diplomatist in a public street would be a fatal blunder, and while Jacobi stood, violently excited, with his cane raised ready to strike another blow, Mr. Ratcliffe suddenly turned his back and without a word, hastened away.

When Sybil returned, not long afterwards, she found no one in the parlour. On going to her sister's room she discovered Madeleine lying on the couch, looking worn and pale, but with a slight smile and a peaceful expression on her face, as though she had done some act which her conscience approved. She called Sybil to her side, and, taking her hand, said:

"Sybil, dearest, will you go abroad with me again?"

"Of course I will," said Sybil; "I will go to the end of the world with you."

"I want to go to Egypt," said Madeleine, still smiling faintly; "democracy has shaken my nerves to pieces. Oh, what rest it would be to live in the Great Pyramid and look out for ever at the polar star!"

CONCLUSION

SYBIL TO CARRINGTON

"May 1st, New York.

"MY DEAR MR. CARRINGTON,

"I promised to write you, and so, to keep my promise, and also because my sister wishes me to tell you about our plans, I send this letter. We have left Washington—for ever, I am afraid—and are going to Europe next month. You must know that a fortnight ago, Lord Skye gave a great ball to the Grand-Duchess of something-or-other quite unspellable. I never can describe things, but it was all very fine. I wore a lovely new dress, and was a great success, I assure you. So was Madeleine, though she had to sit most of the evening by the Princess—such a dowdy! The Duke danced with me several times; he can't reverse, but that doesn't seem to matter in a Grand-Duke. Well! things came to a crisis at the end of the evening. I followed your directions, and after we got home gave your letter to Madeleine. She says she has burned it. I don't know what happened afterwards—a tremendous scene, I suspect, but Victoria Dare writes me from Washington that every one is talking about M.'s refusal of Mr. R., and a dreadful thing that took place on our very doorstep between Mr. R. and Baron Jacobi, the day after the ball. She says there was a regular pitched battle, and the Baron struck him over the face with his cane. You know how afraid Madeleine was that they would do something of the sort in our parlour. I'm glad they waited till they were in the street. But isn't it shocking! They say the Baron is to be sent away, or recalled, or something. I like the old gentleman, and for his sake am glad duelling is gone out of fashion, though I don't much believe Mr. Silas P. Ratcliffe could hit anything. The Baron passed through here three days ago on his summer trip to Europe. He left his card on us, but we were out, and did not see him. We are going over in July with the Schneidekoupons, and Mr. Schneidekoupon has promised to send his yacht to the Mediterranean, so that we shall sail about there after finishing the Nile, and see Jerusalem and Gibraltar and Constantinople. I think it will be perfectly lovely. I hate ruins, but I fancy you can buy delicious things in Constantinople. Of course, after what has happened, we can never go back to Washington. I shall miss our rides dreadfully. I read Mr. Browning's 'Last Ride Together,' as you told me; I think it's beautiful and perfectly easy, all but a little. I never could understand a word of him before—so I never tried. Who do you think is engaged? Victoria Dare, to a coronet and a peat-bog, with Lord Dunbeg attached. Victoria says she is happier than she ever was before in any of her other engagements, and she is sure this is the real one. She says she has thirty thousand a year derived from the poor of America, which may just as well go to relieve one of the poor in Ireland. You know her father was a claim agent, or some such thing, and is said to have made his money by cheating his clients out of their claims. She is perfectly wild to be a countess, and means to make Castle Dunbeg lovely by-and-by, and entertain us all there. Madeleine says she is just the kind to be a great success in London. Madeleine is very well, and sends her kind regards. I believe she is going to add a postscript. I have promised to let her read this, but I don't think a chaperoned letter is much fun to write or receive. Hoping to hear from you soon,

"SINCERELY YOURS,
"SYBIL ROSS."

Enclosed was a thin strip of paper containing another message from Sybil, privately inserted at the last moment unknown to Mrs. Lee—

"If I were in your place I would try again after she comes home."

Mrs. Lee's P.S. was very short—

"The bitterest part of all this horrid story is that nine out of ten of our countrymen would say I had made a mistake."

A Contemporary Review

[With] all due respect to the clever author, [*Democracy*] seems to us not to have caught the best or the fairest view of what its title intends.

[The] judgment to be passed upon the book itself is that the author makes a mistake if it is intended that we shall take this story for a real exposition of American life at its core. Mrs. Lee, with all her equipment, was scarcely qualified to discover the secret of democracy. She had not the esoteric initiation. Again, it may be doubted if Washington presents, after all, the true point of view. The book itself very clearly displays the essential masquerading character of life there, and strongly prejudices us against accepting a judgment founded exclusively upon observation formed within one circle of political life. If we could divest ourselves of sensitiveness we should find it easier to praise this book. As it is, we confess its skill and adroitness. In one point especially it shows ability. It sketches public characters without unerringly pointing to men actually occupying public positions. One thinks he is on the scent of some particular person, and is presently thrown off in the most skillful manner. Able as the book is, it lacks the essential quality of the higher truthfulness. The writer has left out of account forces which, if wisely considered, would crowd back the life here presented into narrower bounds.

The Atlantic Monthly, September, 1880.

READING GROUP GUIDE

1. Mrs. Lightfoot Lee moves to Washington, D.C., in order to live amid "POWER." What sort of power does Mrs. Lee believe she can find in the nation's capital that she cannot find in her native New York? Why is she in pursuit of power? Is political power accessible to a woman like her? Is Mrs. Lee an archetypical figure in American politics?

2. Is the Washington, D.C., described by Adams different from our nation's capital today? Why or why not?

3. Many critics describe *Democracy* as a satire, yet, as Henry Aiken has written, "Henry Adams was a realist." What do you make of these two diverging opinions?

4. Adams sets up Senator Silas Ratcliffe as the novel's villain. However, does the context of Adams's Washington make the senator more complex than that?

5. The novel is an exposé of corruption. What kinds of corruption is Adams revealing?

6. *Democracy* was published anonymously in 1880. Speculation over the author's identity became a furious parlor game throughout Washington and the nation, and the book became a bestseller. A similar event occurred in 1996 when Random House published *Primary Colors,* an anonymous roman à clef about President Clinton and Washington. (It was later revealed that its author was the journalist Joe Klein.) Why do you think Adams published his book anonymously? What freedom did this provide the author? Is this a courageous or cowardly act?

A NOTE ON THE TYPE

The principal text of this Modern Library edition
was set in a digitized version of Janson, a typeface that
dates from about 1690 and was cut by Nicholas Kis,
a Hungarian working in Amsterdam. The original matrices have
survived and are held by the Stempel foundry in Germany.
Hermann Zapf redesigned some of the weights and sizes for
Stempel, basing his revisions on the original design.

MODERN LIBRARY IS ONLINE AT
WWW.MODERNLIBRARY.COM

MODERN LIBRARY ONLINE IS YOUR GUIDE
TO CLASSIC LITERATURE ON THE WEB

THE MODERN LIBRARY E-NEWSLETTER

Our free e-mail newsletter is sent to subscribers, and features sample chapters, interviews with and essays by our authors, upcoming books, special promotions, announcements, and news.

To subscribe to the Modern Library e-newsletter, send a blank e-mail to: sub_modernlibrary@info.randomhouse.com or visit www.modernlibrary.com

THE MODERN LIBRARY WEBSITE

Check out the Modern Library website at
www.modernlibrary.com for:

- The Modern Library e-newsletter
- A list of our current and upcoming titles and series
- Reading Group Guides and exclusive author spotlights
- Special features with information on the classics and other paperback series
- Excerpts from new releases and other titles
- A list of our e-books and information on where to buy them
- The Modern Library Editorial Board's 100 Best Novels and 100 Best Nonfiction Books of the Twentieth Century written in the English language
- News and announcements

Questions? E-mail us at modernlibrary@randomhouse.com
For questions about examination or desk copies, please visit
the Random House Academic Resources site at
www.randomhouse.com/academic